THE
BRAVADOS

PARRIS

AFTON BONDS
NEW YORK TIMES
BESTSELLING AUTHOR

The Barons – The Texicans, Volume Two
The Brigands – The Texicans, Volume One

Answering The Call	*Love and War on the Rio Grande*
When the Heart is Right	*Reluctant Rebel*
Blue Bayou	*Made For Each Other*
Blue Moon	*Midsummer Midnight*
The Calling of the Clan	*Mood Indigo*
The Captive	*No Telling*
Dancing with Crazy Woman	*Renegade Man*
Dancing with Wild Woman	*Run To Me*
Deep Purple	*Savage Enchantment*
Dream Keeper	*The Savage*
Dream Time	*Snow And Ice*
Dust Devil	*Spinster's Song*
The Flash Of The Firefly	*Stardust*
For All Time	*Sweet Enchantress*
Kingdom Come: Temptation	*Sweet Golden Sun*
Kingdom Come: Trespass	*The Wildest Heart*
Lavender Blue	*Wanted Woman*
Love Tide	*Widow Woman*
Wind Song	*When the Heart is Right*

THE BRAVADOS

THE TEXICANS ★ VOLUME THREE

NEW YORK TIMES BESTSELLING AUTHOR

PARRIS
AFTON BONDS

MOTINA BOOKS PUBLISHING

Text copyright © 2024 by Parris Afton Bonds
2nd Edition
All Rights Reserved. Printed in the United States of America
Published by Motina Books, LLC, Highlands Ranch, CO
www.MotinaBooks.com

Library of Congress Cataloguing-in-Publication Data:

Names: Afton Bonds, Parris
Title: The Bravados:: Volume Three of The Texicans
Description: First Edition. | Highlands Ranch: Motina Books, 2023

Identifiers:

LCCN: 2024948586
ISBN-13: 979-8-88784-051-2 (paperback)
ISBN-13: 979-8-88784-053-6 (e-book)
ISBN-13: 979-8-88784-052-9 (hardcover)

Subjects: BISAC:
FICTION/Romance/Historical/American
FICTION/Romance/Western

Cover and Interior Design: Diane Windsor

Dedicated to Cindy Nord,
Whose essence and novels sparkled like champagne.

THE TEXICANS
GENEALOGY
THE BRAVADOS

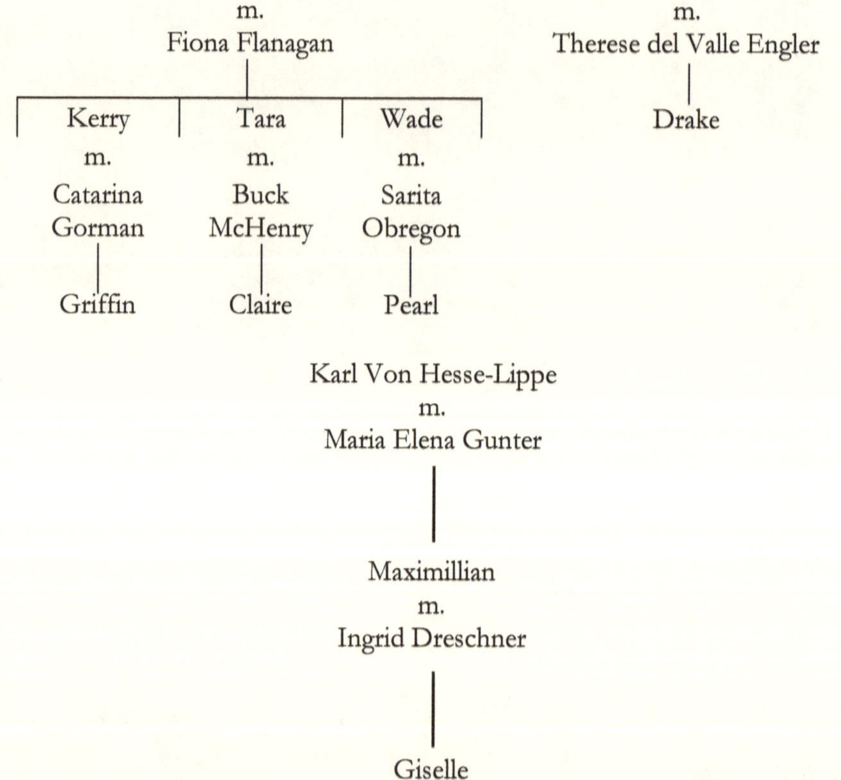

Amarillo
Red River
Brazos
Fort Worth
Dallas
Nacogdoches
El Paso
Austin
Brazos
Trinity
Houston
Rio Grande
San Antonio
Galveston
Nueces
The Barony
Corpus Christi
Gulf of Mexico
N
Rio Grande
Rio Grande City
Brownsville
TEXAS

THE BARONY, SOUTHWEST TEXAS
THANKSGIVING 1890

With trembling fingertips, Alexander de la Torre y Stuart, Baron of Paladín, gently closed Niall Gorman's eyelids. The man had been his best friend for an unimaginably long fifty something years.

Niall had fought fearlessly alongside him on the San Jacinto battlefield when the Texas Republic won independence from Mexico. Together, they had persevered over the years to build their Barony Partnership into a transportation and cattle empire. And Niall had loyally stood fast beside him as best man when Alex was about to wed the woman Niall loved, the Spanish aristocrat Rafaela Carrera.

Alex rested his forehead on the heel of his palm. His heavy sigh sounded more like a guttural groan. At his feet, his old coonhound, Blue, bayed mournfully, its fur bristling. Outside the sprawling hacienda, a banshee wind mimicked both Alex and Blue. The man swallowed hard. It was time to let the Irish Traveler go.

It was also time to let Rafaela take over. Niall's wife and his own, Thérèse, could take care of the burial arrangements. But then, there was little Thérèse couldn't manage. As his second wife, the still vibrant Frenchwoman had seen him through the best and worst during all the years since his lass Fiona's too-early death.

Even now, Thérèse was in the sala attending to the stunned, close-knit families—the Paladíns, the Gormans, and the Von Hesse-Lippes—who only that afternoon had gathered to celebrate, as they had through the preceding decades, The Barony's traditional Thanksgiving celebration.

A few hours earlier, Niall had taken up his guitar to entertain everyone. Midway through a plaintive Gypsy ballad, he collapsed, crushing his cherished guitar as his fatal collapse crushed Rafaela's heart.

Alex rose from the bedside chair. His carriage remained ramrod straight despite his eighty years, its military bearing carrying him from Quebec's windswept heights as a British Redcoat lieutenant to Punjab's impoverished majesty as a Raj—but these days, his bones protested the effort it took him merely to stand erect.

One life leaves, another arrives. Alex moved his creaky bones to investigate that recent and most astounding arrival waiting in his office.

FROM OUTSIDE THE OPEN DOUBLE doors of the sala, crowded with grieving family members, Alex paused and nodded at Thérèse. She was giving Rafaela a consoling sisterly embrace. Thérèse nodded back, then whispered in Rafaela's ear.

He heard Rafaela's congested gasp. With the old dog padding at his heels, Alex continued past the sala, along the colonnaded hallway. He closed his office door behind him, folded his arms, and stared at his seventeen-year-old son.

Drake was passed out on the leather-hide sofa, his long, lean body sprawled in sonorous repose. His dusty Stetson lay over his crotch, his Peacemaker still sheathed in its holster. He had obviously not bothered to shave in days. The devil knew when he had last had a haircut. Alex's nose wrinkled. 'Drake the Rake' reeked of alcohol.

Good god, the sins of the father revisited.

Drake was barely literate. Nevertheless, the Paladín name—if not its money—could get him into the Texas A&M College or the University of Texas. But since Drake had no interest in college, Alex had tried getting him more involved in The Barony's ranching issues.

Only last week, he had sent Drake to Sierra Blanca's ten-year-celebration of the driving of the silver spike that commemorated the nation's second trans-continental railroad.

But instead of representing The Barony Enterprises portion of the Galveston, Harrisburg, San Antonio Railway, Drake had drifted eighty miles farther west of Sierra Blanca to Sin City.

Bankers, merchants, real estate sharks, cattlemen, miners, railroad men, gamblers, prostitutes, and sporting people of both genders all flocked to Sin City—especially into El Paso's Tenderloin District. Apparently, the mother of the child nested on the sofa's cushioned arm next to Drake's disheveled dark head was one of those sporting people.

"Your name, girl?"

"Angel." Her eyes lit at the sight of the hound.

"Angel?" He crossed to the sofa. "Angel what?"

She shrugged tiny shoulders. Her sun-drenched pigtails looked as if they had not seen a comb in weeks.

With a stifled groan, Alex slumped down before the little girl onto one suffering knee. "You have a last name."

"Smith, I think."

Surely that wholesome-goodness smile hid a lie. "How old are you?"

"Ten, sir."

Another lie. She could not be a day over eight, on the outside. Maybe even seven.

"What's your dog's name?"

"Blue. Listen, Drake mentioned—" it was more of a mumble before he passed out, "—that a woman in El Paso left you as a marker for her bet."

"But the dog is black," she pointed out in a tone reserved for dunces.

He admired her play for diversion. "One of its eyes is black, the other blue. Who is she, the woman?"

"My mother. But she croaked."

"She . . . what?"

Long black lashes touched cherubic cheeks. "After my mother lost at Three Card Monte to Drake . . ." the moppet paused and tears suddenly spiked those lashes, " . . . she went to the International Bridge. They said she shot herself."

"And so now you're my son's possession." Alex combed fingers through his thick silver hair. "What in God's name was Drake thinking? And to haul you all the way back here to The Barony?"

Cupid-bow lips dented a dimple in each rosy cheek, and her lollipop green eyes gleamed. "Why, I reckon he was thinking that he will marry me after I grow up."

Alex had heard of violin virtuosos at ten and a few chess champions at nine, but this angelic Angel was a mistress of mendacity at seven.

NIALL'S FUNERAL WAS A GRAND state affair held at the Campo Santo cemetery east of San Antonio. Despite the chilly temperature, dignitaries and friends had come from places as distant as Mexico City and Washington, D.C.

A horse trader, Niall always believed in the inherent value of transportation. The Irish Traveler had first grown his trade by providing carriage horses for San Antonio's elite. Then he began contracting wagons for the Army during the Mexican-American War. From there, it was on to establishing stagecoach routes to contain Texas's wide-open spaces. After that it was, for Niall, a mere leap to becoming a credible railroad magnate.

Early on, the Gorman name meant 'expert horseman' not only in Texas but across the Southwest. Niall was known far and wide for his honorable dealings.

From a gypsy, that reputation said a lot. In keeping with his gypsy heritage, Rafaela had organized the huge bonfire, already blazing behind their caliche block-walled homestead in San Antonio.

Their homestead? No, alas. Now simply hers.

People, both friends and a few newspaper reporters, described their homestead as a rambling Territorial Spanish-Colonial ranch house. For Rafaela, every tile, post, and shutter held some resonance of Niall. His capable hands, juxtaposed by his romantic's imagination, had created their home especially for her.

The bonfire's smoky, woodsy aroma transformed the cool autumn air. Its dancing tongues of ghostly light illuminated the ranch house's rear veranda.

It also illuminated the grieving faces, most belonging to the immediate family, who decamped from the cemetery to gather around the fiery mound of logs and branches.

Among the faces was her and Niall's daughter, Catarina, her eyes red from weeping. She clung to the arm of her husband Kerry, Alex's oldest. On her other side, their son Griffin, Alex's grandson, held his mother's hand.

Alex and Thérèse both stared numbly into the crackling fire. Their wayward youngest was certainly not at the side of his parents. Where was Drake?

Rafaela's gaze swept past them to Alex's middle son,

Wade, and his wife Sarita. Their sixteen-year-old daughter Pearl's countenance was gripped with utter fascination.

However, standing next to Pearl, her cousin Claire's puzzled expression displayed wariness toward this peculiar gypsy bonfire tradition. The fourteen-year-old offspring of Alex's only daughter Tara and her husband Buck McHenry, was a reserved child, much like Rafaela at Claire's age—until the magic of Niall's love changed her, making her joyously aware that there was more to life than any unaware eye could ever see.

Of course, Max and Ingrid von Hesse-Lippe were there. But Max's father Karl, a widower now, stood off to one side like an Old Guardsman on watch. All these years, always seeming to be in the background—yet always there for Rafaela.

During the Middle Ages, the spread of the plague by contamination— *marimé* in gypsy cant—meant death, so all personal belongings were burned. That night, in keeping with his Gypsy heritage, each person present held a personal belonging of Niall's. A shaving strop, his long-barrel Colt, a pair of brass eagle spurs, his chaps.

Rafaela held his smashed guitar, pressed tight against her chest.

Head bowed, she blinked back tears. Memories stuttered through her. For over fifty years, she had shared the most intimate of aspects with this man. The faces of everyone blurred. Everything fell away. Noise ceased. All but her keening, a low sound of heart-crushing lamentation.

When her time to contribute to the blaze arrived, her

keening erupted into the Texican battle cry, a chilling combination Indian war-whoop and wolf howl. She flung Niall's battered guitar onto the pyre. Momentarily, bright orange-red flames leaped higher. When at last they abated, she swung away.

Tugging her hip-length black velvet jacket tightly around her, she strode blindly toward the solace afforded her by the cottonwoods running beside the San Antonio River. When she nearly collided with one old cottonwood, it was there she slumped beside its gnarly trunk. Brow propped on updrawn knees, she cried deeply for the first time since Niall's death—great, heaving sobs that racked her body.

How long she cried, she was not sure, but at some point, she became aware of the solid body aligned with hers. Karl's arms cocooning her, comforting her as he always had through the years.

KERRY PALADÍN WAS CREATING A Texas Democrat dynasty.

His three consecutive terms as first-born native Texas governor, then his stint as a U.S. senator, followed by his present term once again in the governor's office, now thrust him into take-charge mode. That, or sheer perturbation with his much younger half-brother Drake.

Following the bonfire, the family had gathered in the crowded sala. Kerry paced its confined center, his good arm locked behind his back, fingers fisted. His sharp gaze sighted in on Drake.

His half-brother, the exact age of Kerry's own son, Griffin, was slouched in a rawhide arm chair in utter indifference to this current family drama of his own making. At seventeen, Drake possessed the dark, moody, and dangerous good looks of his other half-brother, Wade, derived, of course from the Baron of Paladín himself.

Kerry fired another question at Drake. "Well, did you notice what the mother looked like? Was the woman well-dressed?"

Drake smirked. "I wouldn't know. I only notice the undressed ones."

"Drake!"

All eyes swiveled toward their father. Alex ruled from a leather-padded wingchair, placed between two brocade-draped arched windows. The patriarch was frowning at his court jesters and no hint of humor softened his sharp gaze.

Kerry's French stepmother, Thérèse, stood regally and solicitously beside Alex's throne. Beneath her white lace cap, with its black ribbon bows, her features tightened, declaring she, too, was displeased by their son's behavior. But then, she readily conceded she had too often coddled her only child, arriving so late in her life.

Kerry's narrow-eyed gaze shifted toward the little girl camped on the armrest of Drake's chair. Her arm was propped atop its back. She looked like a Cheshire cat perched on a tree limb—a cheeky combination of attitude and curiosity. "What are the names of your parents, child?"

"Mom and Dad."

He barely refrained from rolling his eyes. "Exactly

where do you live?"

"On the hill."

Just dandy, since El Paso wrapped around the ragged tail-end of the Rockies. It enveloped a veritable composition of increasingly higher hills.

Kerry's searching gaze found Cat. His wife, the only person who gave total meaning to his next breath, flashed him a reassuring half smile. Despite this unanticipated death of her father, she remained stalwart.

Lovelier at forty-nine than she had been at fourteen, she was his rock. She had rescued him from depression's dreaded doldrums after the amputation of his left arm following an irritatingly inconsequential Civil War skirmish.

She nodded at Kerry.

That was all he needed. Often, she had sat in the Senate gallery when he was offering a bill. Just the knowledge that she was there, believing in him and his ideas, was enough. So much faith she had in him. At times, it almost seemed a burden, demanding of him more than he feared he had to give.

"All right," he began, addressing his family, "the girl—" he inclined his head again in the direction of the precocious Angel Smith, or whatever her name really was, "—has to have gone missing from El Paso. I suggest we put up posters, distribute flyers, saturate the area with handbills. Surely, someone will take notice and contact us about her family."

Surprisingly, it was Max and Ingrid von Hesse-Lippe's nineteen-year-old daughter, Giselle, who spoke up. While

not bona fide Paladíns, the von Hesse- Lippes were inte-
grated into the Paladíns through half a century of loyalty.

To Kerry—adoring as he did her grandfather, his
surrogate Uncle Karl—Giselle displayed the best qualities of
the von Hesse-Lippes. Fluent in German, she was warmly
engaging, astoundingly clever, and—as an only child—quite
determined to preside over what she considered her nest of
the Paladín offspring.

"Such a poster would draw an unwarranted and bother-
some amount of interest from those eager to capitalize on a
grieving family's funds," she calmly pointed out. "Either
hers or ours. To avoid plowing through a host of imposters
and opportunists, may I suggest another strategy?"

"And that would be?" Kerry's sister, the always capable
Tara, who practically ran The Barony Ranch operation,
lifted an eyebrow.

Next to Tara sat her fourteen-year-old daughter, Claire.
His niece had inherited Tara's dark brown hair, a startling
contrast to Claire's pale blue eyes, a legacy of her father's—
that and his deadly calm disposition. That disposition
undoubtedly had gone toward making Buck McHenry the
feared Texas Ranger he once was.

Giselle shot a pointed glance at Buck now. "Why, we
hire someone to track down the girl's relatives."

After a maddeningly long moment of consideration,
Buck smiled laconically. "I still have a few connections with
the Rangers. I could get word out." A brilliant tactic. Kerry
should have been satisfied by the step toward the resolution
of being saddled with the tyke Angel—except for the

dangerously yearning glance he caught Pearl casting at Griffin.

The sixteen-year-old was a sweet girl, but she was the daughter of Kerry's brother Wade and Sarita. The dusky Pearl was his niece for God's sake. His son's first cousin.

Damn it, the Paladíns had enough on their plate right now without having to worry about incest.

★★★

WADE STOOD IN THE GUEST room doorway and, from behind, watched Sarita repack the small trunk for the train trip back home to Houston.

With Niall's death following on the heels of the Thanksgiving holiday, they all had been away far longer than they had anticipated. But in their absence, Billy Wheelwright was fully capable of running Paladín Navigation's barge business and his wife, Natty, and his sister, Becky, the Buffalo Bayou household.

When Sarita bent over to retrieve a dropped shawl, her inviting position snatched back his meandering mind.

Childbearing had not affected that petite, girlish figure that some twenty-five-odd years before he had sprawled over inside a Paladín chuck wagon during a fire raging without. And since then, the fire had not ceased to rage within—for either of them.

She might have been the daughter and twin sister of the Paladín's implacable foe, the Obregons, but she had devoted herself as totally to his family as she had once devoted herself to putting the ring of matrimony through his nose. And, godawlmighty, was he thankful he had surrendered up his bachelor status, however reluctantly he had done it.

Silently, coming up against her, he nailed those hips against his crotch and she yelped in surprise.

"Hush." He nuzzled her bejeweled ear. "Our daughter's the next room over."

"I can only hope she's not thinking what I am." She now squirmed that firmly rounded rump against him with explosive sensuality.

Instantly, his cock began to wilt. "Gawd, hon, she's barely sixteen." He couldn't even imagine Pearl engaging in such lustful thoughts.

"The same age as I when first you seduced me." She turned in his arms to arch her pelvis against his thighs. She splayed her hands up over his shoulders and smiled playfully.

At that, he laughed out loud. "Little lady, you chased me from Brownsville to Rio Grande City and from there to kingdom come." He could feel himself growing randy once more.

She stiffened with feigned indignance. "I most certainly did not. You came to find me. And speaking of finding, Wade Samuel Paladín . . . ."

His cock croaked. He knew when she used his full name, she was losing her amorous focus. "Speaking was not exactly what I had in mind."

Her expression grew solemn. "This girl that Drake

found—"

"Won," he corrected, cutting his eyes at his half-brother's latest fiasco. The devil-may-care kid was seventeen and irresponsible. Only a few years older, at twenty-one, Wade had already been saddled with the responsibility of heading up Barony cattle drives.

"This girl," she persisted, her brow knitting. "There's something about her. I can't put my finger on it, but I sense trouble nipping at her heels."

"Like this," he teased and nipped at her earlobe.

Shivering, she laughed lightly. "No, like this." Her fingers loosed the rivet of his denims' fly.

His cock was back in business.

**EL PASO
DECEMBER, 1890**

"God damn it all to hell!" When Rod Obregon slammed the Lone Star Smelter ledger on his desk, it sounded like a cannon shot. "Don't you tell me you can't find a green-eyed, blonde, seven-year-old girl among 10,000 people, when most of them are greasers and redskins."

The Pinkerton man worked nervous fingers around the narrow brim of the bowler clamped between his knees. During his seventeen years with America's most respected detective agency, he had seen a lot. He understood both his clients' and his own objectives, often for better or worse in each instance. Even so, he remained uncertain which side of that often-illusory line Rod Obregon was occupying.

The forty-three-year-old scion of the now deceased, once-powerful Brownsville steamboat magnate Liam Obregon, Rod had married into El Paso's wealthy Gilbert family. The illustrious Gilberts were founders of the smelly, smoky Lone Star Smelter Company.

Apparently, Obregon's beloved wife, the plain-featured Alice Gilbert, may not have been so lovable. Or maybe she had simply not felt lovable? Rod's wife was two weeks buried now. Yet the man with the sharp cheeks and chin, piercing eyes and hawk-like nose, had yet to evince so much as a modicum of grief. Of course, he did have that local reputation for being cold-hearted.

The Pinkerton reports claimed he had largely ignored his wife's presence throughout their marriage. At some point, her predilection for booze became an obvious full-blown craving—so had her addiction to gambling. But to gamble away their own daughter . . . .

Even a stranger would have to credit Obregon for his devotion to their daughter. He was leaving no clue untapped in his frantic efforts to locate her. Just that morning, he put out feelers in El Paso's Chinese community.

Chinese had arrived in El Paso as contract laborers for the transcontinental railroad. Besides laying tracks and ties, the coolies also constructed tunnels connecting their opium and gambling dens. Rumor suggested that the tunnels also connected with Juarez on the Mexican side of the border to foster human smuggling as well.

If that was what happened to Angelica Obregon, better her mother had put the derringer to her daughter's head, not her own.

And if he did not find the little girl, he might as well put a pistol to his own head. Because if he did not, Rod Obregon would.

AUSTIN

APRIL 1891

Seventy-four-year-old Baron Karl von Hesse-Lippe's gaze lingered over each face of the Paladín families crowding his law office. It was standing room only.

Naturally, that monolithic male, the irreverent young Drake, had not bothered to appear for the will reading. Nor had his ward Angel, who surely must feel like she had fallen through a rabbit hole upon her arrival at The Barony.

Karl had suggested that analogy once and she had started at the name of the novel's protagonist, Alice. Then she had turned silent, unusual for the precocious scamp, and vanished for a while among the hacienda's nooks and crannies and The Barony's array of outbuildings.

His firm had handled Barony business affairs for nigh onto half a century, ever since his arrival in Texas. When he emigrated from Germany, he already had been an earnest, albeit optimistic, young man.

And now? Well, now he was merely old. As was the seemingly indomitable Alex Paladín, who, arms folded, watched from one corner. As Niall's best friend, Alex had to know of the surprise couched in the terms of Niall's will. And most likely did Thérèse, seated just in front of her husband Alex, as well.

But did Alex's daughter know? Tara, who ran The Barony Ranch as efficiently—or perhaps more so—as any man? Her long figure, clothed in boots and buckskin skirt and jacket, reposed at one end of the leather sofa alongside her husband. Buck McHenry rarely spoke, but when he did, people listened.

Karl adjusted his wire-rimmed glasses. Time to get on with the will reading. Austin's snail-crawling court system had taken over five months to get the complicated will probated.

"The heart of the will is simple enough," he told the clan. "All net proceeds in Niall Gorman's stock in The Barony Enterprises—namely Gorman Transport—are to be funneled over the next four years to Rafaela Carrera Gorman's personal account."

He kept his gaze from skittering to her lovely aristocratic face. She was not ready yet. He had waited a lifetime for her. He could wait a little longer. But time was clearly running out for them.

With Niall's death, a portion of William Henley's recently published poem had plagued Karl—"Beyond this place of wrath and tears lies but the horror of the shade."

There had to be more to his life than this. For all his scholarly aspects, he was aware of how abysmally ignorant he was about life. He sensed he had squandered it away by playing things too safe, by playing by the rules. All but that disastrous one time.

"During that four-year period" he continued, "the Von Hesse-Lippe Law Firm will continue its administration duties."

He looked up over his shoulder at Max, standing slightly behind him. Dashingly good looking, with longish blond curls in the style of the late General George Custer, Karl's adopted son and law partner possessed a natural flair for managing businesses—and people. He possessed Karl's own caution when it came to risks, even calculated ones. Max went one step farther, though—only banking on shoo-ins and only those that served his own purpose.

Karl cleared his throat, knowing the shocker that was coming, and read in a steady, firm voice. "After which time of said four years and upon the graduation from college of my grandson, Griffin Alexander Paladín, my estate in its entirety is to pass to him to administer, with the provision his grandmother Rafaela Carrera Gorman is to be supported in the manner previously hereto stated."

This time, Karl's gaze homed in on the two riotously red-headed Paladín males—Kerry and his son Griffin, Alex's son and grandson.

Karl had surmised Kerry might be caught off guard but not necessarily displeased by the information that the Gorman portion of The Barony Enterprises, Gorman Transport, had bypassed both Niall's daughter Catarina and Alex's son Kerry.

But it was Griffin's reaction that astounded not only

Karl, but everyone else present, as well.

Absurdly, Griffin looked like a Jack-in-the-box, popping to his feet. "No. Not only no but hell, no." He stalked from the office. His emphatic refusal, so unlike his easy-going personality, startling each of his relatives into momentarily bewildered paralysis.

All but his cousin, Pearl.

SEVENTEEN-YEAR-OLD PEARL PALADÍN was slow to close her lavender-flowered parasol, angled diagonally both to board the streetcar and to shield her identity. She found a seat two rows behind Griffin's orange-red blaze of hair. His "Hell, no!" back in Uncle Karl's office had blazed with the same heat.

She almost missed catching this trolley. Her body's more leisurely rhythms didn't seem to match the fast-paced world beyond Houston's Buffalo Bayou. Too often, her mom complained of her tardiness for classes, for meals, for appointments.

The trolley floated along Austin's only paved street, following electrical wires overhead. Delighted with the ride, Pearl sat in awe of this newfangled mode of transportation. The gentle sway of the trolley, with its clicking and sparking from above, was pure enchantment—much like the steamboats that floated along the twists and turns of Buffalo Bayou.

When the trolley paused at the recently constructed

University of Texas campus, Griffin swung off along with several other passengers. Although reluctant to desert her magic carpet, so did she, keeping a discreet distance from his tall gangling frame.

For a while, he appeared to wander aimlessly along the stone path meandering around the majestic Main Building. With its multiplicity of turrets, it looked to Pearl like a castle. Occasionally, she encountered other students, almost all of them male. Shyly, she would nod before dipping her parasol between herself and them. Then, she would hasten to catch up with Griffin.

At one point, he flipped back the tails of his brown frockcoat and slid onto an unoccupied wrought-iron bench beneath a stately live oak. He fished a notebook and pencil from his matching silk vest. He appeared to be making notations, but she couldn't move close enough to see the pages. She paced a goodly distance, always keeping within sight of his nobly sculpted features.

After about a quarter of an hour, he tucked the pad and pencil back inside his vest pocket. When he hopped on the next passing streetcar, she almost did not make it aboard. A few stops later, he swung off again in front of the Capitol, a new pink granite building towering over the town from atop one of Austin's highest points.

Once again, Griffin repeated his previous action—found a bench, plucked the pad and pencil from his vest, and began scribbling. How odd. She mingled among the politicians and visitors climbing the Capitol's flight of steps. Hovering behind one column, she observed him below.

He was so confident, so at ease with Austin's milieu of wealth and policy-makers. True, she occasionally caught a glimpse of well-off passengers boarding ships at the Galveston wharves. They sometimes disembarked from ocean liners with evocative home ports like Lisbon, Shanghai, and Sydney. But her own fanciful imagination got her no farther than the front door of her parents' modest home, tucked away in an oak-shaded bend of Buffalo Bayou.

Until now. But this imaginative adventure would be one she would pay for dearly when her mom and dad learned of it. Were they still at the Von Hesse-Lippe law offices or already back at Uncle Kerry's stately mansion, where all the Paladíns were staying for the duration? And how long before her absence was noticed among the mass of relatives?

Fifteen or twenty minutes passed, when Griffin abruptly stood up. Pearl's high-button brocade boots fairly flew down the steps to catch up with him. This time, he ignored the trolley, briskly walking several blocks before entering the Driskill Hotel.

Snapping closed her parasol, she too entered the crowded lobby. The hotel was acclaimed as the finest south of Saint Louis. In its open rotunda, she craned her neck to view the domed skylight four floors above.

Slowly, she pivoted, her gaze skimming faces of the rich and the riotous—from women in pearls to men packing Peacemakers. Where had Griffin disappeared to?

Long fingers relieved her of her parasol. "Looking for

me, Cousin Pearl?" She swung around to stare up into Griffin's beautiful face. Her own, not beautiful—by her standards—flushed with guilt. "Griffin," she stuttered, "what a surprise."

He raised a brow, much darker than his flame of hair.

"Yes," she conceded, abashed. "I was looking for you."

"You have been following me. Why?"

"Your grandfather's will . . . I could tell that you were upset with its reading."

He sighed, grasped her elbow with his free hand, and steered her into the dining room, off the lobby. "I would say a High Tea is in order."

"Mr. Paladín, good to see you again, sir." The pompous maître d' inclined his head. "Jules will escort you to your usual table."

Muted conversation and the soft clink of stemware and silverware declared elegance. Her eyes widened. Mounted on the dining room's wood- paneled walls, the gas lamps lit tables draped in pristine white linen. How posh—gas lamps!

His hand still at her elbow, Griffin guided her as a black-liveried waiter led them to a secluded table, graced by a single long-stemmed red rose in a crystal vase. No sooner had she settled onto the chair the waiter pulled out for her, than another waiter appeared holding a tray bearing a tea service and two crystal flutes.

She felt terribly gauche. Would the waiter fill her champagne glass or would Griffin? She pointed toward Griffin's vest. "So, what were you writing about?" She tried to divert his attention from her. The finger sandwiches on the three-tiered stand . . . did she help herself? And those biscuit-looking things . . . ?

"Scones," Griffin supplied, sliding a table knife beneath a scone's doily and depositing it onto her blue Delftware plate. "You will love the cream served here. And, no, I was not writing. I was sketching."

With her the focus of his attention, her absorption with the hotel's refined trappings evaporated. She leaned forward, careful not to place her elbows on the table. Her mother had drummed into her that much etiquette, at least. "Sketching what?"

"Buildings." He waited, apparently expecting her to scoff, before continuing. "Their pure lines . . . their strength and stability . . . their endurance . . . well, I'm fascinated by architecture."

"Show me."

Tentatively, he produced the notepad. While the waiter poured the champagne, she flipped slowly through the pages, studying each, comparing the Capitol and the Main Building's drawings with what she had observed.

Even though he appeared preoccupied with buttering a scone, she could tell he was edgy, waiting for her response. For the first time, trying to express what she was feeling, she realized her lack of education. Perhaps her mother was right in insisting she attend a college.

"Griffin, your sketches . . . inspire me to . . . make me look at things differently."

He relaxed into the spooled-back chair, leaning his weight onto one arm. Enthusiasm for his subject lit his brown eyes. While she lavished strawberry jam onto her scone, he lavished on her phrases like Victorian Gothic, Renaissance Revival, cupolas, Doric columns, spires, and many more terms until her head was spinning.

Noticing her reaction over the rim of his flute, he smiled. "I've overwhelmed you, haven't I?"

The way his mobile lips so easily shifted into a lop-sided smile captivated her. Always had. It was like watching a see-saw. "Are you planning to get an architecture degree?"

What she really wanted to know was how far would his higher education take him from her? Out of Texas? Out of the country? Oh, heaven forbid, no! Bad enough she only got to see him half a dozen times a year at most.

"My father and Uncle Karl want me to get a law degree at Baylor—to be a public servant like they are. But something in me bucks against conformity. I want to build. My way."

Now she relaxed. Baylor and Waco were not so very far away. She took a sip of the champagne. A first for her. It tickled the back of her throat but tasted heavenly.

He scowled, wrinkling his nose, and his scattering of freckles emerged. Gold coins, she had imagined them when she and Griffin had played as children—games like Hide and Seek, Blind Man's Bluff, Cowboys and Indians. Because of her coppery coloring and jet-black hair, she was always designated the Indian.

"As a senator," he growled, "my father's motto is, 'I live to serve.'"

"What do you want, Griffin?"

"I know what I don't want—and that is to manage The Barony Enterprises and its empire."

Bucking Grandfather Alex was unheard of. She said nothing but paid inordinate attention to consuming a second scone she had also spread lavishly with strawberry jam. After a long moment of what for her felt like strained silence, she glanced at him. He was sketching her! She snapped her head away to one side. "No, please don't, Griffin."

"Why not? Pearl, look at me."

Face still averted, she slid him a sidelong glance. "Because I . . . I want to look my best, freshen up."

His pencil continued to skim over the page. "Seriously, Pearl, you are refreshing, as it is." He hooked her a quick grin. "And that smidge of jam just above your lip does add a touch of elegance."

"Ohhh!" she groaned and quickly whisked her napkin at the offensive morsel.

"You remind me of beautiful buildings."

"Buildings!" She grabbed up her flute and downed its remnants. "That is the best you can do, Griffin Paladín?"

"Easy on the champagne, Pearl. Like I was telling you earlier, about a building's pure lines. Its strength and stability. Its endurance. That's how I see you."

"I want you to see me as a desirable young woman." Maybe the champagne had gone to her head.

His pencil skittered to a stop. He stared at her. She licked her lips nervously. "Pearl." His tone was much softer. "We are cousins."

She leaned forward. Her voice sounded raspy in her ears. "I don't care."

He shoved the pad and pencil back in his vest pocket. "I have to get you back. It's getting late."

She threw her wadded napkin on the table. He stood, but before he could pull out her chair for her, she shot to her feet. The gas lamps seemed to multiply, separate, then dance back together. Oh, God, please don't let the champagne make me sick.

But deep inside, she knew it was a soul sickness she was suffering from.

THE BARONY
JANUARY 1892

Feuds and range wars raged throughout the West, but the Lone Star State waged the most—and the Paladins weren't far behind.

Clashes erupted from Civil War biases to cattle rustling, from homesteaders and watering holes to family disputes.

Tara Paladín McHenry was waging her own war and Buck was no help. Not when it came to Claire. Their daughter was close enough to perfection for him.

Moreover, he was war weary. Tara's husband had just returned from Fort Bend County, where a war raged between the Republicans and the Democrats, the Woodpeckers and the Jaybirds. As the election drew close, both parties had armed themselves and began shooting.

Tara's brother Kerry, as governor, had to order in the Texas Rangers.

True, Buck had retired—several times over—from that elite force. And true, with Kerry as both governor and his brother-in-law, Buck could have taken a rain check. But he never flinched from a fight—unless it came to one with their only child. Then he was like putty in his daughter's hands.

Sixteen-year-old Claire, with her dark looks, sun-browned face, and stringent frame, might be a duplicate of Tara, but she had neither Tara's nor Buck's confrontational approach to problems. In fact, it was difficult for Tara to ascertain what was going on behind the girl's serene countenance.

She sat seemingly placid in one of the leather-bound chairs in The Barony's office, once the seat of power and authority of Tara's father and now Tara's own, with Alex Paladín presiding as ruler emeritus.

Right hand lightly resting on the Colt holster at his hip, Buck paced, head down, his shaggy gray hair mingling with his thick gray brows.

"Well, do you agree with me, then? That it's time our daughter spread her wings?"

His old soul blue eyes flicked from Tara's fretting expression to Claire's composed one. "Pumpkin, you've never been addle-headed, but your ma's right about this. West Point gave me a leg up —" he glanced back at Tara with a wry smile, "—at least in recommending me to your ma, and an education would go a long way with getting you through life."

"I have an education, Pa." Her work-gloved hands lay lightly, one atop the other in her lap. Unlike Tara, she did not prefer the overalls and dungarees but just the loose, casual smocks. "Mr. Jamison taught me admirably."

Tara sighed. "Yes, but you need a higher education than what you and our Paladíneños' children received. We are insisting you attend a college this coming year. I don't care where it is or whether it's public or religiously affiliated."

She later thought how that last part of her declaration would come back to haunt their family all too soon.

THE BARONY
JULY 1892

That Sunday, the old coonhound dozed in the shaft of sunlight next to Drake. He sat, knee hiked, on the sawdust and caliche floor of what had once been the blacksmith's domain. The need for ranch machinery repair—windmill blades, carriage springs, even something simple as a gate latch plate— had coopted the smithy and farrier shop into a full-scale machine shop.

Riding the Barony range the week before, he had stumbled across an old, wooden water-well drilling machine. The wagon drill rig had to have been lying in the sand at least fifteen years or more and was so rotted he could barely figure out what it was. Lassoing the unwieldy, four-foot long temper screw, he managed to drag it back.

He puzzled over this elongated, rusted screw. As a kid, he had scaled windmills to help old Diego repair them, so he knew a little about water wells.

But nothing about ink wells. Nor writing and reading—or else he'd be able to decipher what was engraved at one end of the screw link. For him, it was a brain strain.

Despite how hard he had tried in the schoolhouse provided for Barony and Paladíneños offspring, he had fallen far behind even those Spanish-speaking kids, unfamiliar with English. His illiteracy had sparked many a schoolroom fight and later more than a few barroom brawls.

Hell, he could speak his mother's French, the King's English, and *mercado* Spanish but still could not read a simple sentence.

For him, the letters and numbers in the primers disappeared and reappeared in a different order. Sometimes letters and words were never visible to him. But read a passage aloud to him, explain something to him, and he could recall exactly what he had heard months, even years, later.

His illiteracy exasperated his father and worried his mother. When he was younger, he occasionally had heard them arguing about it. One particular exchange, only the night before, would not be one easily, if ever, forgotten by him.

"Our son is not an idiot!" his mother had shouted. "Do not treat him like one."

His father had raged. "I don't. You do. Drake is just

damned lazy because you cosset him."

And then there was always Griffin. Griffin the Golden Child. His half nephew, the same age as he, but leaps and bounds ahead of him in schooling and everything else, for that matter. Griffin knew where he was going and what he wanted and how to get it.

Damn it, there had to be a way to drill for water without the need of a clamp or a temper screw assembly. He returned to tinkering with the screw. As a kid, he could dismantle and reassemble his mother's Singer Sewing Machine as easily as he could a rifle.

His fight-scarred fingers paused. The fine hair at his nape stood on end. Without moving his bent head, his eyes peered out through his hank of blue-black hair that had fallen across his forehead. His gaze roamed from one side of the tool bedecked shed to the other.

Nothing.

Still, his gaze reconnoitered again, this time higher. Past the shed's open double doors. Past its open window and onwards—and back to the window and the giant mesquite outside.

Hanging by her knees from a limb, like a possum with its grinning mouth open, pigtails flopping past her head, the upside-down Angel watched him.

"What the hell are you doing?" Was there no place he could escape the pest? The week before last, she had popped out of the outhouse and scared the piss out of him.

She grinned. She had lost a bottom front tooth since he had hauled her off to The Barony. What a monumental blunder that was. "Waiting on you. You swore."

Only that morning she had hidden his Peacemaker and wouldn't tell him where until he promised to teach her poker. "But not now, damn it. Come here."

Her grin expanded. At once, she did a flip from the limb that took her out of his view. Gravel crunched beneath her running feet and she soon appeared in the open doorway, her fairy's body framed by brilliant sunlight. Despite his mother's best efforts to persuade Angel otherwise, the girl continued to dress in boy's trousers with knee stockings and, today, a middy blouse.

His crooked finger beckoned her, and, delighted, she hunkered beside him. She patted Old Blue's muzzle. "What?"

He pointed at the engraving on the screw. "What are those words?"

She squinched her eyes at the maze of markings, then shifted her gaze to stare up at him. "You don't know?"

"Jesus Christ, just tell me what it says."

"You can't read?"

He could feel sweat beading on his chest. "Do you want to learn poker or not?"

She nodded, sending her pigtails in a frenzied bouncing. "Now. I want to learn today. Don't you put me off, Drake Paladín."

"Then what does it say?"

"Key . . . Keystone . . . Drilling . . . Rig."

"That's all? That's it?"

Her head bobbed again.

He grunted, disappointed. "A card deck is on that shelf over there. Above that long metal table."

She scrambled onto a wobbly wooden stool next to the table. While she stretched to retrieve the deck, he held his breath. She was agile as a monkey. Clambering down, she lobbed the packet to him.

"Sit down opposite me."

She plopped in the fragrant sawdust and sat cross-legged.

He riffle shuffled the worn cards. Jesus, he loved gambling. Walking the edge of life. He'd won his palomino in a game of Spanish Monte with a couple of the Paladíneños. Fortune. Misfortune. It was all the same to him.

"All right, kid, the basics. The cards are ranked from high to low, beginning with Ace, King, Queen, Jack, ten, and so on."

She gave him her innocent gap-toothed smile. "Sort of like Old Maid?"

He swatted at a fly buzzing around his forehead. "I don't know Old Maid. Look, let's just play a round for practice. Matchsticks for chips."

He had planned to go lightly on her, let her win a hand or two. When she took the third one, he realized she had learned at her mother's knee. "You are one hell of a card sharp, Angel."

Beneath those saucer-round eyes, her lopsided grin was more of a smirk.

"Well sharp is not something I can say about you, son!"

Drake's head snapped up. His father, as tall as the door frame, stood silhouetted in the sunlight, arms akimbo.

"But I can say shiftless and self-indulgent."

A furnace heat blasted through Drake.

"Pepe's waiting for you to help him string wire. Now get up and get out there and make yourself useful."

But Drake was already rising—like his temper. His combative stance mirrored Alex's, fist on hips and his full height easily matching his father's. He could break his old man open like a shotgun—and was doing everything he could to hold back.

"Pepe can wait. As a matter of fact, the whole damned Barony can wait for eternity, because that's how long it will be before I lift a finger to help it or you."

He shoved past his father, heading for the stables and his horse. His ears were ringing with his pounding heart, yet he still heard of Blue baying and the girl screaming, "Come back. Drake, come back!"

★★★

ANGEL'S HEART WAS STOPPERED IN her throat and no breath was getting in or out. She sank to her knees in the sawdust and covered her ears, feeling the backed-up blood pounding there like one of those gongs in El Paso's Chinatown. Tears spurted from the corners of her eyes as she doubled forward with the pain.

She was being abandoned all over again. Her father. Her mother. And now Drake.

But no, she refused to believe it. She belonged to him, even if he didn't want to accept the obvious. He would come back for her. She just had to wait for him, as she had patiently waited for him to claim her as his winnings in the Caballo Negro's upstairs room while listening to the strange groaning of the man and woman in the room next to hers.

Arms hefted her from her knees, cradled her against an iron-plated chest. From far away, it seemed, came Mr. Paladín's gruff and oddly nasal voice. "He's not worth crying over, girl."

BAREFOOT, ANGEL SLID THROUGH THE bedroom door's narrow aperture. When she couldn't sleep at night, she would sometimes sneak into Drake's room and lay spread-eagle, face down atop his bed. She was always careful to rearrange the quilted coverlet and restore any items of his she touched to its exact position.

His mother had left everything in his room as it had been the day he left, as if it were a shrine, so in the dark Angel easily negotiated a canvas duster he had carelessly dropped on the floor, as well as an old kitchen water pump he had been tinkering with.

Even though he had been gone three months, when she buried her face in his feather pillow and inhaled deeply, she could still detect the faint whiff of his scent, something both leathery and woodsy.

Light seeped into the periphery of Angel's vision. She

shoved to a sitting position and stared up at Thérèse, oil lamp in hand. Carefully, Drake's mother set it on the stand next to a piled cluster of papers on which Drake had been doodling shapes—boxes and cylinders, triangles and darting arrows—the significance of which made little sense to Angel. Her lower lip trembled. "Am I in trouble?"

"You miss him, too, don't you, *ma petite fille?*"

She nodded.

"So do I. His absence is a hole in my heart that can never be filled." She settled on the bed next to Angel and wrapped an arm around her waist, tugging her into her embrace. "I miss my son something terrible."

"Do you think he'll come back?" Her voice was muffled against the sleeve of the Frenchwoman's silk wrapper. It smelled of jasmine and vanilla and other fragrances Angel could not identify. But they seemed a distant reminder of her own mother.

For a moment, Thérèse was silent. "Not anytime soon, Angel. At least, that is what I hope. My son, he must find his own way in life if he is to be his own man." She looked down at Angel. *"Oui?"*

"Oui," Angel parroted, though she wasn't quite certain she understood all that the woman's response implied.

Thérèse's fingers tipped up Angel's chin. "Tell me, *ma petite fille,* do you miss your father?"

Angel was silent, thinking about this question. She had not been miserable with her father—he was a busy, too often absent man, but, as lonely as she had been, she knew he loved her. It was as if . . . as if, she supposed, she just didn't know him.

Not like she knew Drake Paladín. From the moment her pie-eyed mother had drawn her into the gambling room at the back of the cantina to meet Drake and the others, Angel had known she would belong to him only. She had looked into those bleary eyes, deep with their own pain, and instantly recognized him—had known him since birth—since before that even.

"Can you miss what you never had? I think that my father is like your son . . . he must find his own way in life, before he can be a father."

Tears glistened in the corners of the woman's eyes. She dipped her face to kiss Angel's forehead. "And I think you are a very wise little woman."

She perked up. "Like Jo March in *Little Women*?"

Thérèse's lips crimped in a wry smile. "You are like no other, *ma cher*, so uniquely your own."

EL PASO
OCTOBER 1892

After almost two years, Angelica Obregon's trail had grown cold. Still, the Pinkerton detective continued to sniff out not only his usual sources and suspects but also the unlikely.

That the accomplished and influential Alice Gilbert Obregon had been a habitue of El Paso's discreet and elite underworld gambling society had been unlikely. That she would have crossed the Rio Grande with her daughter to gamble at the Caballo Negro, located in the most dangerous part of Juarez, Mexico, was unthinkable.

Yet, he had been thinking just that—and finally he ferreted out a prostitute who, through a haze of mescal and marijuana, vaguely recalled a woman with a fair-haired child a couple of years before in the rancid smelling *cantina.*

Cantina, in this case, was stretching the propriety of the term. Latrine with accompanying gambling tables and brothel beds would have been more like it. The place reeked of urine where drunken patrons had missed their aim.

He sat at a knife-notched table in one corner, trying to hear the puta's slurred voice over the brassy wail of a strolling musician's cornet. He flicked the musician a Mexican 'dobe to move on and leaned across the table toward the brassy looking woman with her heavily rouged cheeks and lips. She had an artificial rose tucked into unkempt black hair. He felt a fleeting moment of compasssion for this woman who had once been someone's infant daughter.

"*Si, señor,* there was such a woman and a child." Maria ran a grimy fingertip over her filthy glass rim. "But I did not see where they went when the Rake left."

"The Rake? That was his name? No other name?"

The black fringe of her cheap sateen dress swayed with her shrug. "I do not know, *señor.* The men, they do not share much."

"What did this man—the Rake—look like?"

"That was so long ago. Young, I think. Tall." She shook

her fingers, as if they had burned their tips. "And, *hijole,* so good looking."

"Did he have blond hair? Dark hair? A beard? Mustache?"

"I don't know. He wore a hat, I think. Maybe not." Her thickly mascaraed eyes were mine shafts against her sickly sallow complexion. *"Pues, señor."* She nodded toward the back room. "You are interested, no?"

He rose and doled out five more Mexican 'dobes onto the table. "Take the night off, Maria."

Standing outside on the boardwalk, he should have felt refreshed by the drizzle, cleansed of the cheapness that human life sold for in places like the Caballo Negro *cantina.* But he began to wonder if the services he sold were any better.

Discreet inquiries indicated Angelica Obregon was a wild child left too much on her own by neglectful parents. What if the child was better off where she was now?

AUSTIN
JANUARY 1893

The Gilded Age, in twenty-one-year-old Giselle von Hesse-Lippe's humble opinion, this was not.

True, in the era of incredible rapid growth and industrialization, every man possessed the potential to be railroad tycoons like New York's Vanderbilt's and Texas's Paladíns. Also, true—in both New York City and Austin, the opera, the theatre, and lavish parties consumed the ruling class leisure hours.

Why, just this past week, Mrs. Jay Stuyvesant arrived at the von Hesse- Lippe's New Year's Eve party with her dog sporting a $15,000 diamond collar—and Giselle had arrived sporting a yellow jonquil in her honey-gold hair, yellow representative of the suffragette cause.

Meanwhile, women and children worked in factories or sweatshops for far less wages and for many more hours than men.

All while Giselle's mother was sleeping off yet another of her bouts of unpredictable rage.

As a child, Giselle had learned to slip through the great house, as stealthy as an Indian scout, during Ingrid's insane periods—or suffer beatings. School was an embarrassment when Giselle showed up with blood-matted hair or a bruised cheek. Her father's obliviousness was almost as painful.

Not only children of the poor suffered. Perhaps that was why she had felt so much affinity for the child, Angel. To have one's mother pawn you like an amber brooch . . . well, that had to be more devastating than any beatings, no matter how harsh.

Liberation for Giselle first arrived the day she left home to attend the Baylor Female College.

This time, she had been away from her beloved Texas for a year, working for the Parisian daily newspaper, *L'Aurore*. Upon her return the month before, she had been aghast at the state's abrupt changes. Texas had gone from a stage of barbarism to one of decadence, without achieving any civilization in between.

Today, yellow ribbons pinned to the velvet lapels of their Chesterfield coats, she and stout Sally Frommes were leading a dozen other women into the Texas Senate chamber on the second floor, east wing of the Capitol. Their intent was to keep pressure on the state government to promote the causes of all women's rights.

Her idealism envisioned her carrying on a Texas crusade comparable to Elizabeth Cady Stanton's national one. The placard Giselle held aloft said it all.

MEN WANT THEIR RIGHTS AND NOTHING MORE! WOMEN WANT THEIR RIGHTS AND NOTHING LESS!

The short Sergeant of Arms hustled after them. Mouths open, their mustaches quivering in indignation, senators shot up from behind their walnut desks. One old, goateed senator winked as she marched by. Her chin ratcheted up.

The women got as far as the Secretary of the Senate's desk when the Sergeant of Arms caught up with Giselle and grabbed her wrist.

Her placard, shaken loose, slammed directly atop the Secretary of the Senate's balding head. The little man staggered and light from the brass chandelier above danced across his noggin. In horror, she stared at the pimple of blood glistening amidst his pate's beads of sweat.

"Merde!"

A whistle shrilled. A phalanx of brown-uniformed guards poured through the doors. The other suffragettes began screaming. Statesmen hurtled from their desks toward the melee.

"Run," Sally yelled, her arms scooping under the little man's armpits to lift him onto his feet.

One sweeping glance at the horde descending on her was all Giselle needed to whirl and bolt through the nearest door. Reaching the head of the stairs, she tottered and would have tripped over her skirts had not a hand clutched her elbow. Her head spun to behold behind her none other than Griffin Paladín.

"This way!" He yanked her along.

She didn't need any more urging. Along the hallways they flew. Behind her she could hear pursuing shouts. In one office door, out its back door. Around a corner, then down a back flight of narrow stairs. An empty corridor. Then he jerked open another door and pulled her inside, shutting it behind them.

"What? Where?" Her heart was trip-hammering. Her eyes darted around the small room, lit only by a high window.

"Supply Room."

Her gaze swerved back up to his merry one. In response to it—and the frightening chase—she erupted in uncontrollable laughter. She quickly stifled it with a gloved hand.

He looked at her as if he had unearthed an unidentifiable fossil. "Guess we ditched the bad guys, eh?"

He was one of her few male acquaintances who was taller than she. Why had she never noticed how attractive he was? A year older than he, she had always viewed him as the Carrot-top Kid—and more like a cousin. Growing up among the Paladín brood, she felt like they were all cousins. "I thought you were studying law at Baylor."

"I am. I'm interning here during the legislature session—Dad pulled strings. I thought you were working for a newspaper in Paris."

"I was. I heard Susan B. Anthony speak on birth control and that brought me back."

He raised one dark red brow. "Back to Austin to

practice birth control?"

"Only for a short time. And no, not to practice birth control for a short time—I meant back to Austin. For a short time." She had to grin at her flummox. "To campaign for women and children's rights."

He grinned back, and she realized he was still holding her by her elbow. "Do you think it's safe to leave now?"

His gaze darted to her parted lips. "I think it's safer out there than it is in here."

He was wrong, of course.

When he opened the door, reporters' cameras clicked away and flashes flared from their trowels.

THE BARONY
MARCH 1893

"In view of the Wall Street pandemonium, I asked Alex to call this family pow-wow." The Baron Karl von Hesse-Lippe clasped his hands behind him.

He stood with his back to the fireplace in Alex's office. "I won't hedge. The Barony Enterprises is on shaky ground. As legal counsel, I am certainly fearful but not daunted. However, I do think some immediate retrenchment is in order."

The Panic was the worst economic depression the United States had ever experienced. One of the first signs of trouble Karl had perceived had come in February, with the bankruptcy of the Reading Railroad in Pennsylvania.

That Panic—and the ongoing drought—brought hard times that cattlemen and their financial backers had to face.

Seven males filled the room—and Tara, who lounged against the wall, knee propped, her scuffed boot planted against the mahogany panel. As always, Buck was at her side. She was tough, all grit. Buck, older than she by a decade and then some, was her buffer. He allowed her softer side to surface out of anyone else's sight.

Karl's gaze shifted to Griffin. His fiasco with Karl's granddaughter had made The *Austin Weekly Statesman*. "Barons' Offspring Cut a Caper at the Capitol" blared its headline. That was another matter to be taken up later, but not now.

He took off his glasses and appeared to be more occupied in cleaning them with his handkerchief than with the summary he was delivering. "The overbuilding and flimsy financing of railroads that marked our Gilded Age has resulted not only in a series of bank failures but a burst in The Barony's railroad bubble. The expenses The Barony Enterprises incurred in railroad building have outstripped its revenues."

What he was telling them was nothing new. The Panic of '93 had wrapped its tentacles around the entire globe, causing bank failures, a dramatic plunge in crop and silver prices, and mass unemployment everywhere in the world.

But the retrenchment plan Alex and Kerry had in mind was something else. He nodded at Alex, indicating the floor was his.

Alex remained where he was, enthroned behind his

massive desk, Old Blue camped at his boots.

One hip hunkered on the desk corner, his son Kerry sat, obviously irritated. The man was so capable that, unless one noticed his pinned sleeve, it seemed there was nothing he could not do.

Behind Alex, Wade watched, arms folded, his chiseled countenance, as ever, noncommittal. Of Alex's four children, only Drake, the youngest, was missing. With both he and his father notable hotheads, a clash of their strong wills and parting of ways had been inevitable, but no one knew where the kid was.

"Our plan," Alex stated in his no-nonsense, gravelly tone, "simply calls for funneling money from The Barony Land and Cattle Company, which itself is shaky, into our floundering Barony Enterprises—plus some consolidation of management."

Tara straightened, swinging her long brown braid off her shoulder. As not only one-fourth heir to The Barony Land and Cattle Company but also as its ranch manager, this affected her even more than Kerry, Wade, or Drake— none of the three possessed the love for The Barony that she did. "Which means exactly what?" Her eyes, beneath arrow-straight brows, narrowed on her father.

"Kerry?" Karl asked.

Kerry ran a hand through his curling red hair, now streaked with gray at the temples, then focused annoyed brown eyes on his son. "Griffin, your grandfather Niall put you alone in charge of the Gorman Transport. You need to place your education on hold and work with Tara—and

Karl and Max here. You need to focus on Gorman Transport, so it can help get The Barony finances back on solid footing."

Griffin, sitting in one of the two cushioned, cowhide-bound armchairs, had the look of a cornered beast. One parr of Karl felt sorry for Griffin. His creative flair could well be extinguished by the dry, day-to-day grind required in managing The Barony affairs.

A muscle in Griffin's jaw twitched. In his father's familiar gesture, he plowed his hand through his abundant, flame-red mane. "And suppose I refuse? Refuse to take up the reins of my father's business?"

Sitting in the other armchair, Max leaned forward, elegant hands clasped between his knees. Karl had to feel just as much sympathy for his adopted son. Max had married for money and had acquired a madwoman. Perplexingly, at times Ingrid simply sparkled. Karl often wondered if Max regretted his earlier forfeiting of Tara for Ingrid. Obviously, Tara had no regrets with her selection of Buck as her mate.

"You see, Griffin" Max said, "it's not merely a matter of taking over the helm of The Barony's finances. Nor is it a matter of simply penny pinching. It is a matter of settling down."

Griffin hiked one brow. "Do you want to explain that, Max? Settling down?"

Max's light blue eyes were frozen pools. After a pause that was a beat too long, he shrugged. "The Capitol scandal has compromised my daughter's honor."

Griffin glinted at Kerry. "Dad? You're part of this?"

Karl knew if Griffin had asked his grandfather, Alex would have counseled, "Go with your gut." But Griffin's father was altruistic. Like his mother, Fiona, Kerry believed family was everything.

"Giselle is waiting."

"IT IS A NASTY DAY out," Sarita observed. She stared out the triple arched windows Thérèse had ordered installed to provide the hacienda's old but large kitchen with more light.

Outside, the wind raged, lashing the giant live oak on the bluff above and scuttling charcoal clouds across the late afternoon sky.

"I would imagine it is much nastier in Alex's office." Catarina rubbed her elbows and paced the terra-cotta tiled floor.

For as long as Giselle could remember, Kerry's wife had spoken her mind. Giselle admired that characteristic in Catarina and figured she might as well do the same. Nevertheless, her stomach was churning.

"So, shall we lay odds on Griffin's reaction?" She eyed the five Paladín women gathered there in the kitchen. "Does he ride out of The Barony as Drake did or does he come courting me?"

A moment's silence bespoke of the other females' surprise at her forthrightness in addressing the elephant in the room.

"The question," Rafaela's voice was barely a whisper, "is what do you want, Giselle?" At one time, the Spanish aristocrat had almost married the Paladín patriarch. How her heart must be hurting over her Paladín grandson being forced to run the gauntlet in Alex's office.

What I want is to be away from here more than anything right now. But she was determined to see this through. She would not flee from fear or fight, as she had as a child.

She thought of Angel, how the child seemed to take everything in majestic stride. At that moment, Angel was sequestered in the music room, where Claire was teaching her to play the harpsichord.

"The answer to that question, *ma chere fille*," Thérèse interposed, a half-smile appearing beneath her elegantly hewn cheekbones, "should be considered lingeringly over a hot toddy with a French twist."

Here, too, was another suffering mother, her son Drake alienated from the family. Maybe Fiona, The Barony's matriarch, had been egregiously wrong in her staunch creed that land—and family—was everything

Skirting the tiled counter and the stool, where a curiously silent Pearl perched, the Frenchwoman headed toward the far wall. It was covered with hooks from which hung saucepans and other utensils. About one foot from the floor was a strong, broad shelf for heavy pots and kettles.

Taking out one, Thérèse turned to the other women. "Rafaela, if you will brew a cup of cowboy coffee, I shall whip up my concoction, which, Giselle, just might make your mother's current headache vanish."

"Or worsen with a hangover," Sarita quipped, her blue-green eyes dancing below thick, sable brows. Wade's wife could have passed for a decade younger than her forty-six years. "Your potions are mighty powerful, Thérèse."

Giselle knew she herself would fare better if her mother slept off the headache in the bed she had taken to in one of the upstairs guest rooms. "My mother doesn't have to face this. I do. So, give me her serving as well, Thérèse. A double shot should make this pending ordeal even more bearable."

"Ah, *chérie*, you will love my French hot toddy." She was heating the Calvados and apricot brandy with sugar on the large cast-iron stove. "Its lovely warming flavors and herbal, spicy tones—well, they will simply add spice to your life."

"I would say that is exactly Giselle's problem." Pearl finally spoke up. "As of last month, her life became a bit too spiced."

Giselle was surprised by the vehemence in Pearl's usually honey-warm voice. Yet the lovely eighteen-year-old was merely stating what they all were thinking. Giselle slid a sidelong glance at Catarina. "I truly am sorry about . . . about that fiasco at the Capitol with your son."

Pale brown eyes regarded her with sympathy. "'The best laid plans o' mice an' men . . . . '" Catarina's voice trailing off, she shrugged thin shoulders. Her aristocratic Roman nose, so much like that of her mother Rafaela, flared. Without looking at Giselle, Catarina reached out and patted her hand.

Giselle understood Catarina's despair . . . holding out so much hope for her only child's future, which now appeared to have been demolished by both financial crisis, not of Giselle's making, and a social calamity, most definitely of her making. "The meeting should be over by now, shouldn't it?"

"If Karl is in charge," Rafaela spoke almost defensively, "it should go on for as long as need be. He is a stickler for details, which is what has kept The Barony from being broken up, sold off, or sacrificed in the range wars."

"'Buy land and never sell,'" Thérèse said, "has always been Alex's doctrine."

Good advice, as The Barony's acreage was now larger than the state of Rhode Island.

Thérèse poured the liqueurs into six balloon-shaped glasses, added Rafaela's hot coffee, then dolloped a tablespoon of heavy cream over the surface of each. She passed around the glasses. "Shall we toast, *mes chères?*"

"I would wait on the toasting," Griffin growled from the doorway, "until Giselle and I have reached an understanding."

OUTSIDE THAT EVENING, THE WIND howled, seeming to isolate the parlor from the rest of the sprawling, red-tiled-roof *hacienda*. Inside the parlor, the wrought-iron chandelier's candles burnt low and sputtered a smoky wreath. In the beehive fireplace, the red-hot, split logs crumbled and hissed. The distinctly sweet aroma of burning mesquite pervaded the room.

Giselle sat on the edge of the padded wingback chair and cradled the rapidly cooling brandy glass between her palms. The hot toddy's spicy-creamy taste did little to lend her the velvet courage she so badly needed. She detested confrontations and yet, that was obviously the life she was creating for herself, if her demonstrations and protests were anything by which to judge.

Hands knotted behind his back, Griffin paced the old but expensive Aubusson carpet like the caged beast he must feel himself. "It seems we have gotten ourselves into quite a peccadillo."

She cleared her throat. "You are referring, I assume, to the episode in which you rescued me from the Capitol guards?"

He halted with his next step and swung about to face her. "I am referring to the notoriety that resulted from our precipitous actions—yours and mine."

"Is it you . . . or our families . . . that feel this notoriety is a problem?"

He scrubbed the hard ridge of his shadowed jaw. "Look, Giselle, we grew up playing Red Rover and Tag. You and I fished crappies out of the Nueces. We Indian wrestled and—"

"And I always won."

He jammed his thumbs in the pockets of his blue kersey trousers. "That's because your legs were as long as a crane's back then. Anyway, the point is I am not Drake, the

Prodigal Son. I am committed—committed to a belief in myself and what I stand for. Call it blind belief, if you will. But I also believe our lives are bound by common threads of respect and loyalty. I believe we could make something meaningful of this unfortunate incident."

She arched a brow. "Is that a . . . a proposal, Griffin?" She knew she was no beauty, but she had always hoped for something more . . . more passionate. Certainly, more heartfelt.

He sighed, rubbing his forehead beneath the tumble of carrot-colored curls. "Dang it, I said it all wrong, Giselle. What I meant is I find you fascinating and . . . and fun. And challenging. I admire your mind . . . and so easily could come to love you as my wife. That is, if you would accept—" his artful hands made the gesture of a juggler, "—this God-awful bungling at my asking for your hand in marriage."

She supposed her present demonstrations and protests were against her past, surfacing from a childhood spent afraid to speak up for herself. She was no longer afraid. She might want Griffin in her life, but not like this—his coming to her out of duty.

She took a deep draught of the hot toddy. She was glad Thérèse had made it a double. She looked up at Griffin through lids burdened by damp lashes and smiled brilliantly.

"As they say in Paris's *bon ton*, Griffin, *allez te faire foutre*. If you need me to translate the French, this should suffice." Her lips curving sweetly, she rose from the chair and tossed the remnants of her drink on him.

THE BARONY
THANKSGIVING 1893

Old habits die hard. Buck McHenry reckoned, at sixty-nine, both his habits and he were old. Though there was rarely any need for it, he still packed iron—another old habit, this one left over from his years as a Texas Ranger.

The weight of the Colt low on his bony hip, the holster's leather strings girding just above his knobby knee, were nonetheless reassuring. One never knew when you might walk up on a dangerous critter, be it on the range or in Alex Paladín's office. After Alex heard what Buck had to say, he figured the patriarch was gonna be plenty riled.

He rapped on the nail-studded door and, at Alex's bark, entered.

As Buck expected, Angel, decked out in overalls and boots, was scrunched in one of the stuffed wingchairs—reading a swashbuckling novel most likely. Last heard tell, she was toting around some French dude's writings, The *Count of Monte Cristo*. He'd lay odds the book was Thérèse's recommendation.

"The Dime Novels make for better reading, kid." He took up the wing-chair's partner.

Angel dogged Alex's footsteps. Buck figured it was because she felt Alex was her best connection to Drake—if the boy ever deemed it fitting to return to The Barony, which was most unlikely. For his part, Alex appeared merely to tolerate Angel.

Without preamble, Buck turned towards Alex. "I'm here about the girl." She snapped closed her novel. She fixed those innocent gumdrop-green eyes on him. "You heard from Drake?"

He crossed one dusty, spurred boot, worn at the heel and splitting at the seam, over his knee. Nodding at her, he looked at Alex. "Little pitchers have big ears."

Elbows braced on his chair arms, Alex interlaced his fingers and stared over them—first at Angel, then Buck. "If it's about her, then she should hear it, whatever it is."

He shrugged. "A Ranger friend finally tracked down her family."

Her book tumbled to the floor. As he shifted to retrieve it, his can-openers clinked. When he passed the book back, he looked into her eyes and saw the determination there, hard as rock candy.

"Well?" Alex prompted.

"Angel here, Angelica actually, is the daughter of none other than your lifelong nemesis, Rod Obregon. 'Pears his detective has been combing the countryside for her since her disappearance three years ago."

Next to him, he heard Angel gulp and clear her throat.

Alex said nothing, but his face grayed. He could have been a statue, he sat still and silent so long. What could be going through the Baron's mind? Surrender up the girl? Hold her for ransom? Adobe wall her out of revenge?

One never knew what to expect with Paladín. The aristocratic old devil gave no quarter. He was both autocratically opinionated and big heartedly generous.

Yet Mexican-Americans had shady recollections that muttered of filched lands and missing inheritances. When it came to an issue with The Barony and what was his, his lack of scruples was unsurpassed by anyone on either side of the Mexican border.

Well, it might just be a toss-up between the Baron and Obregon.

"I'm not going back," Angel announced, shooting to her feet, chin jutting, and her hands fisted at her sides.

Alex's black eyes nailed the scamp. Many a grown man had cringed under that glare. "I don't think that is your decision."

"Why not, gal? Did your pa mistreat you?"

She shook her head and her pigtails swished across the rigid line of her back.

"Buck!" Alex snapped.

"Now, look, Alex, don't put on your war bonnet. Her feelings should be given some consideration."

"My father is a good man," she interrupted, "but, like I said from the first, Drake won me, and I belong to him."

Scrubbing at his horseshoe mustache, Buck managed to clamp off a snort.

Alex shook his head and groaned. "Hell's bells, girl."

He shifted his bullet stare back to Buck. "Sooner or later, Obregon's detective is going to put two and two together like your Ranger friend did, and the sheriff will be busting down our gate with a warrant for her."

"That's what I'm thinking. With the family all here gathered for Thanksgiving, now would be the perfect time to send her away with her aunt."

"My aunt?" she squeaked. "What aunt?"

GRIFFIN FELT THE "PARABLE OF the Prodigal Son" alluded to him even more than to Drake. It certainly was prowling the back of his mind as he led the so-called biblical fattened calf he had lassoed toward the whitewashed mud-brick houses that made up *La Baroncita,* the medieval-like village of his grandfather's *Paladíneños.*

Under a gray, cloud-scuttled sky, the caliche road followed the mesquite shaded Nueces River that was more of a creek these days.

The tradition of giving The Barony's devoted ranch hands a prime calf the day before Thanksgiving had begun with Grandfather Alex. Though how much longer The Barony could care for its *Paladíneños,* much less evade impending ruin, was in serious doubt.

The last nine months, Griffin had scraped, scrambled, and scratched to keep both its Gorman Transport and its Land and Cattle Company afloat. He had probably made two score trips between his two grandfathers' domains—Grandfather Niall's San Antonio office and Grandfather Alex's The Barony's. Ninety hard miles separated them.

At one time, The Barony had been free of debt. Heavy railroad investment had derailed it. Stock prices continued their downhill slide. Droughts plagued the land and grass was scarce. He had implemented a desperate remedy—culling sick, crippled, and scrub cattle and selling them to the government at savagely sliced prices.

In turn, the government killed the cattle to buoy a depressed market.

He had to hand it to Aunt Tara. Had she not insisted on raising hogs for profit and building the hide-and-tallow works, The Barony would be on the auction block as were so many smaller ranches and farms across America. Fortunately, by tacit agreement, he and she had worked out the touchy subject of management prerogatives. They had established a camaraderie based on both relationship and respect.

He could only hope that his Uncle Wade and Aunt Sarita would be as amenable—as well as their daughter, his cousin Pearl—with the news his grandfather had saddled him with delivering that morning. He knew that for years, both his father and his Uncle Wade had been estranged from the old Baron, but upon Griffin's birth, his grandfather, most reluctantly, had crossed his own line he had drawn in the sand to reunite the family.

God forbid that upon hearing his father's request, bordering upon being a directive, Uncle Wade would balk again, after all this time of armistice.

Uncle Wade and Aunt Sarita rode on either side of Griffin, with Pearl, the lassoed calf, and Old Blue bringing up the rear. That past year and a half, Pearl had all but ignored him at family affairs.

And now he not only graced Pearl's poster of Wanted Dead, forget alive, but also Giselle's. Her wide and temperamental mouth ticker-taped across his mind. He really had a way with women. *Oh, yessiree, I do.*

Leather gloved hands stacked on the saddle horn, he leaned into the brisk wind. "Aunt Sarita, Uncle Wade . . . I have some news for you that might be . . . uhh, a little startling."

Wade turned up the collar of his shearling jacket. "I guess the word 'startling' rules out good news, then?"

"Depends on how you feel about what I have to say." For a beat or two, there was only the creak of saddle leather, the jingle of bridles, and the whinnying of their mounts. Reluctantly, he continued. "Look, there's no use beating around the bush. Aunt Sarita, we have discovered Angel 'Smith' is your niece—Angelica Obregon."

Palm braced on her buckskin's rump, Sarita shifted around to shoot him a blistering glance. "What?"

"She refuses to go back to her father." He tugged the brim's fold of his Stetson downward. "Claims Drake won her, and she belongs to him."

"God almighty," Uncle Wade drawled.

"Seems the worthless strain runs in more than one brother," Pearl spoke up in a dry, withering voice from behind.

So, his cousin still held his adamant rejection of her against him. Good God, as comely as she was, she was still his cousin.

"Pearl!" Sarita admonished, never taking her gaze off Griffin. "You're telling me, nephew, that I am actually this girl, Angelica's, aunt?"

"Yes, by way of your estranged twin, Rod." Hell, were all families pitted with estrangements?

"I would assume the invitation to accompany you today," Wade drawled, "bears direct significance for us on that far-flung relationship?"

He hunched his shoulders, feeling Pearl's eyes scalding the skin between his shoulder blades. "Yeah. Given Obregon's power of influence, it won't be long 'fore his men track Angel—Angelica—here to The Barony. Knowing you're Drake's half-brother, Uncle Wade . . . well, Angel might acquiesce to living with you and her Aunt Sarita for a while. If you'll have the kid."

He was hoping for a 'Yes' from them and dreading a 'No.'

He got neither.

Wade was not a yapper, so his silence was understandable. A long, uncomfortable moment crawled by before Aunt Sarita looked at Griffin. "I haven't seen or heard from my brother in thirty years, not since I ran off with Wade."

Griffin's shoulder blades lowered a little from his ears. "That is what we're counting on—that you won't hear from him."

THÉRÈSE'S CELEBRATED CULINARY FLAIR drew the Paladín clan and its guests from far afield for the annual Thanksgiving dinner. The women clustered in the tiled kitchen, chatting and gossiping as they carried out the tasks Thérèse assigned them.

"Rafaela," she directed, "if you will make the gravy, we can began putting the food on the table. Catarina, get the flour canister down for your mother, *s'il te plait.*"

Rafaela took the ancient wooden spoon that had a flat spot worn on its bottom from stirring and began blending the ham drippings and flour her daughter doled out into the large cast iron skillet.

"Sshhh," Charlotte Solomon whispered at their side.

Rafaela glanced askance at her old friend, their friendship dating from decades before in Matamoros, Mexico. "What, Charlotte?"

The stout woman, her gray hair carelessly knotted in a bun, clutched a small flask to her ample bosom. Her seamed lips stretched into a conspiratorial grin. "Sherry," she murmured, uncorking the glass stopper from the decanter and splashing a generous amount into the simmering red-eye gravy.

"You're doctoring Thérèse's gravy?"

"Don't tell Thérèse or she will have my hide. When she and my brother would have Moses and me over for dinners,

I would doctor her dishes." Charlotte winked. "She got the credit all those years for my secret ingredient."

Catarina feigned shock. "Why Charlotte! And you, a parson's sister."

Smiling, Rafaela passed Charlotte the wooden spoon. "In that case, I shall let you and Catarina complete doctoring the gravy while I flee the kitchen's hellish heat and your wicked sherry fumes."

Untying her apron strings, she draped the ruffled, starched linen across her startled daughter's shoulder and made good her escape.

Dinner would be served soon, but she so needed a moment's respite. As she had helped with the Thanksgiving dinner, the realization fully and painfully washed over her that exactly two years earlier, Niall had died.

In the hallway, Rafaela purposefully circumvented Moses Solomon and Karl, who had driven her in his buggy from San Antonio. The two men were deep in conversation.

She headed for the veranda. A chilly wind swayed the veranda swing, its chains creaking as she sat and began to swing. Just gently, the kind of rocking one does when hugging the body in unbearable grief. Yet it was no longer grief so much as loneliness that assailed her.

In San Antonio, she rambled alone through the sprawling ranch house that had been hers and Niall's, with all its attendant ghosts of memories—unbridled laughter and petty fights and seized moments of lovemaking. With both Niall and their son Jamie dead, Rafaela had only their daughter Catarina. And, alas, Catarina and her husband Kerry lived in Austin, a two-day's ride.

Since Rafaela's grandson Griffin had taken over Gorman Transport and was co-managing The Barony Enterprises, the days her grandson spent at the ranch in Niall's office alleviated her loneliness somewhat.

But a grandson was not the same as a husband. And alleviate was not the same as vanquish. Only one man could rout this longing, this restless yearning. And for all the love and devotion Karl bore her, she suspected his Old-World nobility would never allow him to presume upon their deep friendship.

Yet, there had been that one time . . . .

FOLLOWING THE TRADITIONAL Thanksgiving dinner, the extensive family, amounting to nearly a score, had gathered in the parlor and had even spilled out its double doors.

Mellow would be a good word Claire would use to describe the late afternoon.

Mellow was the music piece, "Beautiful Dreamer," Aunt Catarina was softly tinkering out on the harpsichord.

Mellow was the apricot brandy Claire's parents, Tara and Buck, allowed her to drink for the first time.

Mellow might even describe Giselle's mother, although one never knew when the frowsy blonde Ingrid von Hesse-Lippe might lurch into one of her snippety tirades. Her husband Max usually coaxed his wife to lie down after delivering a draught of laudanum.

What was not mellow were Claire's insides. Rapture was more like it. She took a sip of the nerve-numbing brandy, then stole a glance over her glass's rim from her Windsor chair at David Solomon. He stood behind the oak rocking chair in which his grandmother sat.

The grandson of Charlotte and Moses, who were all visiting that week from Brownsville where they owned a mercantile store, David carried his medium height with a proud grace. This afternoon, he wore a three-piece charcoal suit and Ascot tie with conservative, sartorial elegance. Olive-skinned, with curling russet-brown hair, he had incandescent silver eyes and laughter that was infectious.

Just then, his teeth were flashing white at Giselle. To a group of family member's, she was humorously describing her introductory bout with a bicycle at the Chicago World's Fair.

"My bloomers caught in its spokes and I tumbled head over heels into the Great Basin, camera and all." Exhaling a sinuous eddy of cigarette smoke, Giselle smiled wryly. "I thought my career with *the Austin Weekly Statesman* was over before it had even begun."

Bloomers, bicycles, cigarettes . . . all scandalous for the female and all making the lovely Giselle utterly fascinating. As long as Claire could remember, she had adored and admired the four-year-older girl. Not for Giselle the prerequisite corsets that defined the hourglass figure, immortalized by artist Charles Dana Gibson.

Claire clutched her brandy glass against her chest to

conceal its woefully flat topography.

Residing next to the fireplace, her wine glass on the mantle, her cigarette dangling from between tapering fingers, Giselle went on to describe unimaginable sights: magically glowing bulbs . . . a 264-foot high wheel that revolved more than 2,000 people in boxes simultaneously . . . a moving sidewalk . . . replicas of the *Nina, Pinta,* and *Santa Maria.*

What was unimaginable for Claire was venturing outside the comfort of The Barony with all its inhabitants. Everything she needed was here with her parents.

Or so she thought . . . until David Solomon arrived, the same age as Giselle's twenty-one.

Doubtless, he looked upon her as an infant. He possessed a beguiling quality of being oblivious to his good looks. Nevertheless, there was an air of quiet arrogance about him. And when he talked, his low voice as smooth as her apricot brandy, she couldn't remember listening to someone so knowledgeable.

Well, maybe Giselle.

David's blunt fingers grasped the ears of the rocking chair and gently rocked it for his grandmother, although the robust Charlotte looked strong enough to dismantle the rocker.

David's grandfather, Moses Solomon, much shorter than he and completely bald, hovered protectively to one side of Charlotte, a cheroot in one hand and a whiskey glass in the other.

"I would imagine the bicycle has done more to

emancipate women, Miss Von Hesse-Lippe," David smiled, "than all their marches and speeches and pamphlets."

"Absolutely," Giselle smiled back. "With the bicycle, I have a newfound sense of freedom of movement."

Claire was not sure if it was David or the apricot brandy that made her feel nigh giddy, but, obviously, her cousin Griffin did not share her bliss.

He had been observing both David and Giselle through half-mast lids. "I am quite sure the Great Basin's bystanders," he cut, "appreciated the full view of your newfound sense of freedom. Bloomers and all."

Around the room, eyebrows raised. The pianoforte's music stopped.

Giselle delivered a saccharine smile and purred a stream of smoke toward him.

Around the rooms, those eyebrows raised even higher. Mouths gaped.

That was not like Griffin. To Claire, her cousin represented his name's medieval symbol—the strength of the lion and the wisdom of the eagle. Nor was Giselle's posturing reflective of her down-to-earth, sensible disposition. Whom was this for? Griffin—or David?

Unfolding her stork-like, denim-clad legs, Claire rocketed from her chair. Her gaze swept over relatives and guests alike, garnering their surprised attention. "Well, I admire Giselle's bravery to buck authority and do what she wants."

And that outburst was so unlike Claire. As she stomped from the parlor toward the terrazzo, she could feel the others' astonished stares heating her back.

Outside, just beyond the stone-laid patio, awaited her childhood's imagined castle, the gazebo her Grandfather Alex and old Diego and his son Pepe had built. She looped an arm around one of the gazebo's old cedar posts and pulled into her lungs the chilly but calming air. What a fool she had made of herself.

And what would she make of herself? Was she fated to be born and to die here on The Barony? Was that all? She wished she were like her mother, impassioned about The Barony, but, Claire knew, as capable as she might become in running the famed ranch, her spirit seemed to stand aside and merely observe dispassionately.

She heard a plank creak. Like an owl, her head swiveled nearly one-hundred-eighty degrees to find David, his gray eyes sweeping her from her polished boots to her single braid that had swished over one calico-covered breast. Drat. The one person she wanted to hide from.

"That was courageous." He crossed the wooden planks to gird his shoulder against the far side of her cedar post. "To defend another."

"It was?"

"I would feel honored to have a friend with your courage and loyalty."

She craned her neck to peer around the post at him. "Your friends don't have courage and loyalty?"

He folded his arms. "Most gentiles do not when it comes to speaking in defense of a Jew."

"Oh." An awkward pause. "I didn't know you were Jewish, Mr. Solomon."

"David, please." The way he was watching her made her innards flip-flop. "And does it make a difference, now that you know?"

Mr. Jamison, who taught ten months a year at The Barony's one-room schoolhouse, had described Jews as stingy and Christ killers, but then the strict teacher was unbearably old and just as unbearably opinionated.

Since the Panic of last year, she had heard talk that many blamed the Jews, with their international financial policies, for the collapse of the economy, soaring unemployment, and the failure of farms and ranches.

She shrugged. "I figure our human race must be like cattle breeds—you got your Herefords, your Brahmans, and your Charolais. Each is great at what they're created for. And then you always got a maverick or two like a Longhorn to change up things. It's the mavericks that I kind of cotton to."

He laughed. "I think I'm going to enjoy the rest of this week at The Barony far more than I anticipated."

She blurted, "Do you have to go back to Brownsville so soon?"

She knew his parents had died in the hurricane of '86 that had blown Indianola off the Texas coastline. As the fantastic tale went, at fourteen he had survived when he resourcefully deserted his wind-lashed tree perch, with seawater rapidly rising, to take up occupancy in a horse trough that floated by.

"I'm not going back. I'm heading for Dallas."

"Dallas? Why? Because it is the largest city in Texas?"

"Partially that, partially that race thing you talked about. Ever heard of the Rothschilds?"

She shook her head, feeling really ignorant, especially when compared to the worldly-wise Giselle, who had lived in Europe that past year.

"Let's just say the Rothschilds are a successful—a very successful—Jewish banking family. Generations ago, they started the practice of having family members establish branches in different financial centers. Frankfurt. London. Paris. My grandfather believes in that practice."

"But Dallas is definitely not Paris." But oh, what she would not give to see Paris . . . and London . . . and Rome.

"I agree—although I have seen Paris only once and I have yet to see Dallas. My grandfather believes Dallas has the potential to be the cosmopolitan trade center for the Midwest and wants to capitalize on it early on. He recently acquired a clothing manufacturing plant there that he wants me to manage."

She thought of her family. The Paladíns had distilled a substantial mass of their wealth with the Panic. They were surrendering parcels of land while the Solomon's were acquiring money. "Is it always about money? What do you want?"

He stared out into the gathering autumn darkness and she had the opportunity to observe his strong profile—the aquiline nose and squared-off chin, the half-lowered lids, their thicket of lashes as long as a child's. At last, he slid her a side-long glance. "No, for me it is about accomplishment."

"But doesn't money measure accomplishment? Doesn't cold, hard 'cash' gauge how high you've risen in business?" It was said his Grandfather Moses, who had started out with the small Emporium in Matamoros, had gone on to finance vessels for the Republic of Texas navy, its sum total amounting to a paltry five ships during the navy's apogee.

At that, David's narrowed eyes peered at her over his sharply slanted cheekbones. He smiled dryly. "You make the word 'cash' sound crass. Cold, hard cash. Well, cash is neither cold nor hard. It is soft and warm." The texture of his voice was nigh seductive. "And as to your question regarding what I want . . . what I want is you as my wife, Miss Paladín."

His wife? Her stomach felt like the circus acrobat who missed grabbing the oncoming trapeze bar. He wanted her as his wife? When there was gypsy-exotic Pearl and vibrant, exciting Giselle? She couldn't bring herself to meet his steady gaze. She inspected the gazebo railing's peeling paint. "Why me? Why me as your wife?"

"Why you? Because I need someone with your kind of quiet, steady courage at my side. Because you will need that courage if you marry me. And because you—" his olive-skinned fingers reached for her callused, sun-browned ones that poked at the peeling paint, "—you, Claire, see with fresh eyes, eyes that see the good in people. I need that, Claire McHenry."

Her palm, nestled in his, tingled. Marriage? David Solomon moved that quickly to claim what he wanted? What she wanted, had expected, was something like a romantic courtship from the man she would one day marry. "And why should I marry you?"

At that, his beautiful mouth broadened into a smile, and she realized, like the trapeze artist, she was falling fast . . . and without a net below.

He pulled her clear of the cedar post to which she clung and into his arms. "Because I have been watching you watch me. Because no man will ever make you feel like this when he kisses you." He bent over her, one arm beneath her head, the other around the small of her back, supporting her, and sealed her lips with his, smothering her gasp.

Her lids fluttered closed. The salty taste of his lips . . . the feel of his hand splaying into across her braid to cup the back of her head . . . her body pressed intimately against the length of his. It was both frightening and exhilarating. What riding Chicago's Ferris Wheel must have felt like to Giselle.

Lost in the kiss, Claire skated her palms along his raspy, beard-shadowed jaw. Her heart thumped against her rib cage, demanding to be given away. When he released her abruptly and stepped back, she was deliciously disoriented.

Perhaps he was, as well. He shook his head, scrubbed his long fingers over his brow. "I shall be courting you this week and wanting your answer before I leave."

"I can give you that answer now," a man's voice grated behind them. Her father held the screen door open in one hand, the other rode the ivory grip of his shooting iron.

People claimed she had Buck McHenry's pale blue eyes, but surely hers had never looked that deadly. When he had married her mother, he had left his Ranger days behind, but not his killing ways.

"The answer is no. I will not let me daughter consign herself to hell—either here on earth or in the afterlife—by marrying a Shylock."

"That may be your answer, Father, but it is not mine."

True, she was enthralled with David Solomon, but marrying him without a longer courtship—a romantic courtship, where their love could develop—was not what her heart wanted. Nevertheless, that desire weighed against her father's tyranny. She knew now she had to grasp that trapeze bar swinging toward her and escape the precariously high, isolated platform that was The Barony.

THÉRÈSE STOOD ON THE VERANDA, hugging its cedar post with one arm, waving goodbye with the other. *Merde!* Goodbyes were so damned difficult, especially as she grew older. One knew that the waning years left so little time to rectify earlier years' mistakes—and these had to be two huge mistakes.

She blinked back tears and gulped as she watched Angel—Angelica, she mentally amended—roll away in the surrey with her Uncle Wade, Aunt Sarita, and Cousin Pearl.

There was something about the set of that stubborn little girl's mouth that announced Angel would yet prevail. Thérèse had delighted in having the half-child, half-vixen at The Barony, which sorely needed a revitalization of younger blood. Besides, Angel kept the image of Thérèse's son Drake vividly alive in her heart.

But even worse was watching Claire depart with David, Moses, and Charlotte. Thérèse had helped Tara birth Claire, had cradled her step-granddaughter in her arms before even Buck or Alex got to view the squalling infant.

Thérèse, in all her smug French arrogance, had assumed she could teach Claire how to become *la femme*. Instead, her young step-granddaughter had showed her how to become *du vrai*, the real thing. Totally natural and totally individualistic.

Yes, prejudice was as natural as breathing, and as lamentable. But acting on prejudice was sheer folly. Presenting Claire with an either/or choice was an act Thérèse's son-in-law Buck was probably already regretting, yet too muleheaded to change his ways.

Tara was so distraught at their daughter's enforced choice that, after giving Claire a wrap-around mother bear hug, she had retreated to her bedroom and burrowed in her bedcoverings, refusing to talk further with Buck.

And Thérèse's dear friends, Charlotte and Moses . . . she had known them since she was brought from New Orleans to Matamoros as a sixteen-year-old French bride of a captain in the Mexican army. She understood that the Solomon's had to be hurt by Buck's behavior, although they were too polite to make things worse by confronting Buck's prejudice. Tragically, the couple were most likely accustomed to dealing with prejudice.

Years before, both Wade and Kerry had broken off

relations with the family. Yet time had healed their wounds. If only this time . . . .

From behind, Alex's clever fingers cupped Thérèse's shoulders and drew her back against his solid, protective body. "Come to bed, *mi amore,* " his gravelly voice grated at her ear. "My heart needs your loving and you need my solace."

DALLAS
JANUARY 1894

Dallas had leaped from prairie town to bustling city—bustling, at least, until the Panic last year. And in this new year, Claire likewise was struggling with the leap from the realm of The Barony—that seemingly stretched endlessly in Southwest Texas—to her present habitat, a two-story, unimposing frame mercantile building in Dallas.

Nonetheless, she was glad she had bound herself to David that bleak Thanksgiving Day, five weeks earlier. In a quick civil ceremony performed by an Austin judge, she and David had wedded, before resuming their journey with his grandparents from The Barony to Dallas.

That she wasn't a Jewess obviously made no difference to her husband. David's grandfather Moses had found no problem in marrying Charlotte, the sister of an English Presbyterian parson. If anything, Claire, who had been reared with no particularly structured religious philosophy, admired and respected David's reformed Judaism.

Although he did not adhere to most of the Jewish

practices, not even observing the Jewish Sabbath beginning at sunset on Friday evenings, in their first month in Dallas, he was already rigorously involving himself with the Temple Emanu-El, its rabbi, and its small congregation, many with whom he had started doing business.

He was steeped in his Jewish heritage and thereby sure of himself and his place in the world. Yet she felt as displaced as those historic Jews, with their ancient wounds they prized as medals.

Her own wound was the loss of her large family, all of them, but especially her father, Buck. The choice to break with him had been hers, and as much as she terribly missed him, she could no more imagine life without David than she could imagine the sun failing to rise.

Their bridal night, their first night unaccompanied by his grandparents, had been spent in the dry goods store. David had sold the clothing manufacturing plant to make a down payment on the building because of its prime location. It faced Dallas's turreted red sandstone courthouse on Main Street. Both floors of the dry goods store were packed with inventory from Grandpa Moses's Brownsville Emporium, leaving only the aisle space for her and David to sleep.

Their marriage had not been consummated that first night in the store, because they were hurriedly unpacking and stocking shelves with the freighted merchandise—ranging from saddles and crockery to ribbons and perfumery—for opening of business the next day.

Late that night, they had dropped exhausted and fully

clothed onto the cornhusk mattress wedged between the aisles and slept as if comatose. She awoke, smelling of sweat and dust and morning breath. With the store's opening only an hour off, she silently crept from the mattress to the trunk, a mere few feet away, competing for space with saddles.

As quietly as she could, she began to change, peeling off her knitted stockings, flecked with straw. Next, her fingers flew to her blouse buttons and then her corset's lacing . . . only to pause midway. She looked over her shoulder. Head propped on one fist, David was watching her.

"You have beautiful shoulders." His voice was raspy and his eyes were dark with a languorous look, both of which could come with just awakening.

Yet she felt suddenly skittish. "My corset . . . I was just undoing it."

"You have me quite undone. Come here."

Step by careful step, she approached the mattress, her heart pounding as rapidly as a hand-cranked butter churn.

He reached up a hand and took hers, drawing her down to kneel before him. "You light matches in my mind and under my skin."

"The store opening . . . it's soon . . . we need—"

He grabbed her arms and yanked her down alongside him. "*I* need, Claire. You. Now."

Their coupling was hasty, born out of both their desire for one another and the time restraint, which in turn heightened their lust. Frantic kisses, hands searching, her body welcoming even that first moment of stabbing pain, then surging toward his vigorous, hard-driving thrusts.

Then, all too soon, they were finished, each hurrying to dress again, with the opening only minutes away. Their gazes locked. Her smile was shy, his grin supremely male.

Later, when she found time, she reflected on their fevered, furious mating. Naturally, she was aware that the rutting of The Barony's livestock, while frenzied, was brief, so her untutored body was not shocked by the lack of romance or seduction.

With no courtship, no real knowledge of one another, they were only now learning that delicate see-saw balance the intimacy of marriage required. She and David got along quite well, given that their familiarity with one another was still tantamount to a formality, though nightly refuted by their furtive bedding in the darkness.

Yet a sense of disappointment niggled her. She made excuses. Working seven days a week and all too often into late in the evening, because of the farmers who trudged in after sundown, naturally left them little intimate time and little energy.

Then, too, she did not know how to ask for something she could not even identify. And she sensed that David, also, was still ill at ease with their relationship. But knowing him as little as she did, she had no idea how to remedy it.

If only she could ask Giselle, Claire thought that afternoon, as she stood on the counter stool she had dragged to the store's back wall to hang unpacked bridles. Or Thérèse. Or ask her mother. All three females exuded confidence around the male sex.

Claire had started a letter to her mother about her bafflement with marriage's intimacies and, at a loss as what to say or ask, had thrown her letter into the trash in exasperation.

The door's bell rang, announcing a customer, and she whirled . . . swayed precariously. Only by clutching wildly at a merchandise hook on the plank wall did she maintain her perch. She glanced over her shoulder, expecting the abyss below her—and saw David's upturned, darkly impassioned face—and felt his hands, steadying her stockinged calves.

She gulped. "Oh, it's you."

"Yes," came his voice, unusually husky, "your husband." Slowly, his hands rose farther, rustling the single petticoat beneath her long narrow skirt to clasp behind her knees. "And a man. A man needing your love." His fingertips kneaded the indentures there.

"You have that." She was uneasy. She sensed something more, something inexplicable, was expected of her, though there was another reason for her uneasiness. The way her stomach was free-falling again, with no trapeze bar in sight—it was a feeling that was a heady combination of both excitement and fear. Fear of the unknown . . . for David was the unknown.

"No, I don't." His arms locked around each leg, and his fingers climbed above her knees and tunneled under her long drawers. "I don't have it." He dug his hands into her soft flesh. "Not the kind of love I want." His face nuzzled the tweed fabric of her dress, bunched at the wedge of her thighs. "But I will soon," came his muffled inhalation. His fingers moved higher, to other indentations—the small creases between her thighs and her private place.

She dared not move, fearing his hands would stop their exploration. Her breath rasped, and her nipples tightened. She bit her lip, holding back her gasp of pleasure.

Stroking fingers found her crevice and dipped inside. His mouth issued a low, animal growl against the folds of her skirt. "My God, Claire, you're wet for me."

Her knees buckled. She tumbled into that abyss and his arms caught her, lowered her, and backed her against the wall where he held her captive. While his thumb rotated relentless pressure at the apex of her crevice, harnesses jingled, horse blankets toppled, and hemp rope unspooled over them.

At any moment, a customer could enter—and for all she cared, the customer could wait and watch until her husband finished pleasuring her. The elongated knot of his body thumped against her abdomen in time to the erotic rhythm of his hand. Then, she shattered, and her defenses shattered, as well. His mouth absorbed her outcry. His arms supported her abruptly lax body.

Lashing her waist to his with a length of rope, he whispered against her ear, "I would keep you bound to me forever so that I never need worry you would run back to your Barony."

So that was what had held them at arms distance. "I am not a runner, Mr. Solomon. I'm good for my word." Her groping hands found and looped another portion of the rope around his shoulders. "And I would keep you forever in the prison of my heart."

That night, and the next morning, when she awakened, it was unlike all others. She now knew the ecstasy of two souls as one. She was happier than she had even contemplated being—until that afternoon, when she noticed solemn and serious spectators gathering to watch the ghostly processing of Ku Klux Klansmen marching past the courthouse. The Klansmen, those heroic defenders of white women and civilization, were singing "Onward Christian Soldiers."

Fear's talons grappled her. Tears springing to her eyes, her stomach dropped, and her hands reached out uselessly at a life she had barely just grabbed a hold of.

CONROE'S SWITCH, TEXAS
FEBRUARY 1894

Drake knew the cowboy's days of wrangling had long been over with the encroachment of the hide-ripping barbed wire and the gut-blasting range wars.

As a hired gun for either the cattleman or the sheep raisers around Del Rio, his days would also be numbered. He was lightning-fast unshucking his gun, but there would eventually be someone faster.

Hungry and homeless, he had boxed a couple of illegal matches staged by Judge Roy Bean on a sandbar in the middle of the Rio Grande—while three frustrated Texas Rangers looked on, helpless because of international policy.

But the five-hundred-dollar bank notes per match Drake earned were nigh worthless in view of the cataclysmic collapse of the economy and the U.S.'s return to the gold standard.

He missed his mother's wonderful French meals and his comfortable bed. He had never realized how good he had it. But starving his already too-thin frame on nothing but wheaten biscuits and strong yellow cheese, roasting his brain under a West Texan sun, or freezing his ass in a bitter Texas Norther wouldn't turn his steps back in The Barony's direction.

Rather than make tracks westward from Del Rio, he had nudged his palomino in an aimless easterly fashion. When his cayuse jumped a creek and broke a leg, he had to put it down. For nigh on an hour, he just hunkered there. It had been the closest he had come to tears since he was out of knee britches.

His pockets as empty as his growling stomach, he sought work as a lumberjack in nearby Conroe's Switch, a fledgling town about forty miles north of Houston. Its lumber mill, twenty-five miles out of town in the depths of thousands of acres of virgin pines, was owned by August Jones.

August sat inside the van office, warmed by a pot-belly stove. He was a small, bandy-legged Virginian with a grand goatee and red galluses to support his ample trousers. "Drake Paladín, you say? You any kin to that cattle—"

"Nope."

"Just a saddle bum, eh? You know anything about

lumbering?"

This wasn't going well. He whisked his Stetson across his denim-sheathed thigh. "I grew up on the plains of southwest Texas, so if they aren't mesquite, I know diddly squat about trees. Still, I'm handy with an axe. Split many a fire log."

But lumber camps, isolated deep in Grimm-fairytale-like forests, were something else.

August wedged his pencil behind his ear and fished a battered card deck from a lower drawer of the desk. "I'm a gambling man, Paladín. High card draw—you're hired."

A man after his own heart. Drake leaned across the desk, cut the deck with one hand, then drew and flipped over the top card. A Jack of hearts.

"The Knave, eh?" August thoughtfully popped his galluses. Then he took his turn, glanced at the card he had drawn, and grinned. "I win." He tossed his six of diamonds back on the desk.

"But I had the highest card," Drake protested.

"When I pay attention to what the cards have to say," the man stated flatly, "I always win. You're hired. But I warn you, within three months' time you'll be wishing you had drawn the boxcar."

AUSTIN

MARCH 1894

It was time for spring cleaning at the white columned Governor's Mansion.

Trailing her fingertips along the highly polished banister, Catarina could feel its regularly spaced holes—once filled by tacks Kerry had nailed to keep Griffin, six at the time, from sliding down it after cutting his chin during one such escapade.

So many memories made here in the Governor's Mansion over Kerry's interspaced terms—pumping water into the enormous, eight-foot long tin tub that had been Sam Houston's, when governor back in the '50s. Chunking coal into the antebellum home's little iron grates for heat—ineffective, considering its seventeen-foot-high ceilings. Sleeping in Sam Houston's ponderous four poster bed of black walnut, alone, while Kerry was called away to various parts of the state on gubernatorial duties.

And had he slept alone all those times of separation?

Over their thirty years of marriage, she had worked diligently not to let herself think about that one time of separation of which she was certain—most certain—that her beloved had taken to bed another woman.

Catarina rationalized the affair. He had been reeling from the amputation of his arm. He had been drinking. His liquor had been most likely drugged. The woman had been a prostitute at the cantina.

Still, the memory stung like a betrayal.

Excuses. Was that not what her rationalizations were, in

truth?

And then there was the election night he had spent at his headquarters at the Capitol Hill Hotel, waiting for the results—while in the Governor's Mansion, she had nursed Griffin and waited for momentary news of Thérèse's difficult birthing.

For the umpteenth time, Catarina put her gnawing suspicions behind her. Lately, why was it she couldn't remember the pleasant times? Singing hymns at the Methodist Church at 10th—and Kerry's bass voice that couldn't carry a tune in a basket. Evenings at the Millet Opera House, listening to a Shakespeare performance or Lily Langtry sing or John Phillip Sousa play or watching an absurd medicine show.

She knew if she did not let the past go, it would destroy her future.

She went below to meet with the painters and carpenters. The Greek Revival mansion was nearly in as dilapidated state as the Greek's Parthenon. Her First Lady's predecessors had made only patchwork interior upgrading.

Her secretary following behind her, pad in hand, Catarina told the bespectacled spinster, "First on the list, Liz—we need to modernize the bathroom. And we will need to replace the worn furniture in the parlor and library. Get me some pamphlets on rattan furniture."

Statewide editorial columns often took her to task for her tastes that ran to the avant-garde. Nevertheless, the constituents considered an invitation to one of the First Lady's teas like an invitation to Buckingham Palace.

Her secretary of some twenty-years trotted off to Catarina's office and her accumulation of Early Texas artifacts, among them the recent mourning embroideries she had acquired from Chapel Hill. Kerry accused her of being a collector of people. They met her, and they stayed.

She set about directing the workmen waiting in one of the two parlors. Innumerable receptions had been held there and she had done her best to showcase the mansion with warmth and hospitality—and to showcase Kerry. She knew how to sugarcoat her singlemindedness with layers of charm.

But, after all these years, she still didn't know how to charm her husband. At fifteen, losing her brother Jamie to Yellow Fever, she had quickly matured beyond her years. Take charge, she could, but charm? Not Kerry, it would seem.

When it all came down to the bookkeeper's bottom red line, had their relationship evolved into a marriage of convenience?

She felt her doubts, despite the overpowering, knee-weakening passion she still felt when he entered a room. But, then, how could one not overlook the giant?

True, his 6'3" frame had put on a surplus of pounds, his girth not the rock-solid muscle it had once been. His golden locks had receded at the temples, with a cluster of curls in the center to tumble over his forehead. And the weight of worry for his great state had added lines to his face. Yet, it was still a dearly beloved face to her.

She sighed and, passing a window, noted that the bed of

azaleas looked woebegone, like herself.

She would have to remember to have Liz make note of this for the gardener. Three to four times a week, the Governor's mansion was used for receptions, and in good weather, they were held outdoors in garden spaces that would accommodate anywhere from twenty-five to two hundred guests and an area from which Kerry could speak.

Then, too, she needed to address the need for a new concert hall. There were also the fundraiser letters she was writing. She gave city councilmen, congressmen, and newspaper editors no rest. She reminded herself to do something about the orchestra. The strings in Brahms Fourth were a bit ragged.

She never made it back to her office. A glowering Kerry in a matching gray three-piece suit strode through the door, slamming it behind him. Beads of sweat, despite the mild weather, dampened his temples.

"What is it now?" She turned to him with an automatic sympathetic smile.

"Demagoguery!"

"What?" Picking up her gingham skirts, she followed him into the kitchen, where the four members of the kitchen staff prepared reception dinners.

He grabbed the dipper and downed the cedar bucket's fresh water. "I am accused by the Republican National Committeeman as being a rabble-rouser—whipping up the passions of the crowd and shutting down reasoned deliberation. Well, by God, I won't betray my ideology. Not that I am unwilling to cross partisan lines, but, by damn, I am a hawk and—"

She reached up to frame his florid face. He smelled of bay rum men's cologne. "Because of you—and your Paladín forebears—Texas is the empire, geographically and history-ically, that mere men like this dull-witted committeeman could never envision."

He paused to look at her, really look at her. He set aside the dipper and caught her up against his chest, leaving her toes dangling. "Did I ever tell you what a tiresome old woman you are?"

Smiling, she bussed him on the cheek. "Did I ever tell you what a pompous ass you are?"

His wide grin was so warm, so welcoming, that it gave her strength to voice the one doubt plaguing her lately. Inhaling fortitude, she stared deeply into his eyes, watching for any dormant emotion that might surface. Boredom. Denial. Reluctance. "Kerry, if you didn't wear the yoke of governorship . . . would you still . . . would I still . . . . " This was more difficult than she thought.

Setting her back on her feet, he waited, his head canted, his brow furrowed.

She cleared her throat, feeling the sting of tears in the back of it. "Would there be something of value between us . . . you know . . . other than the deep affection nurtured by years of propinquity that long-married couples share." She knew she was rambling and tried again. "I'm not talking about that first flush of romantic love. We're too old for that, but, oh, something more like—"

His hand lapped around her neck and he drew her to

him, leaning down to silence her with a dominating kiss. At first, she was too startled to react and then she was lost to the heady sensation. Her lips parted, and her hands slipped beneath his suitcoat, her arms wrapping around his waist's vest. Avidly, her tongue joined his in that simulated mating of their bodies, straining against one another for fulfillment.

But again, he surprised her, withdrawing to lift his head and stare down into her eyes. His hand slid from her nape to cup her chin. "Know this, Cat. Without you, there is no me." His hand deserted her chin to sweep the kitchen. "All this, the Governor's Mansion, the power the position holds—it's nothing compared to the power you hold over me, my soul. You always have, and you always will."

Crying and laughing, she managed, "Maybe you're not such a pompous ass after all."

CONROE'S SWITCH, TEXAS
APRIL 1894

Long before the morning stars deserted the sky, Drake shouldered his felling axe along with thirty other men on the timber crew. They climbed aboard flatbed wagons bound for sites where selected trees were to be felled, scaled, and cut to transportable size. Then, the trees were loaded on a small tram line that connected to the International Great Northern Railroad running from nearby Crockett to Houston.

The men were divided into gangs—choppers, sawyers,

and skidders. The choppers went in advance, cutting the roads as they proceeded. Of course, there was always danger of falling trees or rolling logs, but this job ranked near the top of danger because of the deadly varmints still inhabiting the area. Naturally, this job was bestowed on new hires.

Taking the lead that first week, Drake swung the broad axe for ten hours a day until he was certain every bone in his body had pulled loose from its joints. Despite the leather Calcutta gloves, his hands blistered and bled. There were no baths, other than washing the hands and face once a day, and often he had to boil his underwear to kill off the vermin.

At the end of the day, he would return to the company's board-and-batten cabin, thirty by sixty feet, and collapse in his tiered bunk. He would be too exhausted to even make his way to the cook's camp dining room. Only the hearty breakfasts of flapjacks, molasses, biscuits, and sausage the next morning preserved his worthless hide.

New hires—greenhorns—were subject to practical jokes. One frigid morning, he awoke to find his long, woolen socks had been stolen off his feet. A goliath of a Cajun with Medusa-brown hair, Monty Gallier, smirked from the neighboring bunk. With one blow of his ham-hock hand, the thirty-year-old Cajun could squash Drake's scrawny six-foot frame as flat as the cook's flapjacks.

Drake said nothing. Just waited for the opportunity to strike back—and strike was what he had in mind when he sighted the three-foot viper, just stirring out of hibernation.

He didn't need to be able to read sign warnings to know. "Red on yellow, kill a fellow. Red on black, won't kill Jack."

His job was both to notch trees to be felled and clear underbrush for the sawyers, with their long, cross cut saws. Monty, and another sawyer, Gimp Tucker, followed a little behind the trail Drake scored. Circumventing the deadly coral snake, he attacked a towering pine whose girth was as large as Monty's.

Within a quarter of an hour, he heard Monty, dragging the crosscut saw through the pine needles, with Gimp's log-pole frame lagging back. Drake paused, wiping the sweat frosting on his temple with the back of his hand while tracking Monty's progress from the corner of his eye. Yep, the Cajun oaf had it coming to him.

The snake made a warning pop' sound. Drake's axe spun head over haft. A split-second later, the snake lay in two pieces. Monty's brown eyes, as big as biscuits, gaped at the snake, then shifted to gape at Drake.

"Couldn't decide which of you two snakes to kill," Drake drawled.

Monty dropped the saw and charged toward Drake.

The sore muscles ridging his shoulders and corrugating his stomach tightened for the wallop.

Instead, the giant clamped his arms around Drake beneath his armpits, hoisted and lobbed him into a mattress of underbrush.

His ears ringing, he rolled to his feet. He shook his head to clear it and shifted into a crouch, prepared for the next onslaught.

The giant grinned wide, displaying a gold tooth. "You gonna make one hell of a lumberjack, *mon ami.*"

The German foreman, Curt Ackermann, known also as a Bible-Thumping Bulldog, did not hold the same opinion. The middle-aged man's tyrannical rule over the camp made the bad work conditions even more grueling. That evening, he stormed into the dining room. "Gimp tells me you purposefully left a coral in their path."

Drake fired a glance at Gimp.

The man's gaze dropped, and his iron fork began shoveling sauerkraut from his tin plate to his loose lips. Word was his kneecap had shattered when a chain snapped holding a log on a skid.

Drake shrugged. "His call." He chewed on the salt pork, waiting for the tirade to come.

"Drake killed the fucker," Monty defended from the far end and opposite side of the long table, astonishing Drake. "That's all that counts."

"You risked lives Paladín," Ackermann snarled. "Your pay's docked this week."

Drake shrugged again. All he needed for the moment was food in his belly and a place to hang his hat—and a woman.

CONROE'S SWITCH, TEXAS
OCTOBER 1894

Deep in the Piney Woods, Sunday was the only day of rest, which meant come Saturday at early candlelight, the lumberjacks staged their hoedowns. Singing, dancing, and roughhousing roared through the camp until dawn.

Drake thought the sight droll—big, awkward men dancing the quadrille or stag dance in pairs to an old, whiny fiddle. A ruddy-faced fellow named Rufus taught him how to play a harmonica he had found and, after that first week, Drake accompanied the fiddler.

But, dance with men? He refused, though he had no need to, since the only female within twenty-five miles, discounting her mother, was twitching her tail at him— Ackermann's daughter, Margie. She was off limits to the men and they knew to keep their distance or end up hog chow for Ackermann. His Bible and his Winchester were his bosom companions.

Generally, a lumber camp's foreman was a married man. His family would occupy a small log cabin close to the rest of the camp, which consisted of the men's bunkhouse, cook's shanty, a large barn, blacksmith shop, and scaler's office, along with a store or van.

The van, managed by Margie, kept a full line of lumbermen's supplies—clothing, boots, Mackinaws, galoshes, tobacco, medicines, and such. A heavy-set, dark-haired girl with just the faintest shadow of a mustache, she braced her forearms on the linoleum-top counter to parade her buxom wares, revealed by her starched shirtwaist, its top two buttonholes open.

Her molasses-brown eyes followed him as he browsed the aisles. "Need something special?"

He shook his shaggy head, thinking he could badly use a haircut. "No."

"When you stop by, you never say much," she called over the high-stacked shelving he passed behind.

"Don't have much to say."

"I'll need your name for the van bill."

"Paladín. Drake Paladín."

"Paladín? You any relations to The Ba—"

"Nope." With the shoulder-swing walk of a brawler, he moved on to the next aisle. He knew he could gear up the charm, could begin sparking her. It had been a long time between women. Still, right now he needed the job more than he needed Margie Ackermann.

He supposed he was just tuckered out. Angel, that little shaver, would call him out on that flimsy rationalization.

He had been too drunk the evening he had won her as a marker to realize the irksome impact she would come to make on his life—like a little sister tagging everywhere. Hell, it couldn't be easy for her either, what with her mother ditching her to take her own life. And, apparently, Angel wasn't that close to her father . . . not if she preferred to cling to Drake like a tick. He wondered if she had found some other hide to attach herself to.

Finished, he mounded on the counter his two selections—the requisite high-top leather boots and a plaid shirt, brightly-colored to be more distinctly seen through the thick underbrush.

Margie whipped out a pre-printed sheet and began hen scratching. When she presented him the bill, he stared at the printed words, trying to make sense of the many shifting and reversed letters.

Her brows drew together over her pug nose. "Is there a problem?"

His studious gaze deserted the print to trip over hers. "I, uh . . . the cost?" Her brows raised. Her ragged nail stubbed at the bill's bottom line. "There. Thirty-two dollars."

"I know that. Uh, what I want to know why it's so much."

"Well, it says right here—" her nail stubbed at the problematic preprinted paragraph, "—that you agree to be charged for your purchases, and when the time arrives for settling up, your van bill will be deducted from your pay."

"With a hefty profit going to August Jones."

She grinned and instantly became pretty. Her roughened palm stretched out to cup his jaw. "You could use a scraper."

His hand clamped over hers, holding it against his stubble. He relished the mere touch of a female after so long without.

"Honey, it's not a razor I need."

"Whatever it is," her voice was a little breathless, "the van can provide it."

At that moment, Rufus opened the van door. She jerked her hand away, but not before Rufus got a glimpse. After that, Drake became known in the men's camp as the Prince of the Pines.

Better than Drake the Rake.

SAN ANTONIO
THANKSGIVING 1894

Late November saw an early freeze, the most intense in South Texas memory. Branches were brittle with the frost and cattle were buried in snow drifts.

In San Antonio, the temperature plunged precipitously and never got above twenty-eight degrees in the days that followed. High winds and freezing drizzle made the long, traditional Thanksgiving pilgrimage to The Barony unthinkable.

Since Griffin was already in town that week, solidifying relationships with the area's businessmen and plowing through the Gorman Transport affairs with Karl, Rafaela invited Karl to join her and her grandson at the ranch house for a small, intimate Thanksgiving dinner. The house servants had been given the holiday off.

"Does Griffin know you have also invited Giselle?" Karl retrieved wine glasses for Rafaela from her eight-foot-tall Dutch oak sideboard.

"I had expected she would come with you," Rafaela hedged, taking the glass he passed her. *The Austin Statesman* had sent Giselle to San Antonio earlier that week to cover the Anheuser-Busch buyout of the Lone Star Brewery.

"At the last minute, Giselle decided to file a dispatch

with the telegrapher at the depot. You know, Rafaela," he teased, handing her another wine glass, "playing the matchmaker is dangerous. Put those two grandchildren of ours in the same room and you might as well strike a lucifer in a powder keg."

If he only knew to what extent she was matchmaking that afternoon.

The bespectacled German nobleman was so tall, so handsome, even at seventy-seven. Yes, his red-hair had faded and thinned, but there was still that fire that burned in his eyes and in his soul. They stood in the dining room, lit only by the dim wintry sunlight sifting through the double-arched windows and the hearth's blazing mesquite fire. So many memories, so many years, and always Karl, her guardian angel.

The years were hurtling her forward much too quickly. She had never been old before—didn't know what was expected of her. She had a feeling it was now or never if their deep friendship was going to evolve into something more than the years had molded it. She prayed that it would be into an amorous affair.

She passed him the wine bottle, and at the touch of their fingers, tried to keep the breathless tremor from her voice. "Open it for me, will you, please? I'll go pry Griffin from the office."

She found her grandson at Niall's old secretary, his forehead, with its vibrant red hair, propped on one palm as his pencil settled the month's books. For an instant, her heart skipped its beat. Blinking just so, it was like looking at

Niall. The Irish Traveler had wooed her with all his wild passion throughout the years of their marriage. Well, through the few times he was not away from home on business.

"Griffin, my pet, dinner is just about ready, and a visitor will be joining the three of us."

He looked up, distracted. "Oh, who?"

From the far end of the hall came the echo of the foyer door closing and Karl's muted voice. She managed a bright smile. "Come along, our guest is here now."

Giselle was shrugging out of her hooded red wool cloak and handing it over to her grandfather's waiting hands. "Why, I would swear, Opa Karl, the ranch and wagon yard have been swallowed up by the cit—"

Trailing Rafaela, Griffin stopped short in the foyer's arched doorway. "Well, if it isn't our roving reporter."

Giselle tidied up loose strands into honey gold hair, casually bundled atop her head in the fashion of the day and oozed a sugary sweet smile. "Griffin, how nice to see you."

Maybe Karl was right, Rafaela thought, as she listened to their grandchildren spar through the dinner. The boxing gloves were donned.

"How did the Lone Star Brewery interview go?" she asked.

"Quite well. Adolphus Busch's investment will funnel much needed revenue into San Antonio's badly depleted coffers."

"So, did your interview include several rounds of complimentary beer?" Griffin's tone was archly civil.

"As a matter of fact, it did. Yesterday, I hefted my mug in a celebration toast along with Mr. Busch." She switched her attention to her grandfather. "When Mr. Busch learned my surname, we became instant friends. He was also born in the Grand Duchy of Hesse, Opa Karl."

Behind his rimless wire-frame glasses, Karl's eyes lit up. "Really? How fascinating. I had no idea Mr. Busch and I shared the same birth place."

Her gaze swept from Karl to Rafaela and settled lastly on Griffin, whom Rafaela had seated strategically at Giselle's right. "I also shared a round of beer with James Wahrenberger. Have you heard of him, Griffin?"

He canted his head, as if considering, but his eyes were narrow and alert, waiting for the next barb. "Can't say I have."

"Well you should have, even if you grew up in Austin. He is the first Texas architect with a professional architecture degree."

"Is that so?" Griffin seemed to show more interest in spearing his Brussels sprouts than her.

"Yes." She smiled coyly. "He not only oversaw the construction for the Lone Star Brewery, but he also designed the White Elephant on Alamo Square, Dr. Kalteyer's Drug Store on Military Plaza, and, oh, yes, the Joske's Building."

Round one goes to Giselle, Rafaela thought. "Would you care for more gravy, Karl?"

"I am surprised the Brewery had any beer left for Wahrenberger, Grandma, the ham is outstanding."

At Griffins jab, Giselle's lips pursed. Her eyes sparked. Rafaela tensed. Beneath the table, Karl discretely placed a calming hand over hers, knotting the napkin in her lap.

The other two, intensely focused on one another, took no notice.

Laying her fork across the rim of her china plate, Giselle settled back in her chair, her elbows on its padded armrests, her hands clasped. "I talked about you to Mr. Wahrenberger, Griffin." Her tone had softened somewhat. "Told him about your interest in architecture, the house you are designing for your Uncle Wade."

Griffin's dark brows shot up.

"He told me to send you around, that he'd like to see some of your work."

From beneath lowered lashes, Rafaela eyed Karl and flashed him a winning smile.

Later that evening, he helped her with the dishes, while in the parlor, Giselle and Griffin ostensibly called a truce and, over brandy, discussed Wahrenberger, architecture, and journalism.

"You may just make it as a matchmaker, after all," Karl conceded. In his brown double-breasted waistcoat and shirtsleeves, he was pumping water for the dirty dishes she was stacking.

She dimpled. "And you may just make it as scullery help."

He took the dish towel she passed him and focused his attention on drying his long hands. "Rafaela, surely you must know how I feel about you. From that first moment I laid eyes on you half a century ago, I knew no one but you could ever hold my affections. Yet you were married to my good friend, and because of that, I have served you with devotion . . . and loyalty."

He looked at her now. "But my heart—and, yes, my body—grow weary of waiting for some sign from you that you love me as deeply as I love you. I sinfully pride myself on adhering to propriety. But tonight . . . am I picking up on signals . . . that you might possibly wish to move past our friendship?"

She gave him a siren's smile. "Fuck the friendship, Karl."

He laughed outright, surprised, she supposed, by her brazenness, but then he surprised her by looping the dish towel around her waist and drawing her to him. His own smile faded, and his eyes darkened with ardor. "Fucking the friendship was not exactly what I had in mind for tonight."

Her heart hammered against her ribs. She could have been a maiden of seventeen rather than a matron of seventy-seven. Her fingers latched onto his waistcoat lapels. Provocatively, she peered up at him threw her lashes. "I have prepared yours and Giselle's rooms for the night . . . unless . . . unless you would rather share mine, Karl."

CONROE'S SWITCH, TEXAS
APRIL 1895

Ackermann kept a tally of the number of logs each team produced. He drove the teams without mercy until the men were used up.

Over the last six months, he had driven Drake the hardest. Often, he forced Drake's team, and the men varied on it, to light flare torches, cups of kerosene on sticks, so they could work through the night.

Drake did not know if Ackermann suspected his daughter was sweet on him, but Drake refused to cave. Over the months, he became an experienced logger, able to notch, saw, and fell a tree, causing the least damage to surrounding timber. In addition, he was initiated into the dangerous work of transporting logs on skids.

Transportation consisted of hitching the ox teams to the ends of the logs, which were then hauled to skidways, where they were hoisted onto runners of a logging sled, and from there were hauled by trams to the railhead.

One afternoon, he happened to be working with Monty and another logger named Crandall, loading the sleds on the skidways, when Crandall's cant hook swiveled loose. Its jagged peavey spike, instead of anchoring into the log roll, buried itself in Monty's left thigh and skewered to his knee.

"Oh, God!" Blood geysered. At the same time, his knees buckled. He would have tumbled from the twelve-foot log roll had Drake not flung himself across him.

"Hold him!" he shouted at the stunned Crandall, while ripping off his shirt. Buttons popped and showered the writhing Monty. A surprising thrust of energy surged through Drake. Gripping the leg of the much larger man, Drake bound his shirt as a tourniquet above the gaping pink flesh.

Ackermann ordered everyone back to work and had Monty transported by wagon to Conroe's Switch.

That night, gloom pervaded the bunkhouse. The men canceled their usual revelry. Drake, sleepless, tossed on his double bunk. Early the next morning, he stopped by the scaler's office, expecting it to be closed but nevertheless hoping someone might be there with news about Monty.

August Jones was sifting through a stack of papers in his back office. He glanced up, jamming his stubby pencil behind his ear. "Come on in, Drake. Heard about the accident yesterday."

"Any report on Monty?"

August's chest expanded, then dispelled a heavy sigh. "What you would expect. The sawbones took off the leg."

Hands planted low on his hips, Drake stared at the puncheon floor. "Shit " Then he glanced back up at August. "My half-brother lost his arm and went on to—" He shifted his weight to his other leg. "Look, I was up all night, wrestling with this . . . this accident with the swinging cant hook. It could have been prevented."

August raised a bushy brow. "Want to explain that?"

He withdrew the pencil stub from behind August's ear, grabbed one of the report sheets and flipped it over. "See, I know the cant hook needs to be movable, but the way it slips sideways is purely asking for trouble."

He bent over the desk and began to sketch. "Now, if you made a rigid clasp to encircle the cant handle, bolt it with the hook on one side, so that it can move up and down, but not sideways."

Both of August's bushy brows rose in twin arches of skepticism. But, studying the sketch, he nodded. "Not a bad idea, son." His thick fingers tugged on his goatee. "I'm impressed. What do you think about catching a ride on next month's rail freight to Houston? See what you can scrounge up to make this improvement."

Houston. Wade's cocky grin and Sarita's jaunty one skittered through Drake's mind. The longing for family was as sharp as the cant hook, yet his gut knotted at the prospect of getting so close he got caged.

EL PASO
JULY 1895

El Pasoans regarded handsome and wealthy Rod Obregon as eccentric. The description amused him—as did his support of the McGinty Club. It was a musical organization of about two hundred members, one of which, the violinist, was his current mistress.

It also amused him to keep a pet iguana in his Sunset Heights mansion, nestled atop the Franklin Mountains. The six-foot iguana, which he had named after his late wife Alice, was squatting alongside the parlor's wingback chair. Its razor-sharp teeth bared, its mighty tail lashed, warning that at any moment it could launch the prehistoric-looking green lizard at the detective's throat.

The man swallowed, clutching his bowler in his lap. "We . . . well, I . . . I have managed to find your daughter, at last, and she is alive."

The detective's features wore the 'Please, don't shoot the messenger' expression. "And?" Rod inquired calmly over steepled fingertips, when for the past five years he had been practically tearing out his hair. He was striving now not to betray his excitement.

"And . . . and she is . . . ." The man opposite him rotated his bowler between quivering fingers. It was difficult to believe that this unimpressive little man held the Pinkerton Detective Agency record for most crimes solved.

"What? She is what?" All sorts of ghastly scenarios had played over and over in Rod's mind, distracting him at the most inopportune times—whether it was addressing the Lone Star Smelter's board or pleasuring one of his mistresses.

Another gulp. "Your daughter resides in the household of Wade Paladín."

Wade Paladín. He had stolen Rod's twin sister Sarita from him—and now his daughter, as well. Rod settled back in his chair, his fingers now laced low across his checkered black vest. Why had he not suspected that all along? Only the Paladíns were capable of carrying out such an interminable vendetta.

And with Angelica his only heir—between his extensive holdings in both West Texas and the Rio Grande Valley— why, she was worth a king's ransom.

"Send a sheriff to get her. A posse, the Texas Rangers— I don't care who—but I want my daughter back. Now."

"Well, that pre—presents another problem, Mr. Obregon. Angelica is over twelve years of age. Thirteen, to be exact. Legally, the choice is up to her. And from discreet inquiries, sh—she is quite happy with the Paladíns."

Rod's eyes narrowed, a trick he had mastered as a kid to conceal his feelings, which his old man had never taken into consideration. And apparently, Angelica did not either. The love and indulgence he had lavished on her, giving her everything . . . everything that she had taken for granted. The pain ripping through his gut at that instant was as razor sharp as his iguana's teeth.

"In fact," the little man went on, "she refuses to leave the Paladín household until one of them—Drake Paladín, who apparently won her as a marker from your wife— returns for her. Your daughter considers herself as belonging solely to him."

Rod could feel the veins throbbing in his neck. His fingers rifled through their clasp. His thoughts spun like a roulette wheel, settling at last on the slot that would be his plan. He considered himself a fair and just man. But, by God, once crossed, he never forgave nor forgot.

"I want a list of every item owned by the Paladíns. Each of them. Down to the last nanny goat and belt buckle and hairbrush. I want to know every loan each of them has taken out. I want the names of both their friends and their enemies. Most of all, I want them alive and suffering for the rest of their miserable lives."

As they had taken his daughter and sister from him, their daughters and sisters would know no respite.

HOUSTON
JULY 1895

Drake swung down off of the International Great Northern's soot blackened coach into the locomotive's puffing steam. He shoved his fingers through his rumpled hair and resettled his Stetson before taking a gander around, trying not to stare like a simpleton.

Lifting cranes at the confluence of the San Jacinto River and Buffalo Bayou soared hundreds of feet towards a cloud-striated sky. Whistling railroad tugs, scows, and barges loaded with cotton, sugar, rice, and lumber jammed the Port of Houston's most important artery of transportation. Even more impressive was the signage on a two-story red brick building farther along the landing.

PALADÍN NAVIGATION COMPANY

An officious man in rimless glasses, wearing a black-and-brown checkered vest and sleeve garters, led Drake past double rows of desks manned by clerks similarly dressed, and admitted him through another door. Wade, boots propped on his desk, held the new-fangled candle-stick telephone in one hand, the other hand pressing the earpiece against his ear. He was shouting into the contrivance.

"Then we shall look forward to seeing you tonight, Mr. Cordova." He jammed the earpiece back onto the switch-hook and shot to his feet. Skirting the desk to grab Drake into a bear hug. "Brother, have I missed you. Hell, the whole damned family has."

Ignoring the remark, Drake stepped back and surveyed Wade—from the polished boots past his three-piece brown suit to the crisply white detachable collar and cuffs. "You're looking mighty good, Wade." He knuckled him in the gut. "Despite a few extra pounds."

"You look like you could use my few extra pounds," Wade drawled. "You're as lean as a bottle of Lone Star beer. What in the hell have you been doing with yourself?"

"Kickin' 'round."

"You have to come to dinner this evening. Plan to stay the night—or longer. Becky's cooking. You remember old Tom and Esther Wheelwright's daughter. Her cooking will add those extra pounds on you."

"Didn't she have a brother?"

"Yeah, Billy. He keeps our barges up and running. We'll also be entertaining a guest. A prominent—and very shrewd—Galveston broker I hope to do business with."

Wade's drawl slowed, if that was possible. "Besides there's . . . uh . . . sort of been a new member added to our household you'll need to meet."

Drake's head canted, waiting. Surely Sarita had not birthed a second child at what . . . forty-five or so? Or maybe Pearl had married.

"I'll ring up Sarita and let her know you're coming. She'll be excited. Always said she was partial to you because you were the renegade of a family of renegades."

The hours spun by with Wade showing him around the office and its operations. "We sold the Bayou Queen and used its profit as down payment on the three barges. I'm aiming to establish a freight yard near the International and Great Northern's pier terminal in Galveston. Tonight, I just have to persuade Nicolas Cordova to work with me. Though only twenty-three, he already owns a seat on the Galveston Cotton Exchange and Board of Trade."

"Looks like you've done well by yourself, despite the hard times."

Wade shrugged the wide shoulders so characteristic of the Paladíns, male and female alike. "With a lot of railroads crippled by the Panic, our barge traffic has picked up. But so have our debts. That's why I'm hoping to plug our leaking debt dyke by aligning with Cordova."

That evening, Becky greeted Wade and Drake at the door of a new two-story home with a four-pillared facade. Drake's nostrils picked up the familiar aroma of freshly cut timber.

"Howdy, Becky." He removed his Stetson and looked around the large foyer with its rose-and-cream, floral-patterned wallpaper and the wide staircase just beyond. "Looks like you're moving up in the world, Wade."

The beautiful woman, her skin as black as polished ebony rook his hat. "Too fast for me to keep up with 'em, Mr. Drake." She wore a gray, trailing skirt and white blouse with ruffled cuffs. For thirty-seven, she was right damned good looking, and he wondered why she had never married.

"Griffin designed the house plans for us. We began building just when the Panic hit, so, as you will notice, we have had to leave rooms half-fini—"

"Drake!" A girl's voice squealed from the top of the landing.

His head swiveled up to the balcony. Surely not . . . but, yes, the summer child-white pigtails swinging wildly above him belonged to none other than the tick he had thought he had gotten rid of.

ONE GLANCE AT HER UNCLE Drake, only a couple of years older than herself, and Pearl thought it was like looking at a younger version of her father. The half-brothers were both long and lanky, with winningly dark good looks.

Memory of Griffin's uniquely flame-haired good looks smote her. Thanksgiving at The Barony could not come quickly enough. It was all she could do to give her attention to the swarthy Galveston broker across the dining table from her.

Of average height, Nicolas Cordova could never be called good looking. Not with his broken nose, a scar slashing one eyebrow, a pugnaciously dented chin, and an upper lip slightly hitched at one end by an old welt. Yet he was stylishly attired in a black dinner jacket with covered buttons no less, matching trousers, a frilled white shirt and black ascot—and, worse, his demeanor was refined and his manners impeccable. The jackanapes.

Her mother had mentioned something about his father being one of the French Emperor Maximilian's loyal Mexican generals. With the overthrow of Maximilian and Carlotta's reign in Mexico, Nicolas Cordova's father and French mother had followed the Empress Carlotta and her royal court to Galveston, where Nicolas had been born.

"I understand you just graduated from Baylor Female College." Nicolas watched her closely over the rim of his wine glass. His fingers were blunt, not tapering and clever like Griffin's, and his knuckles were scarred.

"Yes." She had only consented to attend the college because it was as close to Griffin at Baylor University that she could arrange to get, and then, damn it all, he was abruptly called home to manage Barony business. Oh, God, she knew the feelings she had for her cousin were a sin in the eyes of the world. Yet how did one rip such feelings from the heart?

"Was it difficult living away from home—in the women's dormitory?"

"Occasionally." Especially when she was tardy to classes, a habitual occurrence with her, it seemed. She dipped her soup spoon into the steaming pea soup, preventing further elaboration.

Drake was as monosyllabic as she in his responses to Angel's plying questions. "Did you have to climb the trees?" Her leprechaun green eyes were wide with a mixture of awe and adoration.

The thirteen-year-old had abandoned her braids, leaving her corn silk hair to mantle her thin shoulders, and, for once, was wearing a dress. A bottle green velvet smock with large gigot sleeves and its short skirt falling just below her knobby knees. A wide gold ribbon wrapped around her ribs hinted at burgeoning breasts.

Pearl thought of all her and her mother's fruitless efforts to persuade the ragamuffin to wear a dress—and now this display.

"No." Drake's bunched shoulder muscles straining his ill-fitting brown jacket indicated his work at the lumber mill had to be more strenuous and punishing than he let on.

Easing the diners' strained and stilted conversations, Sarita flashed Nicolas an engaging smile. "Being from Galveston, Mr. Cordova, you may know of the John Sealy Training School for Nurses?"

"Yes, it just recently opened, I believe."

Pearl cringed. She could feel a mother's proud praise coming.

"Our Pearl has received an offer to teach there."

Hoping to escape the attention her mother had focused

on her, she took a drawn-out sip of wine.

"Oh." Nicolas's gaze targeted her once more. "You have nursing experience, Miss Paladín?"

She wanted to groan but managed a polite smile. "I understand that, if I accept this position, the actual curriculum I would teach would be secondary to the students' service in the hospital wards—caring for impoverished patients."

Thankfully, her father rescued her. With a squeeze of her mother's hand, he smiled. "After dinner, my love, we men are planning to hibernate in the study and discuss a little business."

Her mother's delicately rouged lips feigned a moue. "And drink a little sherry and smoke a few smelly cigars."

The scar disfiguring Nicolas's upper lip hiked in a smile. "But the sherry is the best, Mrs. Paladín—Amontillado from Andalusia, Spain. And the Havana cigars just arrived in my warehouse, as well as a shipment of Nestle chocolates from Switzerland. I gave Becky a couple of boxes to distribute after dinner to the ladies of the house."

With the word 'ladies,' his compelling gaze lingered on Pearl. Though he was only three years older, the heart of those dark brown eyes looked as old as time . . . and looked right into her own dark heart, with all its incestuous longing for Griffin.

She shivered.

Later, after the men adjourned to the study for cigars and brandy, and Angel was tucked in upstairs for the night, Pearl's mother retired to read the issue of *Life* magazine that had just arrived, and Pearl retreated to the kitchen.

Humming the popular "After the Ball," Becky was re-shelving recently dried dishes into the sideboard.

Pearl guessed the woman had to be nearing forty, but her cafe au lait skin showed nary a wrinkle. Her wiry ebony tresses were poufed into a lofty pompadour style. Tall and strapping, she was a truly striking woman. "Why have you never married, Becky?"

The woman wiped her hands on her white apron. "Ain't no man can give me what I don't already have."

Pearl settled atop the tall stool adjacent to the sideboard. "And just what do you have?"

"Why, girl, I am my own woman. Got my own money. Got me an education in convent school. Got my family—my parents and Billy and you Paladíns. What more could I want?"

Pearl was nearly as close to Becky as she was her own mother, because with Becky she could talk more frankly. "A man . . . you know . . . spooning with you."

"Had that."

At twenty, Pearl had yet to be kissed even. "You don't . . . uh . . . miss it?"

Becky's gaze had that same distant look she occasionally took on when talking about far-flung exotic places she yearned to see. "Yeah, I do."

Pearl sighed. "Well, I don't guess one can miss what one has never had."

Becky gave her a knowing stare. "You're wrong about that, Miss Pearl."

MAYBE IT WAS BECAUSE HE was in an unfamiliar place for a change. Maybe it was because the mattress was too soft after months on the logging camp's hard bunks, but Drake awoke suddenly, feeling something was awry.

And it was.

Angel was watching him.

The faint moonlight shafting through the window revealed her now dressed in overalls and barefoot. She sat cross-legged in the bedroom's window seat, elbows braced on her knees, her palms cupping her cherubic cheeks.

He propped himself up on his elbows and the bedcovers fell away from his bare chest. "What are you doing in here?" His voice was rough and low.

She folded her arms. "You aren't planning on taking me with you tomorrow when you leave, are you?"

He sighed. "Look, Angel, we've been through this before." Hell, Wade should have warned him at the office instead of springing this surprise on him—that the marker he had won was none other than Angelica Obregon and that, furthermore, the little squirt was now living with his half-brother and the family.

Her capering's could drive a man mad. She was annoying as hell and constantly poking her nose where it didn't belong. Grudgingly, though, he had to admit that he admired her spirit and tenacity.

He plowed his fingers through his rumpled hair. "First off, I can't haul you into a lumber camp. It's all men."

Almost, he mentally amended, thinking of the long, deep kiss he purloined from Margie just before he left. "Second off, I don't want to haul you anywhere. I don't want you. No way. No how. Got it?"

"Yeah. And I also got your gun."

Not again. His gaze arrowed to the nightstand. His holster was empty.

His gaze ricocheted back to the kid. She held his pistol, its barrel pointed at him. "And this time I won't give it back, Drake Paladín. No way. No how. Got it?" In the darkness, her little teeth glinted. "Unless you change your mind and take me with you."

CONROE'S SWITCH, TEXAS
JANUARY 1896

After months of recuperation—and obvious reluctance—Monty returned that Sunday to the lumber mill to collect his gear. The gold-toothed giant now sported an abundant brown beard as wiry as his abundant hair—and sported a crutch propped under his left armpit.

At the sight of Monty, Rufus and Crandall, and several others loafing in the men's cabin called out greetings. Drake dropped both his axe and the whetstone and rose from his bunk at the back of the lengthy cabin. "Well, by God, if it ain't Long John Silver."

Monty hobbled over to him and swiped one mighty arm about his shoulders. "Good to see you, *mon ami!*"

Grinning, Drake stepped back and eyed the pants leg, knotted near the apex of Monty's left thigh, then raised his gaze to meet Monty's merry one. A sham.

He shifted his weight to one foot, braced his hands low on his hips, and cocked his head. "What are your plans, Monty?" Lumberjacking was, of course, now out of the question, as was just about any physical labor.

"Got some family back in Louisiana—on Île Petite Anse. Thought I'd look them up again, scout out the area, you know, 'fore making any decisions."

"Sounds like a good plan." Although Drake pitied the poor fellow, something in Drake yearned to challenge that unknown which Monty was facing.

Perhaps it was lack of blue sky or the lack of heart-stuttering sunsets that was making Drake feel as confined as a jailbird. Or perhaps it was Margie's relentless pursuit of him.

True, he had been a most willing and clandestine part-ner when he had dropped in to purchase a metal file and she had locked the van office door, pinched out the candle, and invited him into the small back room for an all-too-quick hour of pleasuring. But since then, she had hound-dogged him.

It was Sunday, and he could be out and about—and here he hid, sharpening his axe. If the kid didn't kill him for wresting his gun away and then deserting her, Margie would surely kill him with the frenzied pace of her lovemaking.

Monty's sausage-size finger jabbed him in the chest. "I got this feeling, *mon ami*, that you would make a better rambling man than a woods runner." Drake had the same feeling—especially when the cabin door was flung open and a wintery blast ushered in Curt Ackermann. His Winchester was shouldered with Drake as its target. Everyone froze as solid as the San Jacinto River had that past winter.

"You've tainted my Margie, Paladín. Now go down on

your knees and confess your sins 'cause I'm sending you straight to Hell."

Drake's right hand drifted toward the axe on his bunk.

"Touch it," Ackermann snarled, "and you're a goner 'afore you can even blubber the holy name of our Lord an' Savior."

Looking Death in the face, Drake had no resort but to bluff. "Now, listen, Ackermann." His arms spread wide in the universal peace gesture as he took a step forward. "I hold your daughter in the highest—"

Ackermann laid his cheek against the stock and caught Drake in the rifle's sight.

Drake's palms jacked up beside his head. His violently beating pulse hammered in his ears. "Wait. It's not like you think. Margie and I—"

The foreman squeezed the trigger. An eon of time seemed to pass before Drake heard the hollow click of a misfire echo in the deadly silent cabin.

Even as he hurtled the fifty-odd feet separating him from Ackermann, the foreman had pumped the lever, reloading, and was pulling back the trigger.

Only a fraction of a second separated the embedding of the axe dead center of Ackermann's forehead and the bullet in an overhead rafter.

Drake skidded to a halt before the crumpled body, with its head cleanly cracked like an egg. He whipped around. At the back of the room, by his bunk, Monty stood, gold tooth grinning. "Guess we're even, *mon ami*. A snake for a snake."

August Jones was not grinning when he summoned

Drake and Monty to his office hours later—after a burial wagon had hauled away Ackermann's body in a hastily hewn coffin, accompanied by the weeping wife and daughter.

Seated behind his desk, Jones sighed heavily. "It's your utter disregard for consequences that brought this about, son." He braced his palms wide on the ink-stained desk pad and directed a baleful glare at Drake, slumped in a hardback chair alongside Monty's.

Next, Jones's blistering gaze targeted Monty. "I have to report this murder to the Montgomery County Sheriff. If you thought losing a leg was bad, losing your life is even worse."

Drake leaned forward over his clasped hands. "What say we cut the cards, August? I win, I get your mill and Ackermann's death is chalked up as one among many lumbering accidents."

Monty looked askance at him.

August's busy eyes were rising and falling. "And your stake?" he scoffed. "You ain't got nothing, son."

"Actually, I do. When I was in Houston getting your new parts for the cant hook that I designed, I took out a patent on it." No need to tell August that he couldn't read all the words in the form, and that Angel and Wade had to help him. "That redesigned cant hook will be worth far more in years to come, than your timberland after it is deforested. As it is, your mill is barely getting by."

"You don't say?" August's fingers combed his goatee. A long, gut-wrenching moment passed. "A deal." He pulled out the desk's lower drawer and scooped out the playing deck. "As usual, high card wins."

Drake wondered who was sweating more in that little office—Monty, who stood to lose his life, August, who stood to lose his lumber company, or himself, because the patent was all that stood between him and bellying back to The Barony.

It wasn't as if any of his other siblings did what they were told. But it was his inability to perform some of the tasks his father set him to. His mind refused to focus, and his attention would drift.

"Your self-indulgence is lamentable." His father's impatient charge, when at eleven-years-old he had failed to read fully the important instructions on a thresher's oil can and had sent the thresher up in smoke still reverberated in his head. That was why he could not go back.

Ironically, Drake had to prove himself . . . to himself— and do it without his father's approval.

DALLAS

MAY 1896

"I just happen to have a pair of white mousquetaire gloves in stock that I have yet to unpack, Mrs. Bradford," Claire told the banker's wife, who was a few years older and many pounds heavier than she, despite the fact that she was a mother-to-be. "I think they would look lovely on you. Give me just a moment."

Claire clutched the stair railing to pull her bulky body up each step. The gloves were not a stock item but a second anniversary gift from David only that week. A gift they could ill afford. After that visceral march by the Ku- Klux- Klansmen, chanting "Onward Christian Soldiers" two years earlier, the Dallas Emporium had been boycotted.

David struck back by making monthly donations to the various Dallas churches—donations that ate into their meager food budget. Gradually, a few brave and blustering Gentiles patronized the store. Nevertheless, some Dallas businessmen remained unequivocally anti-Semitic.

Still, he had managed to eke out enough to buy the Dallas Emporium's land and building outright. At that moment, he was helping stage a fundraiser for a local orphanage, as well as pushing to bring the Metropolitan Opera to Dallas. His judgment and civic aggressiveness were earning him prestige and respect from the predominately gentile Dallas society.

Yet, the Dallas Emporium still teetered precariously on failure. David was forever figuring out ways to make more money. He had scrimped and scavenged for funds to have a telephone installed and was putting together a mail-order catalogue.

Of course, he could turn to his grandfather for a loan, but David was too proud. They still owed Grandfather Moses for the inventory he had initially given them to stock the store. Only that week, the loan David had applied for had been inexplicably turned down, despite placing the store and its healthy inventory as collateral.

Or she could write her mother for the money in one of the surreptitious letters exchanged between them. But her father would never agree, and David would never forgive her. How wretched that both she and Tara had to place husbands before their own kin.

"Here you go, Mrs. Bradford." Claire smiled, returning with her cherished pair of gloves.

The plump woman's gloved fingers patted Claire's hand. "Despite the fact you are 'in the family way,' you are spectacularly beautiful, my dear."

That was praise Claire greatly needed. With her lanky height and rail-thin frame, she had never considered herself a beauty. As independent as she was, she had always relied on her health and competence. The pregnancy had made her quite ill early on and later, helplessly ungainly.

Instinctively, her hand splayed atop her mounding stomach in a caressing gesture. She was quite certain the baby she carried would be a son, David Solomon, Jr. "Why, thank you, Mrs. Bradford."

"Lila. Please call me Lila. I insist. My instincts tell me you would make a good friend."

When David returned late that night, Claire was already abed and bordering on sleep. He undressed, tidily put away his clothes, and quietly slid into bed, which occupied a small, curtained-off space, along with a dresser, of the upstairs portion of the store.

From behind, he slipped an arm around her waist to palm her distended stomach and whispered at her ear, "Ahh, I feel the babe kicking, my love."

With clumsy effort, she turned into his embrace. How she loved him, loved his inner strength and indomitability. How she gloried in his lean, muscular body, his loving touch, and the clever ways he aroused her, sometimes with only murmured words or a kiss at her nape as her head bent over the store's ledger.

"How did the businessmen's meeting go?" Her words were pillowed by her nose nuzzling his chest's soft, springy dark curls.

He emitted an exasperated sigh. "Not well. The Knights of Labor is boycotting the Stetson Hat Company—and any merchants who sell Stetsons."

"I know better than to ask if you are going to take the Stetsons off our shelves."

"I told the businessmen tonight that to exclude Stetson hats from our establishment would mean I couldn't stock the best of goods and sell them at the lowest prices. Furthermore, I told them that my own self-respect refused to submit to the dictation of our business as to what goods we should purchase or sell."

She pressed a palm against the cool sheath of his chest muscle to raise herself up onto one elbow. Her unbound hair curtained their faces from the window's moonlight and, hopefully, shielded the trepidation in her features. "Speaking of selling, David . . . Mrs. Bradford came in today, asking for a pair of gloves. We need the money . . . uh, she is, after all, the banker's wife . . . uh, I thought it expedient to sell her the mousquetaire gloves."

In the darkness, his eyes were luminous. He was silent

for so long, she feared she had hurt his feelings, but with his next words she realized it was his male's pride she had wounded. "How you must miss the comforts and luxuries of The Barony."

She aligned one hand with his beard-shadowed jaw. "In truth, I only miss you. You are away so—"

She broke off, smelling the smoke. At the same time, David rolled to his feet. "Fire!"

Wispy sulfurous smoke eddied up the narrow stairway. She fumbled toward the edges of their bed. A hand grabbed for hers. Then David was sweeping her up against his chest. She had to be awfully heavy.

Even as he lugged her toward the stairs, the now billowing smoke had thickened. She shrank from the tongues of red fire leaping hungrily from below.

At the bottom of the staircase, he groped his way through the black curtains of dense fumes toward the store's door, so very far away. He was wheezing and coughing. She could feel the heat singing her skin. Her eyes teared and her nostrils stung with each inhalation. Their flesh was bacon bubbling in a frying pan.

And still, David stumbled blindly downward, toward the only door and their only safety . . . until he missed a step and they tumbled.

MURMURING VOICES. A SHARP MEDICINAL odor. Foggy vision that cleared somewhat. David's beautiful face, strained.

Her hand was squeezed. She winced. Feeling pain. Everywhere.

"Claire." His cracked voice reached through the mists as if coming from a tunnel's far end.

She stirred. Her body hurt like she had been bucked from a bronco and then stomped on.

"You are going to be all right, my love." Moisture trickled onto her forehead.

All right? No, something was not right. Her hand fumbled beneath the bedcovering for her abdomen. "The baby?"

Silence. Shouting silence.

"Tell me, David!"

Even if his voice was almost inaudible to her, his bloodshot eyes said everything. "Our baby didn't make it, Claire."

Instinctively, her body wanted to curl into a fetal position, but movement meant pain. Her fingers knotted into the bedcoverings. She had trouble swallowing. She had thought leaving The Barony, leaving her parents, was like dying. But this . . . this was far worse—a living nightmare. She would gladly choose death over this.

SITTING FORWARD ON A PULLED-UP chair, David held Claire's small, narrow hand throughout the night. When he realized he might also lose her, in addition to their baby, he was floored by how important she had become to him in such a short time. Without complaining, she had worked side by side with him to build his dream of a mercantile empire.

What was it she had written in that letter he'd retrieved from the trash that first month of their marriage? *Am I wrong to believe, Mother, that the union between man and wife is the highest one? More important than the one with man and his community? So much of David's time is devoted to his Jewish associates. Should I convert to Judaism in order to be a better wife? But then, a better lover. . . .*

The last word had been slashed out and the letter unfinished. He had pondered that letter over the last two years. While her religious persuasion was unimportant to him, her involvement with his Jewish community was if he was to succeed.

But even those issues were relegated to lesser import by her letter's last word, stricken. Early on, he must have failed her as a lover . . . and suspected he still did. She was always quite willing but reserved . . . as if waiting for some further response from him.

As a twenty-one-year-old, he had experienced little in the techniques of bedding a woman, and even now he was still not clear as to what to expect from his wife. Certainly, not a whore's performance, but a lusty, more uninhibited participation? He only knew he felt inadequate to this wonderful woman who had agreed to marry him.

The romantic aspect of Claire's nature had drawn him to her like a lode-stone. But then, once they were married, it had become . . . what? Childish? Annoying? Lately, even seemingly demanding.

Of course, everyone had ambivalent feelings about their spouse at times. Still, he resolved he would do better . . . if she would just make it through the night. And if the Ku Klux Klan left them alone . . . assuming the Ku Klux Klan was responsible for this latest act of violence.

THE BARONY
THANKSGIVING 1896

Thanksgiving was so mild, a fire was unnecessary.

Thanksgivings, Griffin mused from his observation post near the fireplace's brass firewood bucket, were a train wreck, what with both Drake and Claire alienated from the family.

As usual, the two were the elephants in the parlor. This Thanksgiving, Pearl was even missing, as her teacher's position at the nursing school prevented her absence from work.

True, Giselle was, at least, civil to him, which went a long way toward making the Thanksgiving celebration more bearable. But, damn it, he wanted more than civility from her. He wanted . . . . Damn it!

That afternoon, sitting in the parlor's reupholstered armchairs, she and his father debated on his gubernatorial pardoning of John Wesley Hardin, which she had covered in Huntsville for the *Austin Statesman.*

"Among others, he killed a man for merely snoring!"

Kerry shrugged. "Hardin served seventeen of his twenty-five years, daughter, and while there, he studied theology and law. He was a model prisoner. I could do no less."

Meanwhile, Grandpa Alex, Uncle Max, and other family members discussed the return of the economy.

"With President McKinley's election," Uncle Wade was saying, "the Republican should set things straight after years of Reconstruction."

With two of Paladín Navigation barges being mysteriously sunk and insurance refusing to pay, the last few years had been financially difficult for him and Aunt Sarita.

Grandpa Alex exhaled on his cheroot and smiled drily. "Regardless of the party, Wade, politicians are the second oldest professionals in the world, which shares major characteristics with the first."

Aunt Tara chuckled, which she did not often do these days. Claire wrote home occasionally, Aunt Tara conceded with obvious self-restraint, but her daughter's letters revealed little, mostly about the Dallas Emporium and Dallas itself.

Uncle Buck spit a plug of tobacco into the brass spittoon near the sideboard. "I'm here to tell you that it won't be politicians that restore the economy, but the Klondike Gold rush."

Karl, glass in hand, moved to occupy the center of the parlor's valuable but threadbare Aubusson carpet, and Griffin suspected something was afoot.

Karl paused, his gaze sweeping each person in the parlor, and conversation dwindled. He raised his glass. "I have been most fortunate to be included both as a part of The Barony and its Thanksgiving celebrations for close to half a century or more." At this, he stretched out his palm to Rafaela, beckoning her to join him.

If one could still blush at that age, Kerry's grandmother did. She deserted Giselle's rather plumpish mother, Ingrid—as well as Griffin's mother and Thérèse, both who hugged Rafaela fiercely. Joining the German baron, she placed her palm in his proffered one and bestowed upon him a radiant smile.

"So, the present moment," he continued, "seems like the perfect time to announce that Rafaela has agreed to be my bride."

Shouts of congratulations, Texican war whoops, and applause erupted.

Griffin had his own announcement to make, but he figured that could wait until later.

"When is the wedding?" Max inquired after a sip from his wine glass.

Before either Karl or Griffin's grandmother could reply, a panting Angel hurtled into the parlor, nearly colliding into Sarita. Angel's head swiveled until her gaze found Grandpa Alex. "Coyotes—big ones—they're attacking Blue!"

Griffin, closest to the hallway gun case, grabbed the old Henry from it. Chambering a round, he loped down the hall for the front door and the veranda. Only last week, coyotes had slaughtered three calves. Ripped out their throats and eaten partial hindquarters.

Seventy-five yards away, in the winter-yellow prairie grass, Ol' Blue, tail between his legs, bared his teeth, as he backed slowly toward the veranda. Two snarling coyotes were closing in on him. Rarely did coyotes get that near to the hacienda, and rarely were they that large. Each was as big as Blue, a good sixty pounds or more. Rabid coyotes?

Griffin levered the Henry to his shoulder and fired. The nearest coyote went down. Through the wisp of rifle smoke, he saw the other turn tail. Quickly, he reloaded and got off another shot as the coyote darted into the outlying scrub brush. He thought he may have only winged the coyote's haunch.

Angel lunged past him, her unbound hair flying, and ran the intervening distance to fling her arms around the dog. "Oh, Blue." She pressed her fair head against his black and tan pelt. "Are you hurt?"

Behind Griffin, Giselle spoke up. "Not a bad shot—for a draftsman."

He turned, caught the slight tilt to her lips. "Wahrenberger told you?" He was surprised she would have kept in touch with the architect she had interviewed.

"That he hired you? That you'll be designing the Lady of the Lake Academy? No, it came across the *Statesman*'s tickertape. Congratulations."

Griffin's father, Uncle Wade, Max, and the others were pouring out onto the veranda to gander at the sight. Rifle lugged in one hand, Griffin took her elbow and steered her down its native stone steps and around the hacienda's nearest corner, toward the side patio's tall wrought iron gate.

Bordered by terra cotta pots of shrubbery and flowers, the terrazzo's center featured a three-tiered stone fountain. The lemony-licorice fragrance of still blooming camellias pervaded the secluded nook. He propped the rifle stock against the fountain rim, then propelled her into one of the pigskin chairs. He drew up the other in front of her, seating himself so that only inches separated his dungaree-clad knees from her draping skirts.

Canting her head, she folded her arms over her navy-blue bodice, its corset-like boning as rigid as her attitude. "What is this all about?"

What was it about? Truly? "Us. Our lives together. I have always felt drawn to you, Giselle. I'll admit that pathetic offer of marriage had come out of pressure, out of obligation, if you will. But I've had time to think. I have always been drawn to you. Only you. This offer is coming from me this time."

"What about The Barony?"

"I don't care about The Barony. Aunt Tara and Uncle Buck can take care of it—and find someone to help manage if they need to. I care about you." He clasped her forearms, unlocking them to draw her tapering hands into his larger ones. "You possess a writer's imagination, Giselle, and I realize that you fervently want some knight on a white charger to bust through your heart's walls with declarations of love."

He paused, knowing that whatever he had to say next

better be damned good—and it had to be the truth. His truth. Because if she could not accept him for what he was, then what he wanted with her would never work.

"I am a practical man, Giselle. I don't believe in love at first sight. I believe love is something that grows with time and tears and laughter . . . and commitment and compassion and communication. I feel we are incredibly lucky that we are starting out at this juncture in our lives, when our hopes and fears and strengths and weaknesses can serve as building blocks for a healthy and happy relationship."

As he spoke, one of her brows had been gradually raising, and at this point she broke in, saying quietly, deadly quietly, "A healthy and happy relationship, Griffin?"

He was no fool. He knew he was blundering again, and badly. "Look, Giselle, I know I want you above all other women, because they all pale beside your vibrancy. If I have to pursue you to the ends of the earth to persuade you to marry me—with all my shortcomings—then I will."

The tinkling splash of the fountain muted the outside world. Her gaze dropped, her doe-like lashes concealing whatever it was she was thinking. Gently, his hands pressed hers, unwilling to lose any connection with her, even that of her mind's deliberation.

At last, she raised eyes that flashed. "Your offer is a little too late. While I have certainly developed . . . feelings for you, as well, as you pointed out, Griffin, I am a writer. The bromide that actions speak louder than words is not to be poo-pooed. Your words are eloquent but empty. While you talk, I am taking action. At my own importuning, I am being sent to do a series of articles on the revolution in Cuba."

SAN ANTONIO
APRIL 1897

That warm afternoon inside the Alamo's chapel, eighty-year-old Karl von Hesse-Lippe took to wife the still lovely Rafaela Gorman, also eighty and the Irish Traveler Niall Gorman's widow for nearly seven years.

The wedding was held on that auspicious day that Fiesta San Antonio commemorated the events of the Texas Revolution. The festival had begun when local women, meeting in front of the Alamo and decorating carriages, baby buggies, and bicycles with flowers, began to throw the blossoms at one another. Later that afternoon, when the bride and groom emerged from the chapel, a cascade of flowers would inundate them.

Inside the mission, Wade was serving along with Kerry and Max as Karl's groomsmen, and with the stately and larger than life Alexander de la Torre y Stuart, Baron of Paladín, performing the honor of Best Man.

With eyes glistening, bridesmaids Thérèse, Tara, and Sarita watched as Rafaela bestowed her baby's breath bridal bouquet to her matron of honor, her daughter Catarina. Only Claire and Giselle, somewhere in Cuba, were missing from among the females.

Rafaela then turned and, with a joyous smile, received the chaste kiss of adoration from Karl.

"Grow old along with me," he whispered against her lips, holding their clasped hands against his chest. "The best is yet to be."

"The last of life, for which the first was made," she joined in the quote from Browning's poem breathlessly. All these years of waiting and wanting and reconciling to living out the remainder of her life alone. Karl had shown her differently. His steadfast love with its hope, love and adoration had proven how rich life can grow with the accumulation of years.

With Niall, she had known that kind of irrational young love that soared one high as a kite at one moment and drove one completely insane the next. She knew now you only recognize true love when you are older. When she had been younger, she mostly imagined true love. She felt much calmer about it now, the kind of serenity that came with age, if one was lucky.

Karl drew her hands up to his lips and kissed her knuckles. "'Mine be some figured flame," he finished with Browning's quote, "which blends, transcends them all!"

WITHIN THE CHAPEL'S THREE-AND-one-half foot thick limestone walls, dust motes drifted around the wedded couple like fairy gold dust.

Sarita looked upon the couple and thought the image seemed out of this world, though a lot of things were not of this world—like Sarita's inexplicable and magnetic attraction to her husband. It was just as strong as it had been for the last four decades, when she first set eyes on the cowboy, scion of The Barony Ranch and formidable foe of her father.

Alas, it may even be stronger.

Over that year that followed her first encounter with Wade Paladín, she had used all her feminine wiles—which, in truth were not that numerous, given that she was a steamboat pilot, a manly occupation—to convince him that he was better off marrying his family's archenemy . . . that he was better off with her than without her.

He had willingly done just that—and in doing so, for years he had suffered estrangement from his father, the patriarch of The Barony.

Her husband had forsaken the cowboy's way of life, ingrained in his very breath and blood, to run the river. He had abandoned southwest Texas' vast, treeless horizons and incomparable sunsets for Houston's murky bayous with their overbearing trees. That alone should have convinced Sarita of Wade's commitment and devotion to her.

But throughout that quarter of a century since, despite Wade's commitment and devotion to her, he had yet to say he loved her. And she had too much pride to convince him yet another time that he had quite rightly chosen her for his bride.

Maybe, with aging, she no longer attracted his fancy. Her hair was like the popular song "Silver Threads Among the Gold," except her silver was more a dull gunmetal gray. Her once rosy checks were hollowed now. With child-bearing, her hips were wider, and stretchmarks marred her belly.

Maybe, after all these years, he had grown bored with her. Without the education younger women like their daughter Pearl were receiving these days, maybe Sarita's conversation was not as stimulating. It happened in other marriages—that dissatisfaction that could come from constant propinquity. Like that of Karl's son Max toward his wife Ingrid.

Yet, Sarita still held out hope that Wade did love her, if only because his erotic dalliances with her in and out of their bedchamber still occurred, though not as often as they had when they were young and newly married.

The wedding ceremony concluded, the guests began adjourning outside the mission to attend the reception at the Menger Hotel, within spitting distance. Feeling dispirited—irrationally, she knew—she wandered alone outside. After all, did some people not cry at weddings and celebrate at wakes?

Amidst the crowd, she struggled to open her parasol. Somehow, supremely short of stature as she was, she got tussled among the wedding guests and the carousers attending the Battle of Flowers. The revelers were already rowdy and by evening, would grow quite drunk, and thus the Army National Guard was annually called in to assist.

Like flotsam, she was swept away by the wave of sweaty, boisterous merrymakers toward the Fiesta Flambeau Parade that was preparing to start at sunset. Gone were her pink floral parasol and beaded handbag. Resisting though she did against the human current, the parade's colorful tide bobbled her from the chapel along to the *charreada*.

A centuries old way for landed gentry to prepare horses and riders for war, the *charreada* began about the same date as the Battle of Flowers and had evolved into an equestrian competition. It featured elaborate horse reining, bull riding, and roping skills, much like the rodeos put on by the Paladíneños at The Barony. Only these equestrians were mostly *ricos*.

This year, the *charreada* arena was located on the south bank of the San Antonio River, outside La Villita, the area's original settlement, where the Gorman homestead still stood. La Villita was now populated with European immigrants from Germany, France, and Italy and flourishing with retailers, bankers, educators, and craftsmen.

Sarita was shoved willy-nilly into the crowd gathering for the *charreada* performance. Unable to maintain her footing, she floundered, hands grasping for anything to stay upright.

A mustached gentleman on horseback saw at once her predicament. He was attired in the traditional black and silver embroidered jacket and tightly cut trousers of the Mexican *charro,* the mode worn by the affluent upper classes, especially when on horseback. Leaning down, he swept her up to sit sidesaddle in front of him on his prancing roan.

"You are lost?" he inquired with his heavy Spanish accent.

"And now I am found," she grinned, abashed, while struggling to arrange her cumbersome Gibson Girl rose-colored skirt.

"I understand this lost-and-found thing, I think." His dark eyes peered down at her from beneath his silver concho-studded sombrero. "But you, you are a woman I do not think I would ever understand. Mystery and gold and fire. Aye-aye-aye!" He shook his free hand, as if his leather gloved fingertips had been burned.

Delighted and amused by his blatant flattery, she shifted her weight, turning to tilt her face up from beneath her beribboned chapeau and laugh. She was startled with the passion she saw flaring in the *charro's* dark eyes. He smelled of lavender and sweat. He had to be a good twenty years younger than her fifty, but it did not matter.

He was not Wade—and she was not interested.

"The gal belongs to me."

Both her head and the *charro's* swiveled to look down at the source of the voice. There stood Wade, his balance planted agilely on his back foot, his white gloved hands on his hips. He still wore the wedding attire's black formal cutaway.

The *charro's* hand drifted to his hip and the pistol upholstered there. Having come directly from the chapel,

Wade was unarmed, of course. "You have heard the phrase, *mi amigo,* 'finders-keepers?'"

The crowd milling like mossback cattle around the mounted horseman was unaware of the tension humming so loudly between him, her, and Wade. "I'll settle this dispute." She at once slid forward off the roan.

As if Wade had expected just that sort of reaction, her capitulation, he caught her easily in the loop of his left arm and steadied her on her feet. With a casual two-finger salute next to the narrow brim of his black top hat, he grinned up at the *charro.* "That I have heard. And you, *mi amigo,* have heard the one, 'losers, weepers?'"

Taking one of her gloved hands in his, he tugged her through the crowd toward the path along the tree shaded riverbank. "Catarina said she lost sight of you. We can still make it on time to the reception at the Menger."

She quick-footed it so she could catch up and, blocking his way, turned to confront him. Fists jammed on hips, she seethed up at him. "You haven't asked me what I was doing astride a horse with a *charro's* arm about me."

His head canted, his squared-off jaw tucked in, his thick lashes blinked down at her. "Well, I would reckon he was keeping you from sliding off."

The raw edge of fury rose rapidly in her like molten lava about to blow. "You are not even jealous?"

"Jealous? Why? If I didn't feel I could trust you, Sarita, I would have hit the trail long ago."

Now the hot lava warred with hot tears. "Wade Paladín, in all these years, never once have you told me you loved me!"

Puzzlement knitted the dark slashes of his brows. "I told you the night I married you that I loved you."

"Great God in heaven, that was thirty-five years ago, Wade!"

"Thirty-three by my calculations. And my word should be good enough for you. I shouldn't have to repeat it. Not today, not this week, not the rest of our lives. I'll love you through eternity, Sarita Obregon Paladín. Don't you understand?"

In the distance, celebrants were already lighting booming fireworks. In the river's cottonwoods, the locusts were buzzing—and in the heat of the afternoon, she was slowly nodding and then flashing her laconic husband a satisfied grin. "I understand."

His word was good enough for her.

He held out a gloved hand and she placed her gloved one in his.

★★★

MAX STOOD OFF TO ONE side, Ingrid on his arm, and watched the flower bedecked carriage drive away with the newlyweds, Rafaela and Karl. Max was glad his father had found joy in life's later years.

Was there any hope for himself?

He turned from the jubilant spectacle toward Ingrid, hovering behind him, and collided with Tara. From behind the short, beige veil of her toque hat, she looked up into his bemused face, her own expression startled, then . . . what? Wary? He hoped not. He valued whatever she would give him, even if it was mere friendship.

"Max, so good to cross paths with you and Ingrid here. Buck and I rarely see you these days." With a cordial smile for Ingrid, she stepped back.

He watched her walk away until she was lost in the crowd. The rough-cut cowgirl had turned into a regal beauty.

What a fool he was. Still wanting at his age, nearly fifty-two, the supreme gift of love from someone else, when he himself was not capable of such self-sacrifice. Of such total surrender. Of the compromises such a union demanded. And yet, here he was, making daily, hourly sacrifices, to a wife clearly mad.

Of course, he regretted his choice . . . and Tara's obviously strained marriage offered a glimmer of happiness for him—that potential second chance. To do things over. To make things right in his world.

But there was the greater responsibility of making oneself right. Clearly, he had a lot of work to do on himself in regard to that specific responsibility. Rather than waiting to see if she would ever change, he should be the one changing.

And what about his daughter? He worried terribly about Giselle, off galivanting in Cuba in pursuit of her own goal. She possessed his analytical nature and her mother's vibrancy. He could only pray she did not possess Ingrid's fragility. Both his daughter and he had daily, hourly, tiptoed on eggshells, never knowing what small omission or commission would set off the usually charming Ingrid.

He looked down at her pasty face and patted her gloved hand, agitatedly running up and down his sleeve. She suffered such anxiety in crowds. He still felt something for her, a caring protectiveness, perhaps, but she was long past the point of participating in an active, loving relationship. "Let's go home, my love."

KERRY DIRECTED THE HANSOM CAB driver to the train station and climbed inside. With any kind of luck, he and Cat would make it home to Austin's governor's mansion before midnight.

She moved aside her voluminous skirts to make room for him to settle next to her. "My mother made a beautiful bride, didn't she?"

With a relieved sigh, he flicked loose both his jacket and vest buttons. Either his chest circumference was increasing, or his gut was. But what else could a man of sixty-one expect? He took Cat's gloved hand, gently squeezing her fingers. "And her daughter was an even more beautiful bride."

She leaned her head against his shoulder, her hat's artificial flower's tickling his jaw. She chuckled softly. "That was three decades back. You don't even remember what I wore that night, Kerry Paladín."

He went silent. After all this time, that disastrous night

still haunted him. He might now hold a powerful position as the governor of Texas, but he still suffered at times the cringing memory of the callow groom he had been. A one-armed man who foolishly had equated manhood with virility.

His intuitive wife slipped her hand from his light grasp and slid it down to cup high on the inside of his thigh, its muscle tightening in response to her light touch. Her whisper was just as soft, just as gentle. "Those days are long gone, my love. Cease your worrying."

"It's Rod Obregon I'm worrying about." Which was not entirely a lie. "He's rumored to be bidding on John Rockefeller's Standard Oil. If Obregon succeeds such an alliance on a national scale, there will be nowhere here in Texas safe from his tentacles."

"Ahhh, but an octopus's tentacles can be devoured." He heard her smile more than saw it in the cab interior's dim lamp light as she turned toward him. "And speaking of devouring . . . I am sure you remember the first time I did just that with you."

Before he could fully grasp her intention, she leaned across him to dip her head and nuzzle her face against his crotch. Little electric shocks pulsed through him. When her fingers flicked loose his fly's button, he slumped further against the cab seat's squab and spread his lengthy legs even wider. With luck, the ride to the train station would take longer than usual that evening.

GALVESTON
MAY 1897

Pearl dodged the careening blue-and-white ambulance, drawn by two horses galloping on the crushed oyster-shell paved street in front of the John Sealy Hospital. Built on the outskirts of town, the hospital shared the Gothic looking four-story complex of red sandstone buildings with the University of Texas Medical School.

The weather was balmy, with both the moon and the sun occupying twilight's sky. A salty sea breeze gently stirred the fronds of palm trees lining the boulevard. It was crowded with drays, landaus, and sulkies and even a policeman on a patrol bicycle.

While her students of the first nursing school west of the Mississippi were housed in the Nurses Home, as a teacher she resided in town at Mrs. Linz's boarding house. At that hour of the evening, the streetcars no longer ran. So, med students and young doctors were afoot. The walk was a good thirty minutes, but she did not mind even though her shoulders ached, and her shoes pinched.

Best of all, this particular evening she could use the half hour to ponder over what her response would be to Mrs. Rebecca Sealy, the head of the hospital's Board of Lady Managers.

The hospital founder's widow had cornered Pearl as she was tugging on her gloves, about to leave the classroom. "During your tenure these last two years, Miss Paladín, you have proven to be a most capable, efficient, and responsible teacher."

"Thank you, Mrs. Sealy" She wasn't sure just where this conversation was going.

The director's sparse brows lowered, as did the pitch of her voice, reedy with age. "I met earlier today with the Board of Lady Managers and your name was recommended to replace an outgoing manager. Would you be interested? It would mean a slight increase in salary—as well as in duties, naturally."

Provided the duties did not involve participating in patient care, Pearl could consider the offer.

She had been invited to sit in on a surgery to remove a bullet from the leg of a man shot during an argument in a pesthole called Fat Alley. To locate the bullet, Dr. Morris used an x-ray machine, the first in Texas, which she had urged the Board to order. But before the doctor could complete the operation, she had become violently ill.

Her social life was non-existent, so the time required for the extra duties Mrs. Sealy mentioned was little sacrifice. Certainly, not the kind of sacrifice Giselle was making on behalf of her chosen career as a reporter, somewhere on the revolutionary battlefront of Cuba.

Well, not entirely non-existent. Pearl had also been cornered by a staff intern, a good looking but boring young man who wanted her to have dinner with him one evening.

If her eleven-hour days of teaching did not exhaust her, the intern's interminable monologues most surely would have. True, she was lonely, but compared to Griffin, all suitors fell short, so why bother encouraging them?

"Miss Paladín?"

At the sound of her name, she turned, only just noticing the brougham's pair of chestnuts clip-clopping, heads down, alongside her. She paused. A gentleman with a silver-knobbed walking cane jauntily tucked in the crook of one elbow descended from the stately brougham, its caleche top raised against the remaining sunlight. Only after he removed his straw hat did she recognize that battered face.

Nicolas Cordova.

"I thought that was you." He mounted the high curb and approached her. Dressed in cashmere striped linen trousers that were crisply creased, with matching black and gray vest, a gray sack coat, and a spangled silver cravat, he looked as if he had just stepped off Savile Row.

Their paths had only crossed twice since he had dined with her parents the year before last—once, briefly, at the Paladín Navigation wharf's office she was when going home for a visit.

The other time had been at the broker's office on the Strand, the Wall Street of the South. He and her father were finalizing the deal for the Paladín freight yard. She had been eager to dine with her father afterwards, until she had learned Nicolas Cordova was buying the dinner. She had begged off, pleading fatigue and work the next day.

At both encounters, he had treated her with courtesy . . . almost exaggerated courtesy. On each occasion, she had glanced quickly at his face and would have sworn she caught the mockery in those dark brown eyes, as if he took delight in agitating her.

His powerful fingers settled the straw hat's scimitar of a

brim at a rakish angle. "I am going your way, Miss Paladín. Join me for dinner?"

She tilted her head, her eyes narrowed. "Going my way? How do you know where I am going, Mr. Cordova?"

That scarred upper lip crooked a grin. "I could plead that your father mentioned Mrs. Linz's boarding house, but I believe that in lying one gives away one's power. Dine with me at the Beaches Hotel, and I'll entertain you by telling you everything I know about you."

"That sounds a little scary."

"It should."

"I don't let other people scare me."

"I'm not other people, Miss Paladín."

She was tired and hungry and piqued by his blatant remarks. So, when he took her elbow without waiting for her reply, she let him assist her up the steps into his brougham. Its interior was plush and dim. She sat in the far corner. He settled back, palms comfortably stacked on his cane's gold knob.

She moved her trailing skirts away from his highly polished boots with their sparkling white spats. "So, should I be afraid of you?" The brougham began clattering over the heavy wooden blocks that paved the street in that area. She could breathe in the strength of him and his power—and his danger. At least, to her well-being, and she knew not why she felt this.

His hiked smile was beguiling, and he replied with a cool steadiness. "Only in the sense that what you most wish for is not a wish I would personally allow to be granted."

At that, she blinked. She folded her arms. "Let the entertainment begin, by all means. Just what is it I most wish for?"

"The forbidden love of your cousin, Griffin Paladín."

She straightened, every sore muscle stiffening. "How could you know—" Instantly, she realized she had given herself away. "I told no one. No one but Griffin, and he would never—"

"I know, your cousin is too honorable to ever betray your . . . infatuation."

"Love."

"I cannot imagine why I am interested in a young woman who foolishly insists that occasional propinquity would constitute love. Admiration, respect, pleasure, maybe, but not love."

"I will not let you sidetrack me. Who told you I was in love with Griffin?"

He smiled. "I am not sidetracking you, Pearl, I am enter-taining you."

"I didn't give you leave to call me by my given name."

By that time, the brougham drew up before The Beach Hotel. Four and half stories high with an octagonal dome and painted in broad red and white stripes, the elegant hotel catered to wealthy summer vacationers. On its front lawn, it featured fireworks, high-wire walkers, and band performances. After all, Galveston boasted the nation's second largest per capita number of millionaires, virtually all of whom had made their fortunes in shipping.

He escorted her past the grand staircase, a reading

room, a gentleman's parlor, a saloon, and finally to the dining room, murmurous with conversation. The white-jacketed waiter seated them at a table on the wide veranda. Arbitrarily, Nicolas ordered for them—a seafood dinner beginning with the hotel's famous prawn cocktail, followed by a large platter of oysters.

Once the waiter departed, she leaned forward. "I want to know who told you."

At ease, he inclined back, one elbow braced on the wicker chair's armrest, but his look was attentive, his manner affable. "How can you be oblivious to this panoramic view?"

"Who?"

He shrugged. "I spent many hours with your father, both at his office and your home in Houston. I got to know your family quite well. Angel is astute. She misses nothing."

"Angel would never blab."

He waited until the waiter had filled their wine glasses and left. "She didn't blab. She defended you. When I shared with her that I meant to court you, she sternly advised me to abandon my suit—that I wouldn't stand a chance with you, because Griffin has your heart."

"Oh." That was all she could say. She was at a loss for words. So many questions plagued her. She blurted the first one. "Why haven't you courted me before this?"

"I have been waiting for you to mature enough to know that Griffin is not the man for you."

"And you are?"

He regarded her from beneath impossibly thick lashes.

"I am what you need, Pearl—an anchor to ride out your tempests. However, I am not sure if you are what I need."

"Indeed?" she gritted through a cool smile. She refused to take the bait. Instead, she unlaced the wrist button of her glove, tugged loose each of its fingers, and hoisted her wine glass without waiting for him. "I doubt if you have even a clue to what I need, Mr. Cordova."

Disregarding etiquette, he leaned forward now, braced his elbows on the white linen tablecloth, and moored that pugnacious jaw atop locked knuckles. "I deal in brokering and investments, Pearl. 1 have become very successful at what I do. I know that love is an investment of oneself. Either you are committed to the investment or you are wasting time and money."

A hint of uneasiness prickled the fine hairs at her nape like a faint thrill of danger. "And you think I would make a good investment?"

His steady gaze raked over her—her bare hand, her bare throat, the wisps of hair the Gulf breeze had tugged from her wide-brim straw hat—and returned to her eyes. "Your prejudice lessens your value."

"What?" She sat her glass down, sloshing the wine.

"Admit it," he chided her, "you hold yourself better than the invaders—the Mexican-Americans or, in my case, the Mexican-American-Frenchman."

"Poppycock! I do not!"

"Why? Because we are slovenly? Lazy? Ignorant? My people take jobs your people wouldn't even consider. Most of us are bilingual. Is it because we take advantage of your charity? I confess to that. 1 will take whatever advantage I can to have what I want."

"I am not prejudiced, Mr. Cordova—"

"Nicolas," he reminded her, smiling.

"I pity what your people have gone through, but—"

"That is exactly my point, Pearl. Pity implies you set yourself above the person. When you can feel compassion, then that will most certainly raise your value in my eyes."

"Why, why your arrogance is abominable," she sputtered, tasting the sour defensiveness on her tongue. "And you lecture me about setting oneself above another."

"In the meanwhile, I will entertain you by playing Beast to your Beauty. To be precise, that is how I came about this beastly looking face. I was just coming into mustache growth, maybe fifteen or sixteen, when I became infatuated with the lovely Lenya Krueger. All golden as warmed honey. Her family—blue-blooded German immigrants— were as dirt poor as mine. There is a reason Galveston is called Texas's Ellis Island."

Her prawn cocktail went barely touched as she listened to Nicolas weave his spell.

"I boxed for money to woo Lenya. Oh, as a puny kid I had plenty of alley fights with bullies. But this was different. This was for a noble cause."

"Rebels invariably claim their cause is noble."

"A cause on behalf of love is always noble."

She rolled her eyes. "Infatuation. You said so yourself."

When he paused to spear a prawn, she asked, "What happened to the lovely Lenya?"

His bull-like shoulders shrugged. "The first time I called upon her with a bouquet, her father confronted me at the door, called me a greaser, and told me to never show my face at his door again."

He concentrated on eating the prawn, taking so long, she prompted, "Well? Did you ever see Lenya again?"

"After that, I channeled the prize money I won, not into bouquets, but into bettering my position. The social graces my mother didn't cover, I learned through tutors. I ran errands for George Ball's office—the banker and financier—then graduated to a longshoreman for Ball's Mallory Steamship Line. Meanwhile, I learned about investing. By the time I earned enough to open my own office, I realized the lovely Lenya was just that. Lovely— and nothing more."

His wholly focused gaze speared Pearl now. "It will be interesting to see if you are worth investing in."

She could have told him she wasn't, that she was shallow and self-obsessed and, oh yes, horridly squeamish, but why trouble herself?

PETITE ANSE, LOUISIANA
JULY 1897

Now Drake fully understood the phrase, "worth his salt."

When he wasn't slinging the pick axe or hefting lumps and blocks of salt rock into mule-drawn carts, he was setting blasting caps. All dangerous and tedious and literally backbreaking work.

If he could wangle the job of operating the steam shovel, he would see sunlight more often than candlelight.

The room carved from salt in which he worked was nearly a hundred feet high. Interspersed forty-foot square salt pillars supported the ceiling. With the candles glittering on the salt crystals below, above, and surrounding him, the chamber resembled a cathedral.

The entire three-mile wide island in the Gulf's Vermillion Bay was a salt dome that Monty's cousin, Henri Gallier, claimed was as deep as Mount Everest was tall.

The island kingdom did puff a good 160 feet above the surrounding mainland marsh and supported not only the salt mine, but also a sugar plantation and a red pepper crop for its tabasco sauce. Salt, sugar, pepper—all the necessary condiments for the domesticated man.

Except Drake was determined that he was one man who would never be domesticated.

At the end of his shift, he emerged from one of the cave-like passageways, his skin and hair coated in a fine layer of salt. As always, his clammy skin rippled and puckered after the rapid dehydration that occurred from constant contact with the solid salt enclosure.

Immediately, he collected his gear and, joining Henry, headed for the rusted iron bridge that linked the island's lush canopy of trees across to the mainland. Once on the other side, the expanse of unbroken horizon uplifted his spirits. A nearly treeless prairieland much like southwest

Texas, the landscape was dotted with small round ponds, hand mirrors reflecting the sky's pink clouds. Overhead a crane flapped its wings.

Drake flung his long arms wide to embrace the sunlight. "Hal-le-lu-jah, Henry!"

Henry Gallier turned to him and shook his head. "Why do you do it, *mon ami*, if you hate it that much?" Unlike his cousin Monty, Henry was a small man, no more than five-and-a half feet tall, but cursed with Monty's wild, Medusa brown hair.

Along with some shift workers, the two trod the gravel road snaking toward New Iberia, ten miles to the north. While the owners and managers lived on the island, some of the workers lived in houses perched on stilts, scattered along the muddy bayous eddying through the prairie. Other workers would hop one of the company rail cars transporting salt—and hop off the spur at New Iberia's Southern Pacific depot.

Mimicking Drake, Henry stretched wide his shorter arms. "The island is a jungle paradise of warbling birds and flowers, with their intoxicating scents—"

"—while inside its salt mine, there are no smells, no sounds." Unless one discounted the nauseous sulfuric odor around the dome's top and the dynamite blasts inside the dome that rattled the ear drums.

"I might remind you, my friend, that the temperature is a pleasant seventy degrees year-round down there, with no mosquitoes to suck your very life's blood. So," he prompted, "why do you do it—slave in the salt mines?"

Drake shrugged his bulked-up shoulders. For the last six months, he had been asking himself the same question. That first year, after placing the lumber mill he had won under Monty's capable management, he had drifted, taking odd jobs . . . looking for something. He knew not what.

Definitely something better than the hardscrabble life he was presently experiencing. Something that fully engaged his restlessness, that targeted his bull's eye—something that caught him up in the moment, as, apparently, Giselle was caught up in her reporting from Cuba's revolutionary front, according to Wade.

With the national economy struggling to regain footing, the lumber mill was managing to operate, meet its bills, and show a pittance in the profit column. Not enough for him to live on with any style, but he could have scraped by without taking the job at the salt mine. Although, because of its inherent health dangers, the job did pay better than most.

It seemed during that year of batting about, he had been like a tetherball, circling one way or another around the pole that was Wade's domain, the nearest Drake could let himself get to the Paladín stronghold, but never actually dropping in on Wade and family.

Drake had shrimped for a while, worked cattle on the Allen Ranch just off Buffalo Bayou, and even laid railroad ties, all of which had muscled him up.

What he needed was mental stimulation—not likely to be found at the insular Gallier maison on the Lost Bayou, a tributary of Bayou Teche. He knew he would soon begin to wander, although if eighteen-year-old Valerie Gallier and her parents had their way, he would wed her and bed her, the latter of which he was already doing.

Their home was hidden away among the bayou's palmetto thickets and moss-draped live oaks. Stucco covered the brick-between-post construction and louvered shutters let light in and hot air out. *La galerie* served as a place for the family's social activities and in good weather, the veranda served as an extra room—his room now. He liked it best when the salt breeze was strong enough to sweep away the coastal mosquitoes.

At supper that night, he ate the seafood gumbo while listening to Henry, his wife Felicite, their twenty-year-old son Maurice, and their daughter Valerie discuss their day.

Because Drake's mother spoke as much French with him as she had English, Drake was passable in the Galliers' lyrical Cajun patois.

"Fog, it is a'rollin' in thick from the Gulf."

The young man labored at a nearby foundry, repairing steamboats, while the fetching Valerie worked at the local rice mill along with a comely young woman Maurice was courting.

"Storms are sure to follow behind." Henry ladled another helping of gumbo into his bowl.

"There's talk they may close the other rice mill." Like the rest of the Galliers, nature had bestowed on Valerie the Medusa brown hair, but on her it was not a curse, but a boon.

"Zut alors!" Feisty Felicite's brown-eyes sparked beneath

gathered brows. "Not another closing."

Unlike wife and daughter, Henry's temperament was as placid as the bayou. Drake passed him the shaker. Men who worked the salt mines either overloaded their food with salt or used no salt at all. Drake was of the latter.

Thoroughly tuckered out, he sought the galerie's weather-warped cane daybed, upholstered in ratty black oilcloth.

His long frame was barely settled on the veranda's daybed when Valerie snuggled her voluptuous body against his. She coiled one arm around his waist. Her nose and lips nuzzled the hollow of his collarbone. "I hope a storm will not drive us back inside, *mon grand.*"

Emphasizing her endearment, her hand slipped down to palm him. As usual, her kneading fingers generated a wilding in him. Strange, she meant more to him than just the closest warm body available . . . but not enough to allow himself ever to be fettered.

Later, as they both drifted into sleep, she murmured drowsily, "I forgot to give you a letter that was waiting for you in the New Iberia post office."

Before dawn, feeling somewhat ashamed that he couldn't read that well himself, he cajoled her to read the letter to him by candlelight. She was not much more literate than he, but from the gist of her stammered deciphering, Monty was bringing Drake up to date about the lumber mill operations. Toward the end of the missive, Monty grumbled about oil floating on the water.

"'Stinks like rotten fish . . . water is too soupy to drink.'"

Valerie finished reading and passed back the badly scrawled page.

True, oil was mostly a nuisance, but it could be saved and sold as illuminating oil or medicine. He folded up the page, stuck it in his overall pocket, and set off for work with Henry.

As the Cajun had predicted, the day was gloomy with clouds boiling over the Gulf. Downpour or not, excavation still went on hundreds of feet below the dome with its salt soda straws stabbing downward toward the intrusive workers.

When Drake's shift broke for lunch, the foreman, a Yankee named Roscoe, delivered the good news that Drake could start training on the steam shovel that very afternoon. What took other workers days or weeks to master, Drake achieved in hours. By the end of his shift, he was handling the mechanics of the steam shovel as smoothly as an old hand.

At the shift whistle's blowing, Henry slapped him on the back. "A day to celebrate, *mon ami!*"

The Galliers were overjoyed by Drake's promotion. That night, while the storm raged, the bourbon bottle was passed around—and when it was emptied, a bottle of rum was opened. Maurice broke out a dilapidated accordion and Drake puckered the notes on his harmonica but barely kept up with the Cajun music's fast, infectious beat.

Gaily, mother and daughter danced the jig, ruffling their skirts and flashing their ankles, while a laughing Henry was drinking himself into a stupor.

Later, with Valerie lying cradled against Drake's length, her thigh slung over his hip, his thoughts drifted to his new position. For him, the steam shovel was a novel toy. Yet something niggled in the back of his mind.

The storm, with its rumbling thunder, had passed through and had left rain pitter-pattering off the galerie's cedar shingles. A pleasant, hypnotic sound. Feux follets flitted their lights in and out of the trees just beyond.

Valerie gouged him in his ribs. "You are not listening, Drake Paladín!"

"Ouch! What?"

"With the raise you will be getting," her fingers dallied with the hair wreathing one of his nipples, " . . . now that you're a steam shovel operator . . . we might could find a place of our own. We could lock its doors to keep the rest of the world—and my family—outside."

"That's it!" He jackknifed upright, almost knocking her off the daybed.

"It is?" Her voice amplified with excitement. "We can get married?!"

The heel of his hand smacked his forehead. "The lock—and key." He grabbed her upper arms. "Valerie, Keystone! The steam shovel's cable drill is a Keystone! It's the cable drill. That's my problem."

For an uncomfortable, too long moment, Valerie was Lot's wife, turned to a pillar of salt. Then, *"Calisse de chavirer!"* Her fists pounded his chest. "Get out—now!"

'Crazy fucker' was right. Quickly, he shrugged into his denims and shirt. Dodging the barrage of his boots, holster, and harmonica she hurled at him, he padded barefoot out into the drizzle and mud.

Mud! Glorious mud! The answer to his problem. He stamped his bare feet and danced his own jig in the gelatinous ooze.

The idea he had was fucking crazy, but so was where he was headed.

HOUSTON
AUGUST 1897

Two interminably long years had passed since Angel last saw Drake. She studied him across the dinner table. He was changed.

His tall, lean body had acquired muscle. The shoulders were wider, if that were possible. And his face . . . it now possessed the etchings of manhood.

Even so, the way his blue-black hair tumbled in a slant across his forehead still lent him the look that as a child she had first glimpsed in that Juarez cantina . . . the same look she had heard in conjunction with the sobriquet Drake the Rake. His face was imprinted on that of every hero in the novels she devoured—whether dime westerns or classics.

Of course, she had changed too. Slightly taller. Breasts now instead of buds. Hair bundled atop her head and no more pigtails. Long skirts, not overalls. Now her voracious reading included first year med school texts.

"You're pulling our legs, aren't you, Drake?" Wade laughed. "You actually worked in a salt mine?"

Drake leaned back in the chair, hooking one lanky arm over its top railing. "Yep. And if I never see another salt lick, it will be too soon."

"Does that mean," Sarita scowled, "you won't be returning to the ranch? Alex needs you."

"Father doesn't need anyone."

"Then Tara needs you to help run the ranch."

"Tara has Griffin."

"You didn't know? The San Antonio architect—Wahrenberger—has hired Griffin to work for his firm. But Griffin will still have to manage Gorman Transport."

Drake shook his head. "Nope, didn't know. But I got my own place to care for now."

"You do?" Angel, Wade, and Sarita asked simultaneously.

He cocked a grin. "Yeah. A lumber mill I won gambling."

Sarita shook her head despairingly. "I should have known."

"That is grand!" Angel clapped her hands together.

His sparkling dark gaze swept all three into his swashbuckler spell. "Just stopped by on my way back to Conroe's Switch. There's oil floating atop the water on the lumber company's property."

Wade hiked a brow. "So?"

"So, with some reliable financial backing, I could strike a gusher."

"Wildcatting, huh?" Wade scoffed.

"Working in the salt excavation taught me more than

how to fill a salt shaker. Look, I have this idea that there just may be a relationship between the salt deposits and the sulfur found around them—that it could be an indication of vast oil pools below."

His cupped hands formed a dome. "As the salt dome increases over time, the caprock above is bent and can form pockets where oil pools and gas can collect."

Wade's mouth twisted. He sat back, folded his arms. "Geologists would most likely disagree with your theory. But even if oil is on your property, as it is in a lot of places in this area, you would have to dig too deeply through layers of solid rock. Impossible."

"I saw a horseless carriage on Main Street last week," Angel pointed out, reaching for her wine glass. "Last year, people would have called that impossible."

Drake frowned at her. "When did you begin drinking wine?"

She arched a brow. "If I am old enough to attend college, I am old enough to—"

"Attend college?" He leaned forward, fixed her with a scrutinizing gaze. "You're just a kid."

"She's going on sixteen," Sarita glanced with pride at Angel, "and smart enough to have been advanced twice in school. Come this fall, she is going to live with Pearl in Galveston and attend college at the University of Texas Medical Branch."

Drake did a double-take. "Medical Branch? You studying medicine?"

"She's studying—"

"The point is," she quickly interrupted her aunt, "anything is possible!" This was not going as planned. As much as she loved Aunt Sarita and Uncle Wade, they acted like Drake did—as though she were still a child.

She waited until the household was asleep and then tiptoed to the guest bedroom Sarita had put Drake in. She eased open the door. The gaslight yellow glow did not cast upon a delighted countenance.

Frowning, he sat on the chaise lounge, one booted foot propped on the red-and-gold upholstery, as he spun the chamber of the pistol he held. His eyes, darker than black pearls, regarded her warily. "Figured you'd show up."

"I wanted to tell you what I had in mind."

"Yeah? Last time you told me what you had in mind, you were holding my gun on me."

"And now you're holding it on me," she pointed out, sliding onto the cushioned window seat.

Drawing her legs up against her chest, her muslin skirts clumped around her bare feet, she propped her folded arms atop her knees. Not a ladylike position, but with Drake, she didn't have to be ladylike. "And last time you finagled me out of your pistol by promising you would come back for me."

His grin slid to one side. "I came back, didn't I?"

She was determined he would not wrestle a smile from her. "But not to take me with you this time either."

"Look, Angel, you're only . . . what? Fifteen, sixteen? And I'm a rambling man and—"

"Juliet was only thirteen."

"Who?"

She sighed. "Exactly my point. You can't read well enough to get an education, much less start up a business. You need me to—"

He groaned. "I need you like I need poison ivy, yellow fever, cholera, or snake bite."

She pushed off the window seat to plop on the chaise longue, one palm braced next to his dusty boot. That close to him, she felt breathless. Maybe it was the corset Sarita made her start wearing that caught her breath. "Drake Paladín, you need me to help you learn to read more easily. When you know what your weaknesses and strengths are, you'll want great people to step in and deal with your weaknesses."

"And you would be one of those great people?"

His voice held that usual scoffing tone he seemed to reserve expressly for her. And yet there flashed across his face a vulnerability. An inner wincing because she was so aware of his weakness but wanted to help him with it. In response, she tinted her voice with jollity.

"That would be me. That is why I am going to the medical school in Galveston. Dr. George Hall is teaching ophthalmology there. He has worked with a British ophthalmologist who has diagnosed cases like yours. They call it Word Blindness."

"I don't care if they call it Hell's Bells. You are not going with me. Ever."

"Yes, I am. Not just now, but when I graduate, we—"

"Here," he groaned, passing her the pistol. "Just shoot me now. Please."

DALLAS
JANUARY 1898

"David, Wade writes he can connect us with his broker, Nicolas Cordova. He says that Cordova can give us the opportunity to participate in the Houston-Galveston-New Orleans mercantile market and obtain price discounts."

In that early morning hour, David stood before the Cheval floor mirror, knotting his black grosgrain neck scarf. From their wadded bedcoverings where she reclined, already fully clothed but still barefoot, she secretly admired his looks, the definition of masculine pulchritude. Five years had not changed those good looks.

Five years of strife.

If not strife with the continuing persecution by the Klan, then competition from the four-story Obregon Department Store, one block over, built within months after the fire that destroyed the Emporium. The Paladíns' enemy—though, granted, there were quite a few—had not only set up a departmental system that included accounting for frequency of sale for each item but had installed gas fixtures and electricity.

Despite their being nearly penniless, David had countered with a skyscraping six-story brick building, constructed by volunteers from the same Christian churches to whom he had early on donated goods and cash for which she and he had been sorely strapped. The small loan they had managed to obtain at an enviable rate came from a Baptist banker, Lila Bradford's husband, God bless him. The mousquetaire gloves Claire had forfeited to Lila had been a rewarding sacrifice.

At Claire's cajoling, David had added the convenience of a dressing room for female customers. He had reserved the entire top floor for their domicile—a luxury she truly cherished. True, the space would have been better allocated for precious merchandise, but she and David had no funds for a separate place to live.

He was a booster of the Dallas State Fair and was helping organize the Dallas Public Library. He participated in a bewildering number of civic activities, even establishing a night school for workers.

Despite all his efforts, Obregon's vast resources easily undercut the Emporium's already low prices. Given time, Obregon Department Store would surely drive David and her right out of business.

"No," David glanced at her in the mirror with a distracted smile. "Forget your Cordova's connections. I want to establish a buying office in New York. Grandpa Moses has vast Jewish contacts there. Then I can purchase a wider array of merchandise than is available anywhere else."

"Well, New York is a long distance away," she temporized, "while right now we have every inch of floor space stocked with merchandise. Except the roof. David, I have been thinking that, like your biblical Babylonian Gardens of old, the roof would make an ideal place for a summer tea garden. The Dallas women would—"

"You have exquisite knees." He was staring at her in the mirror.

She had been unaware the soft billowy folds of her black silk dress had bunched above her knees immodestly. At once, she tugged at her skirts.

Stripping off the scarf he had labored so hard to tie, he crossed to the bed and bent over her. Her nostrils flared at the citrusy smell of his cologne mixed with his purely male scent, and her eyes flared at the predatory glint in his.

"But the committee meeting . . . . " she began in token protest.

"Be damned the Dallas Zoo Committee," he growled, hiking her skirts past her thighs. "They and their animals can wait until this animal has devoured its breakfast."

THEIR DALLAS EMPORIUM now employed two drummers. The salesmen hauled their trunks of merchandise samples and thick catalogues to smaller stores throughout north Texas and in the Indian Territory to the north.

It was the salesman, Walter Cleef, who concerned Claire. The same age as she, twenty-one, the earnest and enterprising lad had worked at the nearby Oak Cliff Ice and Refrigeration Company before being hired by David. When in the store to replenish stock samples, Walter's bespectacled eyes gazed upon her with utter adulation.

Rotating his hat brim between his hands, he shifted from one foot to the other before her desk, perspiration dotting his full upper lip. "I . . . I seem to do right well in dealing with Dallas Emporium customers, Mrs. Solomon, but, like as not, I end up as tongue-tied as a shoelace when I check in here."

Somehow, she needed to keep the young swain at a polite distance. She looked up from the orders he had turned in and managed a jocular smile. "Don't let the 'Boss Lady" desk sign intimidate you, Walter."

His head bobbed. "Yes, ma'am."

She watched his rangy frame saunter out the office door and sighed with relief that she had resolved that employee problem, at least for a while. But another employee issue beleaguered her even more.

Only the day before, David had hired Ruth Warsaw, the young Jewish seamstress to alter outfits for the Emporium's general market. The young woman had worked as a child in the New York tenement sweatshops.

Through the paper-thin walls, Claire could hear him in the stock room next door, as he lay out Ruth's duties and her response.

"If I may, sir, I would like to point out that I could also craft high-fashion women's clothes. And have you given any thought to creating special-order wedding dresses and trousseaus?"

"A splendid idea, Miss Warsaw!"

Claire tried to concentrate on her own duties, but when the conversation next door turned personal, she put down her pen and stepped to the doorway of the other room.

At either side of the narrow receiving counter by the ceiling-high bins, the two were conversing. Intertwined fingers supporting her dainty chin, Ruth was leaning forward in passionate discourse. Her expression was one of adulation. "Did you read, sir, about William Jennings Bryant's famous Cross of Gold Speech at the '96 Democratic convention?"

"No, I confess I have been too busy lately to do more than scan the newspaper headlines."

"An agitator, the man is. He truly believes Jews are antithetical to the American way of life."

"Well, that is no surprise." David braced his crossed arms, their muscles banded with sleeve garters, on the counter and leaned forward in equal fervor. "The populace views us Jews as making up a class of international financiers who promoted the gold standard—the chief cause of the '93 economic depression."

"There you have it—we are always responsible for the world's ills, are we not?"

Claire felt very much an outsider—especially when Ruth next said, "But men like you, our Merchant Prince, will bridge that ridiculous ideology."

His reply was fortified with mild humor and warmth. "From your mouth to God's ears, Miss Warsaw."

Clearly, Ruth possessed David's passionate Jewish consciousness. And Claire could only wonder if she had made a mistake by marrying him. Secretly, she feared she was not the right mate for such an extraordinary man.

GALVESTON
FEBRUARY 1898

Why Pearl agreed to see Nicolas Cordova again could only be attributed to faulty reasoning or sheer boredom with her existence. Although, sharing a room at Mrs. Linz's boarding house with the high-spirited Angel generally ruled boredom as out of the question.

But this evening, with her nose in a book studying, the clever girl waved Pearl goodbye with a dismissive flick of her fingers. "You look beautiful, Pearl. And Mr. Cordova will give you a run for your money. Have a good time."

Pearl sighed, grabbed her velvet hooded cape, and descended the staircase to find Nicolas waiting for her in the musty parlor with its fading rose trellis wallpaper.

While he could never be termed handsome, he was certainly handsomely attired in a swallowtail black dress coat and trousers. Broad braids ran vertically down their outside seams. Moonstone cufflinks and studs adorned his white pique shirt. Tailormade for him, the evening wear fit as snuggly as did his white kid gloves.

She emitted another exasperated sigh. Ever the dandy he was. She should plead illness, except she had dressed as he had instructed her—for an evening on the town—so a snit would only waste her preparations. Her French Belle Époque gown, with its heavily decorated bodice in pale pink figured silk and enormous leg-o'-mutton sleeves, highlighted her hour-glass figure.

He grinned, a rather charming expression, despite his scar. Doubtless, that would leave other females heart-struck. From behind, he draped her cape around her, inclining his head close to hers. "You will most certainly turn heads this evening, Pearl Paladín."

The evening was early and Nicolas's black enameled brougham rolled past the Victorian bathhouses, emptied by a bone-chilling wind, and continued farther on, away from the premier part of town—Broadway, with its lush mansions and gardens.

"Just a quick stop I promised to make, Pearl." He smiled, obviously noting her perplexed glance out the window. "Then I swear to sufficiently entertain you to vanquish your profound ennui."

The stop turned out to be a brick and stone, dungeon-looking building at the beach, on an isolated patch of winter-withered grass. *St. Mary's Orphanage* read its salt-blasted sign.

Within minutes, he returned to the brougham.

"What was that about?"

He raked a dry smile. "Some of the well-to-do have second homes by the sea. This is mine."

"You are serious?"

"Serious? Sister Camillus would tell you I am hopeless."

"Sister Camillus?"

"A second mother, you might say. My father died early on. When my mother injured a right knee that never healed, she became fatally ill with gangrene. The orphanage took me in."

"Well, you have certainly vanquished my profound ennui."

He seemed reluctant to discuss it further and she let the matter drop.

The ornate Cotton Exchange and Board of Trade's three-story brick building was one of the most spectacular edifices in Galveston. The floor of the Exchange Hall was inlaid walnut and oak, as was its paneled woodwork. Decorative brackets featuring designs of the cotton plant in various stages of growth adorned the perimeter of the room. That evening the influential *Harper's Weekly* was present to cover the Valentine's Ball.

When not dancing, which Nicolas did skillfully and smoothly, he introduced her to Galveston's leading families—the Cuney's and the Greenwall's and the Moody's. "These are the people you need to know if you wish to make a difference here."

That startled her. She looked askance at him. "Why would I want to make a difference?"

He arched a raven-black brow. "Because you are a Paladín."

A week later, he took her to the newly constructed Grand Opera House. Romanesque Revival in style, it was one of the largest in the country with more than 1600 seats.

Crystal chandeliers radiated prisms of light on every floor.

That night, Lillian Russell was performing Victor Herbert's comedy operetta, *The Serenade.* Enrapt, Pearl sat forward on their opera box's blue velvet-lined chair, *lorgnette* lifted, only vaguely conscious that Nicolas was studying her.

Not that she cared. She was too enthralled with the lavishness of the performance and her heart soared with *The Serenade*'s finale, "Take your choice, my Dolores, marry whom you will!"

After the operetta ended to thunderous applause that swept from orchestra to gallery to the very ceiling, she looked at him through tear-misted eyes. "What?"

"So, you can be moved. You laughed. You sighed. You cried."

"Of course, I did. I am not inhuman. I do have feelings."

He took her gloved elbow and, assisting her into her hooded cape, escorted her out of his opera box. "Just not for me?"

Head down, she concentrated on negotiating the grand, wooden staircase, so he could not study her expression, as he was apt to do. "Oh, I have feelings all right."

"And they are?"

She flicked him a sidelong glance. His smile was friendly and natural, but there was an iron in him. "Annoyance. Excitement. Bafflement. Intrigue."

He helped her into the waiting brougham and climbed in beside her. In the carriage's dark warmth, his eyes glittered. "I would be more pleased if you had mentioned lust."

She stiffened, shrank both inwardly and physically from him, where his knee touched her voluminous taffeta skirts. "You are outrageously ill-mannered, sir!" But in all honesty, she found herself enjoying his company . . . and admittedly, was finding his countenance more than an adequate counterpart to her own. Bold. Brash. Indifferent to others' opinions.

"I am outrageously blunt and honest. You will always know where you stand with me, Pearl. I want you. Can you, at least, accord me the same honesty about your feelings?"

Nervous, her fingers toyed with her pearl-beaded bag as her mind raced. She was twenty-three, an age when most other females were already wed. She had never even known a stolen kiss. At that thought, she blurted, "Then why don't you kiss me? I want one of those romantic kisses like in *The Serena*—"

"No, you don't."

Both her brows shot up. "I don't?" The man's arrogance was insufferable. "Then precisely what do I want?"

"This." He grasped her shoulders and drew her to him. His eyes searched hers, looking for something, she knew not what, before he lowered his head over hers.

She had expected a ruthless, punishing kiss and, worse, groping hands. Instead, his gloved hands gently held her, as if she were an exotic butterfly that might take flight. His lips grazed softly over hers, inviting her response.

Her palms were pressed against his chest, ready to

shove him away, but his lips moved in such an easy, exploratory fashion that she realized she was safe . . . and then realized she was inclining closer to him, that she wanted to feel this tingly, heated rush along her entire length, from her pearl-studded curls to her ivory satin high heeled shoes.

Dimly, she heard the clip-clopping of horses' hooves. "Where are we going?" He lifted his head, his gaze dark and masterful. "My place. It is actually a modest lime-washed bungalow secluded within a shelter of oaks, oleanders, and palms." He paused, as if giving her time to retreat from his sally, then went on when she made no reply. "My bed is enwreathed by a fine gauze netting that keeps out the mosquitoes in the summer—and the rest of the world year-round."

His words flowed over her, lulling her as easily as had his kisses. Here was no silly attempt at seduction, no expectation of sentiment. A part of her cried out in warning, but another part asked how long she would continue to live a banal life. "And it makes no difference that I do not love you?"

"It makes no difference that I do not ask for your hand in marriage?"

At that, she smiled. "I would refuse."

"That is why I shall never ask."

In this, they were perfectly fit, neither expecting from the other anything more than the pleasure of the moment. Yet, in their coupling time and again throughout that night, she suspected they both discovered the one thing they

could do together quite expertly.

CONROE'S SWITCH, TEXAS
MARCH 1898

Drake hunkered beside the small pond, its surface slicked with a rainbow of oil. Its sulfurous stench overrode the clean scent of the pines surrounding the glade.

Across the pond, Monty braced his massive weight on his crutch. "Well, it seemed a good idea, *mon ami.*"

Drake scooped a handful of the oil-sheened water and watched it dribble between his fingers, as his dream was doing. "It still is, damn it."

Frowning, he wiped the oil glaze on his denim-clad thigh and stood up, hands on hips. The oil was down there. Lots of it. His experience at the salt dome agreed with his gut instinct.

The technical difficulties and the shortage of money in tapping it plagued him night and day. Granted, he could be wrong. He could hit a large volume of gas instead, a nuisance and a danger.

He just needed to perfect a better drill than the cable rig if he were going to reach the depth where he suspected he would find a vast pool of oil.

A drill that rotated, instead of merely pounding through the subsurface formations. A drill that churned up rock bits and floated them to the top with mud, not water.

But all that took money. He could not even finance a

test well. He had been to every banker Wade and that broker Cordova could scour up, but every banker had turned him down. That felt to Drake as if word had circulated that he had the Yellow Jack—and be damned if he'd ask his father for help.

Still, he asked himself, as he often did when in a pickle, what would his father do? His gaze skimmed across the black water to settle on Monty's wooly features on the opposite side. "Sell the mill."

"What?" The big man almost lost his balance on his crutch.

"Find a buyer. Put out the word in Conroe's Switch. Everything goes—tractors, trams, tools—but I will retain all mineral rights plus a lease on a one-hundred-acre block in and around the survey of this pond."

He would use the proceeds of the sale to finance the drill he envisioned. He would need a damned good lawyer to draw up the contract . . .not that he trusted any of those fee-chasers.

Oddly, there was only one person he trusted. While Monty could read and write, just barely, his personal code was definitely the Creole's laissez faire. In the oil business, letting details take their course was seldom the best course.

No, there was only one person who knew of his own secret struggle and, damn it all, he could not even write to her for help. And even if he could, he feared to do so would change the dynamics of their relationship.

Bellyache all he might about Angel being full of deviltry, there was something sensible to be said about his uneasiness in regard to her. To be in deeper cahoots with her, he would have to be crazy as a loon. Something requiring more, requiring opening himself and being vulnerable, to a counterpart like Angel—who knew him only too well—even as fired up as he was about the oil well . . . .

Nope, no way. Right?

THE BARONY RANCH
APRIL 1898

The buckboard wagon crested the incline while the seat jounced on its springs over the rocky rubble. Ahead was the windmill and a tank. Tara remembered early on in their marriage, she and Buck had romped a couple of times in that tank. Water had splashed wildly, and a moss horn steer had contentedly watched their amorous contortions.

These days, her and Buck's romps were few. The chemistry was still there, but so was the resentment. Their marriage had deteriorated into functionality. That fateful day of the showdown between Claire and Buck, Tara had been stunned, not knowing how to reconcile the two loves of her life. She still did not.

Buck had driven off their daughter, and, love him though she did, Tara didn't know if she could ever forgive him. That created a standoff between her and him. Neither Claire nor David were ever discussed. As if they did not exist.

But, of course, Tara had never accepted that absurdity. She and Claire had maintained fairly regular correspondence over the years, something she did not reveal to Buck, though she had desperately wanted to share with him about the loss of Claire's baby, desperately wanted to feel Buck's sinewy arms around her, supporting her in her own grief.

A grandchild she would never know.

She could divorce Buck. She was certainly capable of running the ranch on her own. She had old Diego, his son Pepe, and the Paladíneños to assist with the physical labor. And she had Karl and Max's firm to handle the financial and legal aspects of The Barony——and her nephew Griffin, when he could make the time.

What she did not have was any communication with her husband.

He was a good man. He treated her with respect. Hell, he fixed her coffee and brought it to her every morning. But he would not budge on his rancor against Jews.

So why did she not divorce him?

He set the brake, passed her the reins, and went around back.

She twisted on the seat. "Need some help?"

"Nope. I can do it."

Just like him to insist on doing things he was too old to do. He jammed tools in his belt and tugged out the heavy metal blade. Breath held, she watched him scale the windmill ladder. A sigh of relief eased from her after he reached the platform safely.

It would serve the old coot right if he fell off, damn't.

MANATI, CUBA
APRIL 1898

The yellow press war between William Randolph Hearst's *New York World* and Joseph Pulitzer's *New York Journal* raged with shameless sensationalism in reporting the Cuban Liberation Revolution against Spanish rule.

Then, the sinking of the U.S.S *Maine* in Havana's harbor and the death of its 252 men on February 15th meant that United States military intervention in Cuba became likely.

The *Maine's* sinking also prompted the *Austin Statesman* to capitulate to the beseeching of its only correspondent in Cuba. The newspaper agreed to arrange for Giselle to cover the notorious reconcentration camps established by the Spaniard's former Governor General, also known as "The Butcher."

Thus far, as closely as Giselle could calculate from her sources, almost three-hundred thousand people had already perished of disease and starvation in those reconcentration camps. Those still alive were known as the Walking Dead. Skeletons staggering amongst stinking piles of rotting bodies.

Within hours, she hoped to gain firsthand knowledge at one of the larger camps—provided she survived the violent tossing of the sponging schooner that was more a cockleshell of a boat with gunnysacks for sails and coils of rope for seats, the rope's hemp rasping her delicate backside after less than an hour a-sea.

Dressed as one of the crew, she and the dozen sailors bailed and broiled, bailed and broiled, in the nine-hour journey from Havana around Cuba toward its bottle-shaped harbor of Manati. Beneath her feet, the sea took her on a tumultuous ride, and she could not help but wonder if it was a reflection of the state of the Cuban government.

Her stomach rolled with the ocean surrounding her . . . not just from its tossing but with real fear. Not so much from the fear of swamping but of what lay ahead of her. How did one deal with Cuba's autocratic Spanish government? It was a terrifying regime. She, a foreigner, a female, had no clout.

Only a short time before, Charles Govin of the *Key West Equator-Democrat,* while traveling with some rebels, had been captured and macheted to death by Spanish forces. Anyone found carrying arms or even caught outside a concentration camp without papers faced instant assassination.

Even if she survived the sea's tempest, she still had to get past the Spanish forces posted at a great blockhouse bristling with cannon that guarded the entrance to Manati harbor.

While Giselle might not be armed, and she certainly had

papers, those very papers—her own press credentials—might not exempt her from execution. She could be charged with communicating with the rebels, crossing Spanish lines, and traveling without a military pass. Her stomach knotted painfully, along with every muscle in her tense body, at what might be required of her.

The little mulatto Kosmo, his skin as dark as tarpaper, assured her she had no worry. He lolled over the tiller, keeping the schooner's nose parallel to the shore. "We are a good twenty miles from the coast—not even in the war zone of the lanchas. We wait till midnight to put in."

From another crew member, a grizzle-bearded freedom fighter, she learned that Kosmo, the son of a former African slave on a sugar plantation, was a scout for the Cuban revolutionaries' General Garcia and was said to be the most knowledgeable operative on land and water.

At last, where the schooner approached the shoreline, the Caribbean's turmoil subsided to gently lap below the gunwales. The salty breeze kept the worst of the oppressive heat at bay. In the distance, El Turquino—the 8,000-foot-high peak of the Sierra Maestra mountain range—dazzled the eye.

Nevertheless, Giselle felt uneasy. Living with a mother prone to spew like an unpredictable fumarole, Giselle had developed an almost mystical intuition.

Not until nearly midnight, when the schooner's jib-sheet was released, did a favorable wave roller give the craft one last lift, hurtling it onto a secluded beach in a hidden bay just out of sight of the harbor blockhouse.

Waving goodbye to her erstwhile mates who were to rendezvous with her in forty-eight hours, Giselle waded ashore. Her plan was to sneak into the rear of the reconcentration camp just outside Manati.

The sand crunched beneath her feet, sloughing toward the refuge of the scrim of palms. Her stomach sank incrementally with each step. She should be at home, making a cherry pie for a husband or knitting cozy booties for a baby.

Instead, she was plunging into the danger of rape, torture, or even death if she was captured. Her fear felt like the tang of blood on her tongue. She swiped her salt-grimed lips and glanced down at her crimson fingertips. Since setting foot ashore, she had been gnawing on her bottom lip, unaware of her frantic uneasiness.

The jingle of horses' trappings and the rattling of the Spaniards' short sabers from within the palmetto thickets warned that not only would her plan have to be shelved, but that she should have heeded her own intuition.

ON EL MANUECO, A HIGH, conical hill, was a stone castle-fort—its parapets fortified with cannon that overlooked Manati harbor. A closer inspection of the old castle revealed a few crumbling walls. Inside one of the castle's larger rooms, its window shutters were thrown open to a panoramic view of the palm-lined harbor and the turquoise sea.

The fort's chunky commander, a Peninsular Spaniard wearing a blue cotton uniform with gold epaulets, was gazing at the vista, his plump hands clasped behind him.

From Giselle's viewpoint, seated at a chair in front of his large desk, she noted that Comandante Bernardo Rubi was missing a thumb.

Meanwhile, dressed as a sailor, she was missing her usual clothes—and missing Griffin terribly. Missing his innate strength of will and character. If she was to be honest with herself, she had admittedly been afraid of her feelings for him. Afraid that they stood in the way of her fulfilling all that she could be, not just as a woman but as a human being.

She spoke to Rubi in her barely passable Texican Spanish. "I insist that you release me, Comandante Rubi. As a United States citizen, I cannot be held prisoner, and I am entitled to full treaty rights under Paragraphs Two and Three of the Protocol of '77."

He pivoted. Beneath the flourish of his mustache, his smile was about as congenial as her mother's on a good day.

"Then you do not know, do you, *señorita?*" For such a big man, he had a high-pitched voice. "Your country and mine officially declared war on one another today. Technically, you are my prisoner. But you have nothing to fear. I will consider you my guest—I am assuming, *naturalmente,* that you will oblige me by cooperating as a proper guest should? Otherwise, well . . . ." He spread plump palms, a warning smile slinking across his cunning, porcine face.

Otherwise . . . would she be missing more than a thumb?

She could feel the gooseflesh rippling out on her arms and legs. From childhood memories came not only the pain of her mother's precipitous beatings but, worse, the waiting. Never knowing exactly when they would come. One moment, her mother would be fun and frivolous and affectionate, and the next moment . . . .

Giselle knew if she was to make her life meaningful, at least to herself, she had to move beyond this paralyzing fear. Her capture, which at first had seemed to be a disastrous development, she realized now had placed her in an opportune spot to do just that. And, in addition, she might even gather maps and important information about military conditions in the countryside outside the capital of Havana.

"Naturalmente, Comandante. "She flashed the same smile she used to placate her mother's violent wrath, all the while desperately pondering how and where she could find a telegraph office to file her next dispatch.

SAN ANTONIO
MAY 1898

The United States Army had little manpower left after the Civil War thirty years earlier, but America needed able-bodied volunteers to fight the Spanish in Cuba. Even so, Griffin was not scrawling his signature as a volunteer with the cavalry on its regiment recruiting list out of patriotic devotion.

Neither his family nor the *Austin Statesman* had heard a word from Giselle in three weeks—not since April twenty-fourth, when the United States declared war on Spain. There was no forwarding address in her last letter . . .only a vague reference to a tip off about a reconcentration camp that might make for an important news scoop.

His father was using all his gubernatorial influence to get Giselle home safely. Nonetheless, political paperwork and a lack of diplomatic connections stalled Kerry Paladín's efforts.

Enlisting with a newly forming cavalry regiment was the quickest method Griffin could think of to reach Cuba and find her.

Fort Sam Houston's Quartermaster's Depot was willing to issue horses to the new regiment. Therefore, the regiment's leaders, Colonel Leonard Wood and Lieutenant Colonel T. R. Roosevelt, Jr. opted to base its headquarters there in San Antonio.

Responding to President McKinley's call for twelve hundred volunteers to assist the war efforts in Cuba, the two commanders were seeking men mainly from the southwest because the hot weather was comparable to Cuba's.

The very day the regiment opened for volunteers, Griffin headed for its recruiting station in the Menger Hotel courtyard. The open space adjoined the hotel bar and was only about a hundred yards from the Alamo.

The place was jammed with a diverse bunch of volunteers—adventurers, elite easterners, prospectors, hunters, Indians, even a few Ivy League athletes—all of whom said they were proficient in riding and shooting.

"We're too late," grumbled a cowboy in a straw Stetson ahead of Griffin in the line.

"What?"

"Word up ahead is the twelve-hundred-men limit was just met."

Goddamnitalltohell. Griffin scrubbed his jaw. There had to be a way he could wangle his name on the recruiting list.

He spun and strode inside the noisy forty-year-old hotel bar, the center of Texas society. It was a replica of the taproom in the House of Lords Club in London—a solid mahogany bar, mahogany-paneled ceiling, French mirrors, and gold-plate spittoons. Undoubtedly, the stuffed bull moose head on the bar wall had witnessed plenty of tomfoolery and wrangling over the years.

He ordered a beer, chilled by the Alamo Madre ditch, which passed through the hotel courtyard. Morosely, he sipped the beer . . . a Lone Star, which of course reminded him of Giselle. It was her interview with the local brewery that had gained him the position with Wahrenburger's architectural firm.

With the declaration of war with Spain, tax on barreled beer had been raised to two dollars. Beer sales were said to be on the decline. Glancing around the crowded bar, he thought wryly that its guzzling patrons must not be aware of the tax increase or were too well off to care.

At the bar's far end, a stout, bespectacled gentleman

was buying beer for three or four of the lucky recruits. Griffin stared at the vaguely familiar man. Then Griffin snapped his fingers. Of course! He was Teddy Roosevelt of the prominent Roosevelts of New York.

Griffin did not believe in using the Paladín name to gain favors . . . until right now.

He signaled to the aproned bartender. "Send the gentleman in the glasses a mint julep with my compliments. And I want the mint julep served in your finest crystal, not in your usual silver tumbler."

When the bartender placed the mint julep, garnished with fresh mint and a dusting of powdered sugar, before Roosevelt, the officer peered over his spectacles down the length of the bar. Griffin's fingers tipped the fold of his hat brim. Roosevelt waved a beckoning hand. Hefting his bottle, Griffin strolled over to join the group.

"How did you know I liked mint juleps?" Roosevelt's walrus mustache was flecked with powdered sugar.

He grinned. "In '92 you hunted javelinas with my father Kerry—at our Barony Ranch."

"Governor Kerry Paladín? You're his son?" Roosevelt pounded him on his back. "Well, bully, if that doesn't beat all."

Griffin sure hoped it would.

MANATI, CUBA
MAY 1898

The third week of Giselle's capture, she anxiously watched through the decorative wrought-iron grill of her room window, high above the bay, as a monitor dispatched from the U.S.S. *Texas*, floating offshore, made its way toward the harbor.

Daily, Comandante Rubi had a guard escort her to his office for a period of supposed questioning that was more idle discussion. For the Spanish officer, she was a diversion from the tediousness of this insignificant outpost in the vastness of the Caribbean. She would entertain him with her tall tales of Texas or gossip of famous people she had interviewed. Sometimes he questioned her about American policy, of which she professed to know nothing, but more often he merely wanted to chat.

Earlier that day, she had learned that the *Texas*, flying the flag of the oldest neutral country in the world, Switzerland, was loaded with food and clothing the American Red Cross wanted to distribute to the reconcentrados. To this end, Miss Clara Barton, Captain Harrington, and Dr. Lesser and his wife would be coming ashore.

And from the little information Rubi also let slip, Giselle learned that the Spanish government was anticipating the United States military to attack Santiago, a hundred miles south of Manati Bay, any day now.

She knew this was an opportune time to escape. She paced her small stone room, its walls dark stained with leprous splotches and with only a fraying tapestry to relieve its bleakness. Her only recourse, she decided, was boldness.

Pushing up her sleeves, she flung open her door to confront the knuckle-dragger of a guard posted outside it.

"I'm going to see the *Comandante*."

He looked askance but, naturally, was accustomed to Rubi summoning her to his office. So far, so good, but at the door to the *Comandante's* office two more armed guards stood at attention on either side of the doorway. When she went to enter, their rapidly lowered Mausers blocked the door.

"*Comandante* Rubi wants to see me."

The older of the two guards, a man with bristly sideburns, growled. "*El Comandante* left orders he is not to be disturbed."

She blinked. What now?

She did the only thing she could think of—she began to howl like a banshee, one of those Texican war whoops. The guards were startled, and within seconds, Rubi threw open the door. "*¡Caramba! ¿Que pasa. ..?*"

That was all she needed. She shimmied past him and blurted out her predicament to the equally startled septuagenarian Miss Barton and her companions. "Please . .. I am an American. A correspondent for the *Austin Statesman*—and I am being held here against my will by *Comandante* Rubi!"

A furious Rubi growled. "The woman is a spy. Disregard her theatrics. She does not have the right to the prisoner-of-war status and will stand trial." With a flick of his fingers, he had the guard hustle her from his office.

SAN ANTONIO
MAY 1898

The recruits camped south of downtown San Antonio at Riverside Park. Under the scalding Texas sun, Col. Wood and Lt. Col. Roosevelt transformed volunteers into Rough Riders, named for Buffalo Bill's Wild West and the Congress of Rough Riders of the World.

The men who comprised the First U.S. Volunteer Cavalry were given the same basic gear as Regular Army Cavalry. They kept their Fort Sam Houston horses and Roosevelt used his connections with the War Department to get Griffin and the other soldiers the latest Krag-Jorgensen carbines, the same firearm issued to Regular Army Cavalry.

The Rough Riders also packed extra gear to embellish their status. They wore brown canvas stable fatigues and carried machetes instead of sabers. One of the Rough Riders, William Tiffany of Tiffany & Company, arranged for some of the men to be issued 1895 Colt automatic machine guns, an alternative to the Gatling gun usually mounted on a tripod.

Griffin was delighted with the Colt automatic machine gun but a little leery of the Sims-Dudley dynamite gun. That experimental artillery piece used explosion-driven compressed air to loft a five-pound charge of nitro gelatin. Already one of the Rough Riders had been killed when its smokeless powder charge went off prematurely.

Over the next two weeks, when they were not drilling, Roosevelt, Griffin, and many of the Rough Riders idled away their time at the Menger Bar. "Wood took me to task for buying beer for the men," Roosevelt shared, looking splendid in his tailored Brooks Brothers uniform. "He feels my fraternizing with the underlings lessens the rank and respect essential between an officer and his men."

They sat at a back table. Despite the late hour, the bar was shoulder to shoulder with soldiers and civilians.

"Sir," Griffin grinned. "I would never make the mistake of arguing with a man I don't respect. Respecting you as my superior officer, I would be most grateful if you bought the next round, sir."

A hearty chuckle rolled up out of Roosevelt's barrel chest. "You are a damnable ass, Lieutenant Paladín!" But he signaled for two more Lone Stars and then fell to reminiscing about his cattle raising days in the Dakota Territory.

Others joined them—one, a lovely brunette, Julie Britton. The daughter of a former Texas Ranger from San Antonio who now was also a Rough Rider, she was definitely off-limits to the soldiers. "My father," she told Griffin, "saw duty in the West Texas salt flats with your Uncle Buck."

"Is that so?" He could only hope her father did not pass along to Uncle Buck the news that his nephew was a Rough Rider. The less the family knew the better. Griffin was chaffing to get out of the bar, to get out of San Antonio, to get to Cuba.

Even as Roosevelt was holding forth on how he had pressured the U.S. Army to outfit the Rough Riders in khaki rather than the standard blue wool, the brunette was eyeing Griffin rather than listening to the loquacious lieutenant colonel.

At a pause, she leaned into Griffin. "Your red hair is like flame. If I touched it, would I get burned?"

An image of Giselle flashed across the backs of his eyes. Tall, patrician, honorable, cool . . . cool to his ardor. Obviously, her career meant more to her than marriage to him. For a long moment, he hesitated. The need for an immediate companion warred with that irritating, niggling voice coming from his gut . . .can you be any less honorable than Giselle if you want her?

"Yes, you would get burned," he finally replied and, draining in one gulp the last of his beer, he rose from the table and made his goodbyes.

Outside, he stood, hands jammed in his khaki pockets, gazing up at the endless number of stars—and thought what an endless fool he was.

DALLAS
MAY 1898

That beautiful sunlit morning, Claire found two things David had not told her about.

Searching for a pencil, she was rummaging through the littered bills and correspondence on the desk they shared. The leather desk blotter slid sideways. Peeking from below was a sheet of paper, bearing at its bottom the name, Secretary of War Russell Alexander Alger.

Her breath caught. She slipped out the creased letter.

Brief and to the point, it had been dated two weeks earlier but must have just arrived.

The U.S. War Department has received your firm's application to supply our troops in Cuba with uniforms but regret to inform you that it has already contracted to Brooks Brothers out of New York.

She bit her lip. That explained David's gloomy disposition. Her heart hurt for him. She knew how hard he struggled against the prejudice of many gentile businessmen as well as the machinations of the Klan—and Obregon. And for the last, she was solely responsible. Or rather, the feud between Oregon and the Paladíns was. David was merely an innocent bystander.

Letter in hand, she gathered her skirts and descended the stairs. Understanding his prickly pride as well as she did, she was prepared to couch her words of comfort in conversation rather than heartfelt overtones.

She was not prepared to find him in Ruth's fitting room. Between the hand-width slit of curtains, Claire could see David and Ruth, their lips meshed in frenzied kissing.

Quietly, Claire turned away and, hand-over-hand on the banister, blindly climbed back upstairs, her feet weighted with lead. Ruth understood him so well, maybe she could comfort David far better than she herself.

She was not going to start crying. Because if she did, she feared she might never stop.

GALVESTON
JUNE 1898

Mrs. Rebecca Sealy, head of the hospital Board of Lady Managers at the John Sealy Hospital, sat with her age-spotted hands clasped atop the cluttered desk, though Pearl observed the hands appeared to be knotting and unknotting.

"You understand, Miss Paladín, that this has nothing to do with your performance. It is just . . . just that . . . well, you are no longer needed in this position."

"Is there a position in which I am needed?"

Mrs. Sealy picked up her fountain pen, fidgeting with it. "I am afraid not."

Pearl could hardly believe what she was hearing. Her teacher's record was unblemished at the John Sealy Training School for Nurses. If anything, her record was exemplary, with commendations and awards cluttering it.

Incomprehensible!

Unless, somehow, someone had learned of the night she had spent in Nicolas's bungalow. The sweet, intoxicating smell of oleander would forever cling to her memory. It was a night she would remember if she lived to be a hundred—and a hundred times she had wanted to re-experience that night, but pride prevented her from suggesting it.

Nicolas, damn his stubbornness, would have it no other way but her coming to him on his terms.

He had been just as adamant that her anonymity be preserved that night. Both in arriving and departing in the wee hours of the morning from his isolated bungalow, she had worn her identity-concealing hooded black velvet cape.

No, she was certain no one had known of her night spent in the ecstatic comfort of Nicolas's arms. No one but Angel, and Angel would never tell—and Pearl was quite certain Mrs. Linz was snoring soundly when she returned to the boarding house.

So, what, or *who,* was behind Mrs. Sealy's decision to discharge her?

Bewildered, Pearl packed her meager belongings at the school, all the while trying not to sniffle. How would she support herself? She could return home to live with her parents at Buffalo Bayou, but her independent nature rebelled against that.

Unwilling to return to the boarding house and announce the news of her disgrace to Angel, Pearl wondered along the port first. Despite its laissez-faire culture inherited from American-French privateer Jean Lafitte, Galveston was the world's busiest cotton port. On any day, four or five steamers from ports as far as Singapore could be found in the bay, preparing to unload French perfumes, Cuban cigars, or English wool.

On that particular day, cowboys were herding maybe four-to-five hundred cattle down the boulevard toward the docks at 37th Street. Were the cowboys Paladineños?

She remembered reading in a recent edition of the *Galveston Daily News* that cattle shipments to feed the Marines at Camp McCalla, near Cuba's Guantanamo Bay, topped a thousand head that week.

And she remembered reading something else . . . .

Congress had rapidly authorized the military to hire female nurses to serve in Cuba in the war against Spain. Initially, the military's Medical Departments had rejected the idea of using female nurses. However, the male nursing system had been immediately overwhelmed by the vast unanticipated number of disease-related casualties.

The *Galveston Daily News* reported that already yellow fever and typhoid were breaking out in camps like Key West. The camps had been established as training areas for the volunteer troops.

Typhoid and yellow fever, her squeamish system could handle. But only providing she did not see service in some field surgical tent, sawing off a man's arm or some other grisly horror.

The only problem she faced, and it was major, was the standard adopted for a nursing appointment to Army service—graduation from a training school, combined with suitable endorsements.

As she turned her steps toward the Strand and Nicolas's office, reluctance warred with excitement. His office was located between that of a wholesaler's and a commission merchant's. The clerk escorted her directly to Nicolas.

If he was surprised to see her, his countenance gave no evidence of it. He rose and came around from behind his desk to bend over her gloved hand like a chevalier of old. Except he did not release her hand.

She had meant to calmly explain her dilemma and present her request, but she surprised herself by seeking the protective concave offered by the steel plate of his chest and outstretched arm that at once took her in.

Gulping, she blinked back tears and raised her face to his. He looked both startled and pleased. "I have been let go from my teacher's position. Mrs. Sealy won't give me an explanation as to why."

He glanced over her head at his office's still open door. As always with her, he was careful to observe propriety. He led her to the leather upholstered couch and, hitching his pin-striped trousers at the knees, took a seat in its matching chair adjacent to her. Forearms braced on his thighs, boxer-size, swarthy hands lattice-worked between his knees, he leaned forward and fixed her with his imprisoning gaze.

"Pearl, I have noticed a pattern in the refusal of your family members' loan applications. When I pointed it out to your father, Wade remarked that this persecution could possibly be attributed to Rod Obregon. You should recognize the name."

"Of course," she murmured. "My mother's twin. Angel's father." Her mother rarely discussed her origins, only to say the Obregons had been in the steamboat business, that she had lost track of them when she ran off to marry Pearl's father.

"It seems your Uncle Rod's aversion for the Paladíns goes back to the days of his father. Whether their vendetta is justified or not, I don't know. But I do know he is one of the most powerful men in the state. His influence reaches into just about every arena of our state's economy. Apparently, he influences more than financial matters."

"You think he's responsible for . . . for the hospital's decision to let me go?"

He shrugged.

Now it was she who leaned forward, her clasped hands almost touching his. "Nicolas, the army is contracting nurses for field camp hospitals in Cuba. They must be at the General Hospital in Key West by the fifteenth. I want to go."

He rolled dark brown eyes. "You are not a nurse, Pearl, and you get sick at the sight of blood. You told me yourself."

"I have a plan."

His scarred upper lip twisted into a dry smile. "No doubt."

"Listen, the military is arranging to transport Corpus Christi hospital's big x-ray machine to Cuba."

"The what?"

"X-ray machine. It's the latest thing in medical science." She took one of his hands and he raised a brow at the intimate gesture, but she plowed on. "It takes images of what's inside the body. Like the bones in your hand here. It will be used for gunshot wounds, locating bullets by their image instead of by painful probing. I know enough about the machine that I might be able to convince the military medical board to let me go along. But according to the *Galveston Daily News,* I would need a suitable endorsement of good moral character."

"And that would be me, I presume?"

She went to release his hand, but he continued to hold hers. "Your name does carry weight in Galveston, Nicolas."

"Your parents would never countenance it."

"I am of age, after all—but I have thought that through, too."

"Oh, I am sure you have."

"The Surgeon General is procuring the services of immunes—colored women most likely immune to the Yellow Fever—to serve as nurses. They aren't required to have hospital training. I know Becky would jump at an opportunity like this. With her accompanying me, my parents could hardly balk at my idea."

"Yes, they could. And would. Regardless, I foresee a definite impediment to your plan. Being under contract and going along are two different things— namely, money is involved in contracting with the military. Like a salary and travel expenses and food. Going along means you are on your own."

She looked at him from beneath her lush lashes. "That's also why I came to you."

"I see. You need a loan."

At that, he released her hand. He stood, walked the

width of the office, rubbing his jaw. She would have wondered if she had hurt his feelings, but by now she knew him well enough to know he was impervious to others' opinions of him.

"I could warn you," he faced her at last, arms akimbo, "that you are taking a huge risk. You have no idea of the horrors of war. Yet I know you would find a way to go, even if I refuse to agree to a loan."

She bit her lip. Surely, he would not refuse her. And he was wrong about her. She was not one of those indomitable people, like Giselle, who always found a way to make things work the way they wanted. Why, Giselle was already in Cuba, way ahead of everyone else—out of touch maybe, but she would show up with a headline-winning story. That was the kind of person Giselle was.

"So, I'll finance your expedition on the condition that . . . ."

His pause punched her hard in the heart. She knew what was coming next—marry him or forego the loan—and her body recoiled. Marry him . . . that she could never do. They had nothing in common. Not like she and Griffin did. Sometimes, she was not even sure she liked Nicolas.

He must have suspected the reason for her wince, because his smile was deceptively like a sneer, but his tone was one of utter dispassion, completely matter-of-fact. " . . . on the condition that, if and when you return, we never see one another again. This is the last time I help any Paladín."

NICOLAS WATCHED PEARL SASHAY from his office, the door slamming behind her. He had to smile, a weary one at that. Despite Pearl's dismay, she had not been so affronted by his implicit rejection of her that she had refused to accept his loan.

He plucked a cigar from the pewter humidor on his desk. Biting off the cigar's tip, he circled around his desk to settle back into his swivel chair. He lit up the cigar, then propped his shiny Florsheim button-ups atop his desk. Casually, he watched the cigar's puffed smoke swirl and eddy about him. How utterly fascinating was smoke—such a feminine thing. Mystical and elusive, like Pearl.

He knew he could never be her knight in shining armor. His was too rusted.

But he wanted her, wanted her like he had never wanted another woman. Had wanted her from that first moment of sighting her—sitting across her parent's dining room table and watching her sparkle, listening to her melodic voice with its dry wit, and observing her spirit to match her looks. He had never met anyone of those looks and temperament. Yes, there was no denying what had been on his mind from that first moment.

Yet once he had her in his bed, he had not been surfeited but addicted. After their illicit night together, he had not expected to fall in love with her. Worse, he was disgusted with himself, knowing she only saw him as a means to get what she wanted.

She had been too good for him. She had beat him. And his rejection of her today was a bitter triumph.

DAIQUIRI, CUBA
JUNE 1898

Even as Admiral Sampson's ships blockaded the pivotal Cuban harbor of Santiago, the First Volunteer Cavalry at San Antonio, Texas boarded railcars for the four-day trip to Tampa, Florida—without their horses.

It was unbelievable—a dismounted cavalry unit! The transport and organization of such a sizable force and its equipment had taxed the abilities of both the military command and the railroads. Only Wood, Roosevelt, and a few of the other officers would be allowed to keep their mounts.

In Tampa, Griffin, along with the other Rough Riders joined some 30,000 soldiers, along with their gear, transporting on a convoy of four U.S. steamers bound for Cuba. He did his best to endure the Caribbean's boiling sun and the cramped quarters of the transport, the S.S. *Yucatan*.

At last, the narrow opening of Santiago, Cuba's harbor came into sight. According to a report issued by Lt. Colonel Roosevelt, the enemy flotilla was trapped inside the harbor. But it was heavily protected by the grim Morro Castle batteries and deadly submerged minefields. In addition to an estimated force of 36,000 troops posted around the city of Santiago.

Just swell.

The American transport ships landed the first wave of American soldiers eighteen miles east of Santiago at the unfortified beach of Daiquiri. As Griffin waited his turn to go ashore, all he could think about was how he was going to locate Giselle . . . and whether or not she was safe.

The surf was running high, so he and the other soldiers waded ashore thoroughly soaked. Each man carried only his weapon, ammunition, and a knapsack holding three days of rations.

The Rough Riders moved swiftly west to the neighboring coastal town, Siboney, with the order to secure that area for additional landings. Small boats moved back and forth across the shallow waters to land load after load of American soldiers. The process consumed the entire afternoon and well into the night.

A camp was set up on a brush-covered flat, bounded on one side by jungle and on the other by a pool of stagnant water surrounded by a few palm trees. No sooner had the Rough Riders built fires for dinner when a tropical rain storm pounded them and drowned their fires.

That night, after the storm passed, Griffin bedded down. He stared up into the immense heaven of stars. Where was Giselle? And how in God's name was he going to survive the disease-infested jungle and the impending battles required to encircle and capture Santiago, much less find her on that God-forsaken island and get her back to the safety of the States?

What a preposterous, irrational, cockeyed plan he had concocted—and what an utter, love-struck fool he was! But that was nothing compared to another thought that continually buzzed around him like a damn mosquito that he fought to swat away . . . what if he was unable to find her or save her? He couldn't let himself entertain that possibility.

He did not sleep that night, afraid to dream. Afraid of a nightmare. Afraid there was nothing left of Giselle for him to save.

The next morning, the all-Black Tenth Regular Cavalry and the Rough Riders moved out. Between Daiquiri and Santiago was Las Guasimas, a Spanish stronghold. Two scouts leading the advance discovered the Spanish lay hidden in the heavy jungle canopying the road to Las Guasimas. So, the Americans skirted the roads' to scale the area's high ridges.

At eight a.m., Col. Wood, astride a mule he had commandeered, ordered Griffin and the other soldiers to fill their magazines.

Griffin's hands shook as he followed the order. His first battle. At that moment, he had never wanted a drink or a cigar more.

Nothing had prepared him for the apprehension of impending death. The relentless pounding of blood at his temples. The profuse sweating beneath his armpits and at his crotch. The dry, metallic taste on his tongue that was fear. The knotting in his gut, like he was about to piss when being taken out behind the wood shed as a nine-year-old for one of his mischievous infractions.

He was intensely afraid. Not of death, exactly, but of not having the choice about how he would live or die. His fate lay in the hands of Colonel Wood and Lt. Colonel Roosevelt, whose orders he was sworn to obey.

Col. Wood placed his Hotchkiss battery in a firing

position nine hundred yards from the entrenched enemy. The Americans opened with their volley and the Spanish returned fire. The denseness of the jungle, combined with the Spaniard's use of smokeless powder, made it difficult for Griffin to locate enemy positions.

With a cool determination he did not know he possessed, Griffin forged ahead. Right and left of him, soldiers went down. A shot in the arm or leg did not seem to deter the young men, who pushed onward with him.

At last, the exchange of gunfire began to subside, and a quarter of an hour later, one of Wood's officers rode back to report that he Spaniards were routed. He was grinning broadly. "Yeah, the cowards are beating a retreat all the way back to Santiago's harbor."

After that, Colonel Wood set an exhausting pace. Griffin felt damn lucky to be among the remaining five-hundred or so Rough Riders. After marching for three days in a row, he struggled along with the rest of them up steep hillsides tangled with thick jungle. Next to him, a soldier dropped his bundle roll out of sheer fatigue, and just ahead of him, another soldier fell, semiconscious, due to the heat.

Only images of Giselle kept Griffin going. The way she smiled jauntily when trying to hide her uncertainty . . . the way her teeth nibbled on her pencil's eraser when she was contemplating something she was writing . . .the way her lips circled her cigarette's tip, a provocative gesture that never failed to arouse him . . . the way her slender arms raised tantalizingly, as she pinned in place an errant curl . . . the way she carelessly displayed her shapely ankles when she hoisted her skirts. Jesus, she was the embodiment of his wet dreams.

They spent another chilly night huddled in their trenches, knee-deep in mud and water from the daily tropical downpours. Those trenches quickly became breeding grounds for mosquitoes. Dysentery, malaria, and yellow fever spread through the ranks. Provisions were either non-existent or slow to reach the men.

"Embalmed beef," the sergeant in the trench with Griffin grumbled, referring to the god-awful canned meat they were issued.

By midafternoon on the fourth day, the Rough Riders and the Buffalo Soldiers built their camp beside a marshy stream, grittily staking their claim—San Juan Hill— buffering Santiago on its other side.

In the opposite direction, to the west of Santiago, Cuban General Garcia and his guerrillas blocked any reinforcement of the Spaniards from inland. When coupled with the U.S. Navy's blockade of Santiago's harbor entrance, the Spanish ground forces, as well as its squadron of ships, would be contained.

That night, Colonel Roosevelt began preparing for the attack. However, after more than a week in the temperamental tropical climate, many of the troopers were ill. He was eager to engage the enemy before yellow fever and other tropical ailments could take an even greater toll on his men.

He felt the key to taking Santiago lay in occupying that high ridgeline that overlooked the city from the east. If the

Americans could take and hold this hill, they would have a commanding view and a tactical advantage over the 36,000 enemy soldiers in the harbor city below them.

Rising from the jungle, San Juan Hill was defended by some 750-odd Spanish soldiers in heavily fortified positions that were additionally protected by large blockhouses. Two modern howitzers provided the Spanish artillery support.

Early the next morning, on July first, the bugles sounded Reveille, opening salvos in the battle to free Cuba. Griffin and the other anxious soldiers quickly ate their breakfast.

He rolled up his bedding, preparing his pack for the march towards the San Juan River to engage the enemy, when what he wanted to do was head north into the interior and search through Cuba's dozen or so reconcentration camps for Giselle. No matter where she was, star-crossed lovers though they might be, he swore he would find her—even if it was in the enemy's nest—and convince her he was worthy of her love, as well.

But first things first . . . he must survive here and now.

Somewhere behind him and the other Rough Riders, the Buffalo Soldiers of the 10th Cavalry were moving at double-time to catch up in the march. At last, his regiment reached the ford of the San Juan River.

This was it.

Griffin swallowed and with sweaty hands, checked his rifle again.

Ahead, astride his pony, Texas, Colonel Roosevelt raised his sword and yelled, *"Charge!"*

Amid the whine of sniper fire and the explosion of Spanish artillery, Griffin plunged knee-deep into the water.

Suddenly, from the canopy, Spanish guns began a heavy shelling and a barrage of shrapnel hit the untested troopers. Those in the forefront not struck down quickly sought cover under the far bank's heavy foliage.

The crossing was so littered with dead bodies that a partial damn was created. Griffin stared at the harsh realities of violence and death. At one point, he floundered over a bobbing body. A bloody stream, leaking from between its shoulder blades, dribbled into the already crimson water.

He gagged, retching with his repulsion. The blood thudding in his ears drowned out the sound of gunfire. His legs threatened to buckle. As his heavy pack threatened to pull him down, he tried to shake off the horror and fear that stunned him, struggling to keep his head above the water's blood-churning surface.

A colored man grabbed his arm. "Heave-ho, mate," the tall, athletic man called out, grinning.

He nodded his gratitude and, in tandem with the Buffalo Soldier, thrashed ashore. Thick smoke from the American artillery behind them had filled the skies and masked the positions of the enemy above.

Along with the others, Griffin determinedly climbed the steeply rising hill. Some of it was snarled with prickly pineapple plants and barbed-wire entanglements, which the soldiers' gauntleted hands plowed through. Amid a recurrent hail of bullets, the furious advance was subsequently reduced to a crawl.

Looking back over his shoulder, he saw the heavy pall of gun smoke that hung over the valley below. He was amazed that not a single bullet had found its mark in his sweaty flesh . . . so far.

Surmounting the hill became a two-hour effort under a blazing sun, though everything seemed to him like a nightmare from which he couldn't awaken. By now, he was shirtless against the heat and armed with a pistol in one hand and a machete in the other.

The highest ridge, known as San Juan Hill, waited just ahead. Zigzagging, he and the blue-flannelled Buffalo Soldier began to rapidly scale the first of the double hilltops, separated by a slight ravine. Its crest was dominated by a blockhouse. Across the ravine to the north, atop Kettle Hill, hunkered another large blockhouse.

He fought his way through the ravine's enemy trenches, using his machete to decapitate a Spanish defender springing suddenly from nearby foliage to attack him. At last, he and the Buffalo Soldier reached the top of Kettle Hill. Breathing heavily, they both sprawled on their bellies beneath a tree hung with wild jungle orchids.

"Your name?"

"Mandrake."

"You gotta be kidding me." Griffin managed to grin, noting only then the other man's shoulder bars outranked him. "My uncle is named Drake, sir."

"No, man, I'm serious. Captain Mandrake Jarvis of the Tenth Cavalry."

"Griffin, sir. First Lieutenant Griffin Paladín, sir."

Behind them, the army's rapid-firing Gatlings rat-a-tatted the air, urging them up and forward. There was no retreat. The final stronghold was the yellow stucco *hacienda* that had been converted into the blockhouse atop San Juan Hill. It had to be taken at all costs.

Off to Griffin's left, Roosevelt spurred Texas forward. A sea of young soldiers followed. Griffin shot to his feet. While other soldiers shouted the rallying cry, "Remember the *Maine* and to hell with Spain," he gave his bloodcurdling Texican war whoop.

He propelled himself through the swarming bees of buzzing bullets, toward the Spanish flag flying over San Juan Hill—and toward the cavernous jaws of death.

SIBONEY, CUBA
JULY 1898

A score of staffers on the army hospital ship, the U.S.S. *Relief,* gathered around the bulletin board on the hurricane deck. A cablegram had been posted with the latest results of the fierce fighting in its third day in the battle for Santiago.

157 dead, 1300 wounded. Daring Rough Riders hard dealt by enemy.

Obviously, the United States had underestimated the enemy's strength and resistance.

Other details were listed, as well as casualty names. But, as more wounded were waiting to be hoisted aboard from hospital barges, the doctors, nurses, nuns, and orderlies made way for other medical staff to view the most recent postings.

Pearl rubbed her eyes, as if she could scrub from them images of the hourly horrors she was witnessing. She turned from the bulletin board and shouldered back through the clustered men and women seeking their turn to read the grisly news.

What insanity. This killing of one another. And how insane her decision to become part of it—to think she could avoid the war's carnage.

But duty called.

She threaded through the maze of steamer chairs, where wounded were convalescing under canopies. She continued past the dispensary, autopsy room, and contagion ward.

The army ship had been converted to five wards, with every nook and cranny occupied. In each ward, iron double-deck bedsteads were fastened securely to the floor. Each bed contained a wire basket for dressing material and medicines.

The water was too deep for firm anchorage, and with the rock of the ship, she half stumbled down the stairwell to the upper saloon deck with its medical ward of eighty-two beds, and then down yet other stairwell, at last reaching the gangway entrance. The large surgical ward with its seventy-four beds was positioned near it—and in a closed-off corner of that ward was the brightly lit operating room.

Often, she was dragged in to assist in surgery. The shock of what she had observed in that room was etched onto her brain like an image on an x-ray negative. It seemed nothing could faze her now. The compassion Nicolas had accused her of lacking, she had acquired. But that deep compassion was now being quickly replaced by a cold, hard clinical detachment.

To one side of the surgery ward was the photographic dark room and large, heavy x-ray machine, the crowning glory of medical science. Only now, under Dr. Gray's tutorage, was she learning fluoroscopy and skiagraphy.

A homely young man with a huge heart and infinite patience, Dr. Gray was overtaxed in evaluating the hideously wounded men constantly wheeled in and out of the operating room. The cranial wounds bothered Pearl the most, even more than the chest ones.

And then there were the soldiers who didn't make it, most of them succumbing to tropical diseases that attacked the disabled immediately. The putrid smell of infection still made her gag. There had been so many burials at sea.

She had to wonder how Becky, who was seeing the worst of the cases, was faring. As an immune, Becky was nursing the ill and wounded at Siboney's general hospital, a pest-house of rows of tents ashore. From the *Relief,* Pearl could see the Red Cross flag that floated over the hospital tents, staked on a narrow rocky strip between the sea and the base of the mountains.

"Nurse Paladín, come look at this radiograph," Dr. Gray called from the dark room.

She did not really want to. She longed to be back in her dry-docked, dull classroom. Yet here she was, as her mother once was, boat bound.

"I'm not a nurse, Dr. Gray," she reminded him, as she had each day they had been anchored off Siboney.

She might be merely a Radiographic Assistant, but she was nevertheless required to wear a starched high collar and cuffs, with a white apron covering to the ankles. Professional but not practical, considering the splatter of blood serum, feces, and *vomito negro* from yellow fever.

"See . . . right here." He pointed at an image with his pen. "The metal jacket—a nickel-encased Mauser—is perfect."

She looked and noted the bullet was lodged behind the tibia about four inches from the ankle joint.

"Entered the calf here, below the popliteal space, and never touched the bone," Dr. Gray noted. "That's the good news. The bad news is, with gangrene setting in, amputation is required."

A month ago, his medical jargon would have gone over her head. Her gazed dropped down to the bottom left hand corner of the x-ray, at the name imprinted on the image— *First Lieutenant Griffin Paladín.*

Despite the electric fan swishing lazily overhead, a blast of heat suffused Pearl, then whirling blackness.

CAMP SIBONEY, CUBA
JULY 1898

The hospital base camp that provided care for many of the wounded was protected by barbed wire and the reek of a stagnant, mossy lagoon—but nothing could protect it from yellow fever. It had overrun the camp, so an offshoot nursing facility had been set up in the nearby hurriedly constructed railroad shed.

Nurses and orderlies were now among the patients, as well as regimental doctors. Even the head surgeon and commanding officer, Major LaGarde, had been stricken by the disease. This left Captain Mandrake Jarvis of the Tenth Cavalry, the colored regiment that had also participated in the siege of Santiago and now had been sent to care for the sick, as the camp's commanding officer.

The impervious Captain Jarvis strode through the camp, filthy from the mass of the sick, and issued orders right and left. Despite the way he had efficiently taken charge of the camp's hospital, kitchen, laundry, and all disciplinary matters, inside and out, Becky Wheelwright found him insufferable—and apparently invincible.

Appeals went out every day for volunteer nurse replacements from among the Buffalo Soldiers. The soldiers still able to stand were cleaning up the place, taking down and putting up canvas tents, moving the ill on stretchers, unloading stores from mules and railroad cars—and digging graves.

At that moment, Becky could hear *Taps* being played over the remains of those who had died during the night.

She had managed to stay reasonably healthy and was feeling all right that morning, despite the tropical downpour of the summer hurricane season—until she looked out and saw the captain sloshing through the mud toward the tent where she was tending to six patients.

She groaned, turned her back, and opened one of the first aid dressing packages to remove its antiseptic powder and absorbent sterile cotton. The pungent smell of the boric and salicylic acids fleetingly overrode that of the arm amputee's putrefying flesh on the last cot.

"Nurse Wheelwright," the captain barked from the tent's doorway.

At the rear of the tent, she closed her eyes briefly then pivoted with a grimace of a smile that was either from the onset of a headache or his abominable presence. He was one of the few men taller than she—and one of the few men she found so aggravating.

Like many other soldiers, he had reshaped the crown of his campaign hat to a four-cornered Montana peak so it wouldn't hold rainwater. He yanked off his hat now and whacked it against his thigh. Water sprayed off it like a wet dog shaking its coat. "Get the patients ready to move. I'm relocating this tent."

"That's impossible, Captain. These patients are too sick to be moved." Even as she spoke, one of the patients began spewing black vomit.

The captain stalked down the narrow row between the squeezed-together cots until he was mere inches away from where she stood at the bandaging table. Green specks fired his brown eyes. "Either my men move them, Nurse Wheelwright, or the rainwater spill-off from the lagoon will."

"Yes, sir!" she snapped, replicated a salute, and shoved her hand against his chest so she could plow past him.

Except his chest did not yield. She glared up at him and saw laughter glinting in his expression.

It was as if she herself had been overcome with yellow fever—hot, weak, her heart fluttering precipitously in her chest.

Surely, not. Surely, she was not so foolish as to be love-struck. Not at her age . . . not at forty-one . . . and not over this haughty officer, however handsome he might be.

At last, he stepped aside, letting her pass.

After he headed back into the rain, she quickly bundled the quinine pill bottles, chlorinated soda, gauze, and other loose medical supplies into one of the wool blankets. Not that there were that many supplies. Disinfectants and sterilizing supplies were meager—and dysentery and bed-sores had become rampant.

Only three of the men were conscious enough for her to explain what was about to happen. "We're moving to higher ground," she consoled one young man who had taken a bullet in the thigh that the attending doctor decided was too dangerous to remove.

In a single night, that doctor, wearing only his regiment uniform protected by a butcher's apron, had operated on more than a hundred patients by fitful candlelight.

By now, thunder was vibrating the ground, lightning was setting afire the sky, and the wind was lashing the tent. It was deeply ditched, but the water was rushing around it in the ditches like small rivers.

Two dripping wet soldiers hustled inside and began moving the first cot. Grabbing another blanket, she caught up with them and trudged in the mud alongside, trying to shield the patient from the rain with the blanket.

While the rain poured in torrents, each patient was loaded into a mule pulled army wagon with a tarpaulin covering its bed. Back and forth between the wagon and the tent she splashed, accompanying and shielding each cot with the sodden blanket until all were loaded.

On her last trip back to the tent to collect whatever was left there, she stopped just inside and, gasping, braced her palms against the bandaging table. Water was swirling around her ankles now. Heat flushed her again and the room began spinning.

Even as she swayed, the reassuring thought crossed her mind that she was not love-struck after all, she was simply ill. And then the floor came up to meet her.

Rain was pelting her face when next she opened her eyes. Through rain-spiked lashes, she could make out the square, determined jaw above her as that of Captain Jarvis. With each of his steps, she was jarred unmercifully. "Put me down, Captain Jarvis."

"When we get to the railroad shed."

"You're wheezing."

"Wet skirts and all, you're no light thing, Nurse Wheelwright."

She felt too weak to argue and closed her eyes. When he reached the corrugated shed, he commandeered from somewhere a dry blanket and laid her down on it amid the multitude of rows of wounded and ill, then he deserted her.

Chilled yet sweaty, she lay there, listening to the groans and retching sounds of the others, louder even than the drumming of the rain on the tin roof. The stench was more overpowering than the hospital camp lagoon.

Within minutes, a colored orderly, looking utterly exhausted, appeared with another dry but hardly clean blanket and draped it over her. "I'll see if I can round you up some water and vittles, ma'am."

She nodded toward the man lying to her right. His ebony face possessed a chalky undertone, and he was shivering uncontrollably despite being covered by a blanket. "I think he needs attention more than I."

Soon thereafter, she drifted off only to awake that evening to the distant sound of a foghorn. With twilight, the wretched sounds made by the ill had hushed somewhat. Here and there, candles had been lit against the encroaching darkness. The ghostly shadows of several orderlies moved and stooped, moved and stooped, among the rows of blanketed forms.

A blanket completely covered the body on her left, and soon an orderly arrived to cart the corpse away to the Dead Wagon.

She felt the weight of someone's stare and realized it was the man to her right. The chalkiness had receded from his face. "You're better?" she rasped. He nodded. "*Sí*. Fever broke. Malaria."

"You're Cuban?" Many of the revolutionaries had fought alongside the Americans at San Juan Hill and she had tended some of them herself.

"*Sí*. A scout for General Garcia. I am called Kosmo. You are only the second woman I have seen in the last few months." His crooked teeth gleamed in the darkness. "For this reason, I stare. I apologize."

"Oh." Being one of the few women, among several thousand males, she was accustomed to this. "Was the other woman a nurse, also, or one of your Cuban female freedom fighters?"

"No. Neither. A war correspondent for the *Austin Statesman*."

SIBONEY, CUBA
JULY 1898

"Goddamnit, you tell those sawbones they are *not* going to take off my leg!"

Pearl splayed her palm over Griffin's chest, pressing him back onto his bed. "What if the gangrene kills you?"

"Then let it, but I am *not* going to gimp around the rest of my life. Amputation may have happened to my father, but I won't let it happen to me. You understand, Pearl?"

"And do you understand that if you continue to cause such a ruckus, the docs will chloroform you here and now?"

She had volunteered to apply intermittently the new treatment protocol of a saline solution of bromine and bromide of potassium dressings to his wound, hoping to battle the gangrene—and amputation.

But medical science did not possess enough documentation on how lengthy the treatment needed to be administered before victory could be certain. She figured the war would certainly provide grim and ample opportunity to test some new protocols.

It was strange, however . . . now that she was attending Griffin in such an intimate situation—he covered only by a sheet—she experienced none of the fiery passion she would have thought. Nothing like she felt when with Nicolas. And it had nothing to do with a patient's weakened state. If anything, the furious Griffin could have taken on the entire occupying Spanish army. Which reminded her of more grim news . . . .

"Griffin, our Becky—Becky Wheelwright—has been nursing the ill and wounded at the army hospital ashore at Siboney. She herself has come down with the Yellow Jack."

"She's here? In Cuba? Goddamnit!" he muttered. "Can you do anything to hel—"

"There's more. A barge incoming with patients has brought news from her. Giselle is being held captive by the Spanish commander at Manati." Another oddity. Any other time, Pearl would have rather swallowed arsenic than mention Giselle's name to Griffin. But this time . . . and the fact that Pearl was genuinely afraid for Griffin's object of devotion . . . loosened her tongue.

Griffin's eyes blazed as brightly as his matted red hair. He grabbed her wrist. "Get me some damned clothes, Pearl. Now!"

Late some afternoons, *Comandante* Rubi, along with his Spanish armada of guards, would escort Giselle down the hill to the culinary and cocktail comforts afforded by the adjoining bar and cafe of the Hotel Inglaterra. Just below the castle, the old-world hotel snuggled with other quaint stores and picturesque bistros on the main thoroughfare of Del Prado.

These excursions were the only times she was allowed out—in clothing Rubi procured from an elegant dress shop on *Avenida* Del Prado.

How could she not like the man? He was intelligent, witty, and he liked to shop for her. Still, after three months of near incarceration . . . sometimes she thought she would surely go stir-crazy. Cut off from news and kept in suspense, her legendary vitality was noticeably reduced.

Foolishly, she continued to hope for some kind of gallant rescue, like in the fairy tales. Since she had tried, and failed, to save herself, she had to be realistic—no noble and valiant rescue would be forthcoming.

Only the finest of Manati's Spaniards gathered at the Hotel Inglaterra's bar at that hour for the piano music and drinks beneath the cool revolving palm fan—while scant blocks away, Cuban children, gaunt in the face and with terribly swollen bellies, lay beneath the blistering sun while being attacked by besieging flies. The reconcentrados' mangy dogs had been eaten long before.

Aware of this suffering and starvation almost within smelling distance, Giselle could not bring herself to touch the tapa appetizer of olive, cheese, and *chorizo* on toasted bread that covered her glass of sherry. That way, the harassing flies did not get into her sweet sherry or into the *Comandante* Rubi's daiquiri, a rum cocktail distilled by the local Bacardi family, which was his preferred drink.

Drink she did. Probably way too much. Drinking was a way of blotting out the cruel extermination of an oppressed people. Over 800,000 Cubans were driven from their homes and forced to live in small, squalid areas where sanitation was impossible. Tens of thousands were already dead.

Sanitation at the castle was also questionable, although its image as a "castle" was taxing the actuality. Plumbing was rudimentary. Electrical lights and fans rarely worked. Scabs on her arms attested that the bedding was doubtful. Ringworm, scabies, bedbugs? Who knew? Piped water was rusty, and its availability often reduced to a trickle. The tarnished mirror in her room reflected a woman few men could find appealing.

Not that she had to worry. Luckily, Giselle soon learned *Comandante* Rubi was not at all interested in women.

Unluckily, she had been unable to send a single dispatch to the States, despite her many pleas and sly ruses.

Heavily armed guards did not permit her to forward any of her secreted messages of troop strengths and armament. She could only leave the castle escorted by the *Comandante*. Then the guards stood watch outside both the Hotel Inglaterra's front door and the bar doorway.

This time in the bar, instead of the usual tapa covering her sherry glass, she saw Rubi's hand, the one missing its thumb.

She could barely hear his voice above the piano music. Puzzled, she glanced at him from beneath the wide brim of her straw boater. He had never before kept her from drinking, or even getting a bit tipsy. Something was troubling him.

"Santiago de Cuba is in its second week under siege by your general, Pecos Bill Shafter."

She frowned. Rarely did he share military information with her. "Yes?"

"Your U.S. artillery atop San Juan, backed by your Gatling Gun Detachment and a dynamite gun, are pounding the city—while the Cuban rebels under Garcia are choking off all its water and food supplies."

Exhilaration winged through her. Nevertheless, she waited, watching him closely. Something felt different.

He removed his pudgy palm from the top of her glass. Despite the whiffing fan, beads of sweat formed on his brow. He patted it dry with his linen napkin, then took a long draught of his rum. He seemed more interested in ogling the dashing bullfighter in the faded poster on a wall near them than talking.

She waited, reminding herself to breathe.

At last, still peering at the time-yellowed poster, he murmured in his reedy voice, "Should Santiago surrender, you will become a liability."

She inclined her head to listen carefully.

"A newspaperwoman," he continued softly, somewhat sadly, "with the knowledge you have gathered here—the reconcentration camps and so on—well, you would be a political embarrassment. For my country. For myself. You understand?" At that, his sorrowful gaze slid from the poster to fix on her.

Had she heard him correctly? A frisson of apprehension rippled her spine, prickling the fine hair at the back of her neck. "No. No . . . I don't. I don't understand."

"If Santiago capitulates, I am afraid you must share the same fate as any spy."

Her gasp was audible, then her face went numb. So, her feckless determination to cover revolution had brought her to this. To die alone, so far from home and her family and friends. She forced her hand to cover his, matted with fine hair. "Surely, something can be arranged, *Comandante* Rubi." She smiled beseechingly. "Surely, I could be exchanged for one of the Spanish captives the Americans have—"

He withdrew his hand. His unblinking gaze was resolute. "Make no mistake, while I find you a charming and diverting guest, I shall have no qualms arranging your execution."

GRIFFIN LIMPED ALONG THE NARROW, winding alleys beneath overhanging wrought-iron balconies and past the *Plaza de Armas.* He started up Manati's cobblestone road, spiraling toward the castle atop El Manueco's summit. Midway up, he noticed a cart rattling just ahead, its oxen hoofing it more quickly than he could walk. The ox cart was almost overflowing with mangos, coconuts, and pineapples.

His guide, the Cuban scout Kosmo, glanced at him with concern. "Your trouser leg, Lieutenant . . . you are bleeding again." The man was sweating heavily, whether from his recent bout with malaria or their present danger—or both.

"How much farther . . ." Griffin paused to bite back the pain, " . . . until we reach the Spanish garrison?"

Beneath his gaping white linen jacket, wedged behind his belt but within easy reach, was a .38 caliber long Colt. Some officers preferred Smith & Wesson's, but not he.

"No that much further, *señor.*" The little man's dark face wore a cheery grin, but his tone was grim.

Griffin hated this rescue plan, but it was all he could come up with. His absence without leave could land him a court martial, but by military law he had a month-long grace period. Besides, there was also the fact that he was merely a volunteer, one even now carried on the hospital roster.

With Pearl's help, it was fairly easy for him to leave the *Relief.* She also helped Griffin contact Kosmo. Even with the Cuban freedom fighter's assistance, finding—let alone rescuing—Giselle would take a hefty dose of sheer Texican bravado and pure Paladín harsh confidence.

Unfortunately, he also had his Grandmother Fiona's luck of the Irish, because heading downhill toward him and Kosmo was a squad of Spanish soldiers.

While a rakish Panama straw hat hid his flame-red hair, Griffin's height might draw the soldiers' attention—and so might the clothing he wore. Scrounged up by Pearl, the typhoid-ill French mine owner's white linen trousers were far too short for Griffin.

At once, he dropped to one knee, gasping at the pain that action induced, to fiddle with his boot lace, as if retying it. The boots, far too small for his longer feet, were cramping his toes painfully. His sweat was soaking his shirt and jacket.

From the corner of his eye, he watched the soldiers pass—and then he looked again. Confined within their core was a tall, young female, of whom he caught only a glimpse.

"That's her!" the Cuban scout muttered. *"Señorita* Giselle."

Griffin scanned the backs of the four soldiers around her. Only three appeared to be armed. The fourth wore an officer's insignia—stripes and chevrons.

"Go get that fruit wagon up ahead, Kosmo, however you can. Whatever it takes. Give me a half hour then meet me back at the *Plaza de Armas* with it. If I don't show, you clear out."

Kosmo looked at Griffin as if his brain were rotting from jungle fever. Shaking his head, the little Cuban trotted off after the fruit cart.

Griffin's mind spun like his Colt cylinder, clicking on an empty chamber. He came up with nothing—no brilliant plan, no creative manipulation—just the idea to keep close and wait for an opportunity. It damn well better happen within thirty minutes.

Griffin followed the soldiers and their captive—his Giselle—from a safe distance. After the group turned the corner at the bottom of the hill, he rounded the corner to discover a noteworthy hotel bordering on swank, the Inglaterra.

Two of the soldiers were posted outside the entrance. The men appeared to be idling, talking quietly, paying little attention.

Fists knotted in his pockets, shoulders hunched, his temples beaded with sweat, Griffin limped toward the hotel's heavy nail studded double doors. Glancing down, he saw fresh blood spotting the trouser leg over his wound.

Shit!

"¡Eh, mano!" One of the soldiers, a doughy-looking guy, jabbed the bayonet of his Mauser in Griffin's direction.

He froze, heart thundering in his ears. Keeping his head down, he peered at the soldier from beneath the brim of his hat. *"¿Sí?"*

"Your boot lace, it is unknotted."

He nodded. *"Muchas gracias."* He knelt and quickly tied it, correctly this time, before hurrying past the guards and through the deluxe hotel doors.

Inside, from a bar/cafe to his left, someone was

banging on a piano, "Hot Time in the Old Town Tonight."

Had to be a lucky sign, since the song was popular with the American troops. The third armed guard posted outside the bar entrance was not such a lucky sight. But with good fortune backing Griffin once again, he hobbled unchallenged past the guard and stood just inside the doorway. Gradually, his eyes adjusted to the soft candlelight flickering on each table.

Probably fewer than a dozen well-dressed couples were seated at the tables. An ornate beribboned and flower bedecked purple chapeau hid the profile of one woman, but when he glimpsed her features, he realized with disappointment that they were not Giselle's.

Then he spotted her, seated at a far table with the commanding officer. Apparently, she had not noticed Griffin. Beneath her straw boater, her features were arranged in a pleasant, albeit strained, smile.

Griffin hunkered a hip onto a stool at the far end of the bar and winced as sharp pain shot up his leg. The Colt barrel poking his groin didn't help either.

In his South Texas-butchered Spanish, he ordered a *cerveza* from the aproned bartender. Then he turned his focus on Giselle and the Spanish officer.

The man was bulky, and Griffin figured even on his good days he could not take him on. Gradually, between sips of the godawful brew, he noticed the officer's mannerisms—not blatant, but nevertheless telltale signs that aroused Griffin's suspicion.

Hell . . . that ploy had once worked for him at the

Menger in San Antonio.

So why not?

He signaled the bartender. "Whatever that officer is drinking, give him another, my compliments." He dug inside his pocket, fishing out from his meager clutch of *pesetas* what he hoped was enough, and dropped them on the counter.

After the bartender set the cocktail before the officer and murmured it was *gratis*, the officer peered across the room at Griffin, eyed his long, lean frame, then beckoned him to the table.

It was then that Griffin played his hunch. He shook his head in the negative, then nodded up, in the kind of gesture that could not be misinterpreted, to the hotel rooms above.

A meaningful grin creased the officer's crafty expression. Muttering something to Giselle, he stood.

Griffin did, too, wincing again, before heading toward the lobby in as steady a stride as he could.

The hefty officer caught up with him at the foot of the broad carpeted stairs. "I shall take care of the room." His voice was a low purr. "Management keeps the first room on the right for me."

Griffin nodded again and headed up the stairs, silently cursing each painful step. He could literally feel his strength seeping away and could only hope the blood seeping from his wound was not leaving a trail.

The first room on the right was dimly lit by late afternoon sunlight filtering through a gauzy curtain, but he found the bed and grabbed a pillow. After less than five minutes, the officer entered.

Both the pillow and the piano banging below muffled the sound of the Colt's discharge.

"Sweet dreams, you pig."

Fervently hoping the Roman poet Virgil was right, that "fortune favored the bold," Griffin gritted his teeth in some semblance of a smile he hoped would mask the agony of his throbbing leg. With a nod, he sauntered past the guard at the bar entrance.

Giselle was glancing around, and he knew her well enough to realize she was wondering if she had time to try an escape. He noticed her shoulders sag from the obvious futility of her hope.

He slid into the empty seat across from her. She looked up and gasped. He grinned, placing his larger hand over her gloved one, leaning close to make himself heard over the ragtime music. "Your companion, the Spanish officer, is taking a long nap upstairs from which he will not awaken."

Her bee-stung lips formed a perfect *o*.

"Giselle, you once told me that my words were eloquent but my actions empty. I am trusting that my request for you to accompany me and Kosmo to the *Wanderer*, waiting only three miles down the shoreline, impresses you as a most eloquent form of action."

"That would depend, Griffin Paladín, whether you can get us past the guards outside and avoid the Spanish cavalry patrolling the beach."

Her teary, arch smile relieved him. Apparently, captivity had yet to dampen her spirit. She had a point, damn't. His fingers drummed the table. As he rapidly considered possibilities, his gaze strayed around the cafe bar. His eyes stopped on the bullfight poster. The matador wearing the funny looking black felt hat with knobs over each ear gave him an idea.

Once more, his eyes scanned the room and its patrons. Then he rose, flinching with the pain. "Give me a moment, sweetheart."

He approached the older woman in the purple hat, so ludicrously decorated with ribbons and flowers and even a tiny straw bird nestled among them. He nodded at her escort, an elderly gentleman sporting a flamboyant handle-bar mustache. Both were drinking martinis, garnished with limes. Quite a few martinis, to judge by their tipsy grins.

With a tip to the brim of his hat, Griffin said in his fractured Spanish, "Pardon me, but my . . . uh . . . fiancée over at that far table adores your chapeau. She has agreed to marry me today, at the last moment, but only if she can wear something as beautiful as the hat you are wearing." Using extraordinary charm—well, at least, he hoped so—he smiled down into the woman's faded eyes, bracketed by crow's feet. "Is there any possibility you would be willing to exchange hats with my fiancée?"

She perked up with obvious feminine pride. Her gloved fingers flittered with her hat's draping ribbons. She slid an assessing glance at Giselle's straw boater. *'Pues*, si. I would be willing. How very romantic. Could we attend the wedding?"

"Uhh . . . a ship's captain is marrying us. Out at sea. It's rather a rushed thing, you understand."

Her companion lifted his frosted glass. "Our best wishes, then. *Salud.*"

While the woman clumsily removed the hat pins from her hair, Griffin summoned Giselle over. "This kind lady has agreed to trade hats, my love."

"What?" Puzzled, Giselle glanced from him to the woman.

"For our wedding," he prompted.

"Oh. Oh, yes." She caught his drift and flashed the older couple a dazzling smile.

Quickly, she removed her hat, the trade was made, and within minutes he and Giselle passed the guards at both entrances and made their way toward the *Plaza de Armas.* Noting his limp, she glanced down, spotted the blood-stained trouser leg, and gasped.

"A mere annoyance," he gritted.

She slipped a supporting arm around his waist. Fortunately, Kosmo was waiting near the plaza's fountain with the fruit cart, because Griffin did not think he could walk much farther.

"Kosmo!" Giselle threw her arms around the little black man. "It's you!"

Kosmo beamed, but Griffin warned, "Time enough later for renewing old acquaintances."

With the little Cuban revolutionary perched on the cart bench, and Giselle and Griffin wedged warily in the cart bed among the prickly pineapple, mangos, and bananas— quite possibly also harboring a passenger tarantula——the three set out for the beach.

No one stopped them as the cart wobbled over the shifting, crunching sand for what seemed mile after heavily forested mile. Still, Griffin would not feel safe until they were aboard the *Wanderer.*

He soon spotted the huge wooden transport, anchored about a hundred yards offshore. Two lighters were ferrying supplies and ammunition to Cuban insurgents, waiting in the nearby jungle—both to provide protection and help unload.

The motley freedom fighters, bandoliers of cartridges slung across their chests, moved to and fro on the beach. Crates and boxes were stacked on the wet sand.

With Kosmo leading the way, he and Giselle arrived just as the last of the supplies were unloaded from the *Wanderer's* lighters. Suddenly, from the opposite direction, a Spanish cavalry patrol charged the landing party. Bullets began plowing the sugary sand from rifles in the surrounding jungle.

As senior officer, Griffin barked the order for the Cuban soldiers in the landing party to lie down and open fire on the advancing Spaniards. Shoving Giselle behind a stack of boxes, he sprawled his own outstretched body over hers and fired his Colt repeatedly at the mounted horsemen.

Around them, men died, but amidst the carnage, plate-size butterflies fluttered like souls taking flight. He prayed that was not a bad omen.

When the Spaniards withdrew into the jungle to prepare another assault, Griffin ordered everyone aboard the two small supply craft, along with several of the wounded guerrillas.

Kosmo chose to remain. "Until our paths cross again!" the little man shouted, waving at their receding boat.

The small craft drew alongside the *Wanderer* and he, Giselle, and the others quickly scaled its ladder. At the same time, the Spanish cavalry charged a second time. They swept the waves with their Mausers and peppered the *Wanderer*'s wooden hull.

Aboard the *Wanderer,* Griffin tried to spot Kosmo, but he was invisible within the pall of gunfire. Had the little man disappeared back into the jungle?

Then, grim-faced, Griffin turned to Giselle—only to find her missing. So like her, not to stay long in one place. Off in search of another adventure. Most likely seeking an interview with the ship's captain or the boiler room's stoker. Titles did not impress her.

What was important—did he? Did he impress her enough that she would agree to marry him?

GALVESTON
AUGUST 1898

"A caller for you, Ms. Paladín," Mrs. Linz yelled up the staircase of the genteel 17th Street boarding house.

Frowning, Angel laid her fountain pen alongside the pad where she had been scribbling notes for her upcoming ophthalmology examination. Who could be calling on her at this time of the evening?

Only the University of Texas office and her family knew where she was living—not that Uncle Wade had not been above threatening to cart her back to Houston when she refused to return on her own after Pearl shipped out to Cuba.

Pearl's expedition had not made him tap-dancing happy either. "Don't any of the females in my family ever listen to me?!" he had thundered.

Someone else looked ready to thunder when Angel descended the stairs to the parlor with its shabby couch and even shabbier vertical-striped wallpaper, peeling in unsightly splotches. "Since when did you start going by the name of Paladín?" Drake demanded.

She was thrilled that he was there but waited until the landlady had waddled off down the hallway, out of hearing, and waited until her own erratic pulse steadied, then gave him her best gamine grin.

"Since the day you won me in that card game." He filled the parlor with his presence. Filled her entire frame of vision. He was appealingly arrogant and wholly unaware of how devilishly handsome he was in his red flannel shirt, denims, and dusty boots. "Of course, when we marry, that will make it legal, but regardless, few—"

He yanked off his Stetson and flung it onto the couch, shifting his weight to one leg, fists on hips. "Damn't, Angel, that's not going—" He broke off, grunted, looked down at the threadbare rug, and then back at her through those ridiculously thick black lashes. "I need your help."

Her lips stretched into a wide self-satisfied smile. "Please have a seat, sir. I would be most willing to entertain your proposal."

"Get that idea right out of your head, Angel. Hells bells!" He grabbed up his Stetson, and she was terrified he was going to leave, but instead he gestured towards the coat rack. "Get your hat and gloves and come with me." Her smile was nearly simpering. "But, of course. However, at this time of evening it may be difficult to find a priest."

He rolled his eyes. "If you keep this up, the only priest you will need will be one to administer your last rites."

"Give me just a moment."

Demurely, she lifted her skirts to climb the stairs until she reached the first flight and was out of his sight, then raced up the remaining steps and into her and Pearl's room. She paused before the cheval mirror to bite her lips until they were a hothouse rose pink. Tiding her upswept hair, she pinned on her Carriage Hat with its wide Leghorn brim curved to suit her face.

Then, recalling Pearl's offhanded remark that a woman should put perfume where she wanted to be kissed, she dabbed White Lilac at her wrists, the base of her throat and behind her ears.

Grabbing her gloves, she descended the stairs again, this time at a stately pace. Her mind was sorting out what was behind Drake's coming all the way to Galveston to seek her out.

"I want to go where we can talk privately and it's not too stuffy," he told her, taking her elbow.

"I know just the place." She had been wanting to go there since moving to Galveston.

The whimsically designed octagonal pavilion known as the Garten Verein was in the center of town and was the center of Galveston's refined social life. Lit at night like a fairy lantern, dancing couples would swirl within the pavilion while German waitresses served beer steins and sandwiches. It also sported a bowling green and ten pin alleys, a tennis court, croquet grounds, and a large ornate fountain amidst its garden's wandering, secluded paths.

Although the membership was modest, she naturally did not have one. Nicolas Cordova most likely did. She would figure out a way to make use of his if she had to. She missed seeing the dandy calling on her cousin Pearl, and she really missed Pearl. Despite the coming and going of the boarding house med students and young interns, without Pearl's exotic presence, the house seemed drab and dreary.

Drake scowled at the Garten Verein's flamboyant pavilion with the bandstand's music filling the sultry evening air. "I said I wanted to go somewhere we could talk."

She stifled a sigh. So much for the opportunity to inveigle a dance out of him. "We can. Just behind it is a lovely landscaped park."

Incandescent fireflies lit the way among the paved stones leading to the back of the pavilion. He asked her about the family, Pearl and Griffin. "Word has it they're somewhere in Cuba, along with Becky and Giselle."

She shared with him what little she knew, which was virtually nothing. When he eyed the wrought iron spiked fence and locked gate, he looked down at her, his brows nearly meeting over the bridge of his strong nose. "Well? What now?"

"Surely you have scaled a fence before?"

"My question is have you? Never mind. I'm sure you have."

She tossed him a cocky grin and held up her arms to him. "Lift me over." His grin, slow in coming, was as cocky as hers, and she realized he really was going to do it. "Angel, you are a hellion."

He slid his hands beneath her armpits and easily raised

her above his head. Her skirts were swishing his face, yet she still was not clear of the fence's spikes. "Tuck up your knees!"

"Don't look!" she warned, drawing her knees up against her chest and clutching her skirts around her ankles.

"Heave ho!"

She landed in the flowered garden bed on the other side with an explosive grunt.

"Hey!" another male voice shouted. "What is this fracas?"

Beyond Drake, she could see a uniformed guard charging down the slope toward them. Drake glanced over his shoulder, braced his hands on the top rail between the spikes, and effortlessly bounded over the fence. He grabbed her gloved hand and jerked her to her feet. "Come on! Run!"

Tugging her along, he raced down one of the pebbled paths, diverting his course through a maze of trails created by shrubbery and trees. Holding onto her hat with one hand, she was running as fast as she could, trying to keep up with his longer strides. Behind them, she could hear the guard calling out for them.

Drake was laughing. She had never heard him laugh.

The guard's shouts faded. When one path dead ended at a small fountain, she yanked on Drake's hand. "Stop. Let's . . . rest. He's not likely to . . . find us now."

He released her and she plopped onto the fountain's stone rim. He sprawled next to her on the grass, his lower back braced against the stone, trying to catch his breath.

"The priest may have to administer the last rites to both of us."

"I prefer the marriage vows first. Next, we grow old together, and only then we receive the last rites and die together, wrapped in each other's arms."

"Look, kid, do you not understand—there ain't going to be any 'together.'"

"Oh?" She looked down at him. "Then why are we here . . . together?"

Only the tinkling of the water and his grumbled sigh interrupted the twilight silence. She broke it, commenting, "Somewhere you've lost your hat in out flight."

"I've lost my mind, that's what." Nonetheless, he began to explain his plan to sell the lumber mill. "You're whiplash smart and I trust you. You . . . well, you know my reading shortcomings."

He cleared his throat and started again. "Like it or not, I have come to realize that you are . . . that is, your knowledge and skills . . . have become valuable to me. So, I just want you to verify," he patted his shirt pocket, "you know, confirm, that the contract I have here is in order."

"You came all the way from Conroe's Switch just for me to review a contract?"

"Not exactly. If this works out like I hope, like I'm planning, there would be other business matters, legal things, and such."

"I see." Near her knee, her gloved hand fingered through his thick black hair while she gave what he had said some thought.

Startled, he shifted a fraction away but then leaned into her caressing hand. "From what you've shared, Drake, you would need me quite often. This sounds to me like a 'together' proposal of some kind. How do you plan to implement it?"

Her fingers worked through his hair, soothing him sufficiently, she hoped, so that he would not cut and run as was his habit with her. For that matter, he was that way, period. A rambling man, he had called himself. Still, instinct told her he missed his father terribly. She knew he had a sharp, calculating mind like his old man.

"Well, what I had in mind was maybe you coming to Conroe's Switch once a month for several days."

He propped an elbow on her knee. She knew he was unaware of his intimate action, so wrapped up was he in discussing his subject while she massaged his scalp. "There's a fine hotel there, and I would pay all your expenses—plus a salary of some sort. If we worked it right, you'd miss very little of your schooling, maybe none at all."

She smiled to herself. She was one step closer. "Let me make a counter offer. I agree to your terms, but only on the condition that you dance with me tonight at the pavilion."

She could feel him stiffen. "I don't know how to dance."

"I'll teach you."

"Nope. Not about to make a fool of myself in front of folks."

"Then we can dance right here."

"There's no music. And just so you know, I am not

going to let you play Delilah to my Samson with this hair mussing you're doing." Nevertheless, he leaned into her, tilting his head for better access to her massaging fingers.

"You said you trusted me, Drake Paladín."

"I do—in all matters but this childish fancy for me that you won't let go of."

"Well, you'll just have to trust me in that matter, as well. I'm not asking you to marry me right now. If not a dance, then I'm asking for a kiss—right now. The kind a fellow gives a girl he's hankering after."

"I'm not hankering after you. Get that through your head, will you?"

"You will be." She firmed up her tone. "But this is my final offer. I want a kiss—and a salary and expenses—in exchange for my monthly review of your business matters. Take it or leave it."

He sighed. His hand caught her wrist and brought her hand down, turning it over, to plant his warm lips inside the hollow of her glove.

She heard him inhale the delicate floral scent she had dabbed on her wrist—and, even more, heard the way his breath caught. In response, her own breath fairly sizzled in her throat. How could such a sweet gesture pack such a wallop?

Abruptly, he raised his head, only just realizing how intimate the gesture he had just administered. "Don't go thinking that means anything. It's not a kiss on the mouth."

"It still counts."

"Get it through your head. You're like a sister to me."

She noted he continued to hold her wrist, his thumb unconsciously massaging the pulsing flesh of its underside. She gestured toward her wrist. "Don't stop, Drake."

He yanked her to her feet. "I'm not stopping until I've hauled you back to your boarding house and I'm back in Conroe's Switch, safe from your scallywag ploys."

MONTAUK POINT, NEW YORK
SEPTEMBER 1898

A steam-powered fog signal swept slowly over the multitude of tents at Camp Wyckoff, occupying a finger of land jutting into the Atlantic. The camp had been hastily established to quarantine the disease-decimated troops returning after their decisive victory in Cuba. The Department of War hoped to prevent the spread of yellow fever stateside. Twenty-one thousand veterans suffered amidst the camp's squalor.

That evening, Becky made her way from the detention hospital to the general hospital where Pearl worked. Becky fretted over the gal as if she were her own child. Miss Pearl needed someone to take her in hand and give her prissy butt a spanking. Her harebrained idea to participate in the war could have cost the girl her life . . . and that of her own, she mentally noted. Luckily, her case of yellow fever had been mild.

She thought it ironic that the Fifth Corps confronted a deadlier enemy at Camp Wyckoff than they had the Spanish bullets in Cuba. Eighty percent of the Corps were suffering from the tropical disease.

The Camp's tents had no board floors with only canvas strips spread on the ground and the soldiers' ragged, bloody uniforms to serve for pillows. Medical supplies were negligible, potable water was in short supply despite the Point's ponds and lake, sanitation was almost non-existent, and the food rations were slow to arrive and when they did, they often had worms.

Nonetheless, that evening the able-bodied soldiers finishing out their quarantine time were strolling along the nearby lakeshore or pitching horseshoes and playing cards by tent lantern light. During the day, they idled their time watching the bronco riding staged by the Rough Riders, who had suffered the greatest casualty rate of any regiment in their battles at Las Guasimas and San Juan Heights.

"Nurse Wheelwright."

She knew well that commanding tone by now. At Camp Siboney, that voice had just about commanded her to recover. Aboard the USS *Miami* transport, that voice had commanded her to rest.

She turned to watch Mandrake cross the narrow road that separated the tents of his Tenth Cavalry from those of the Rough Riders. He strode with military bearing as stiff and straight as his Winchester. "If it isn't the proud and proper Captain Jarvis." He looked uncommonly handsome in his blue wool field service blouse with the captain bars gleaming on his epaulets.

He hooked his thumbs in his leather cartridge belt. "I'm

being shipped out tomorrow. Fort Douglas, Utah."

"Yes?" What now?

"Follow me when your army contract is finished."

She blinked, opened her mouth, shut it, and then managed, "Captain Jarvis, I know you're a man of few words, but do those last few words respectfully imply you be wanting to marry me?"

"They do. Respectfully."

She stiffened. The night draft, bolstered by the ocean wind, whipped her long, starched apron against both hers and his ankles. She had once had a yearning for faraway places, exotic sights. Cuba had satisfied that. Utah never would. "That's it? Not even you have captured my heart, Nurse Wheelwright?"

"I would go down on one knee, here in front of everyone, but I'm on duty, and I was concerned if I waited until I was off duty, you might not be around."

"I do believe that's the most I have ever heard you say. But it's not enough, Captain Jarvis. Not by a long shot. If you want to be marrying me," her brown eyes snapped with indignation, "you'll find a way to get that skinny carcass of yours down to Galveston, Texas. There, you may court me as befits an officer and a gentleman!"

As she spun away, she recalled her ma often scolding her for acting uppity because she possessed a convent education. Maybe she was uppity, because she sure was not going to humble herself, even if the bossy Mandrake Jarvis was a captain in the U.S. Army who had been nominated for a Medal of Honor.

She also recalled admitting to Pearl she missed being with a man. God help her, she hoped she did not miss out on being with this one.

WHILE THE THIRD U.S. CAVALRY band blared "Hail to the Chief," Giselle stood in the summer heat with a crowd of officers and enlisted men at the Long Island Railroad's Montauk station.

Throughout the ten-week war, she had got not one dispatch off to the *Austin Statesman,* but this time, at least, she was prepared with pad and pencil. President McKinley had arrived to investigate the appalling conditions at Montauk's Camp Wyckoff. She had been among the first of those few reporters filing reports. Finally, her big chance had arrived.

Just as the President stepped off the coach, followed by Secretary of War Alger and the rest of the presidential entourage, the pounding of horse hooves and a flurry of dust heralded the arrival of Lt. Col. Roosevelt and his officers to greet the President. Her gaze alighted on Griffin, emerging from the dust like some mythical knight astride his steed.

His getting her aboard the steamship *Wanderer* had been a heroic accomplishment. With sand sprayed by pinging bullets abrading their faces and around them men dying, she had looked up into his intrepid features and realized she was not afraid. Not with him there.

Now he dismounted with the smooth agility of a man accustomed to life on horseback and strode, not toward the platform and President McKinley, but toward her. She glanced off toward the stalwart President. If she missed this opportunity to interview him . . . after all she had gone through to be a reporter . . . .

Tugging at his gauntlet with his teeth, Griffin freed his hand to claim hers. "They say the third time is a charm. It had better be, because I shall not ask again. Giselle, will you be my wife?"

GALVESTON
NOVEMBER 1898

That Sunday, Mandrake hinged opened the screen door and knocked on the wooden one of the shotgun-style house at Avenue Q-1/2 and 28th Street. The morning was warm. Or, maybe, he was warm because of his unaccustomed nervousness.

Out of bullets, he could face without a qualm an enemy charging him with a bayonetted Mauser, but this . . . this was altogether new to him.

A colored man of medium height, about his own age, nearing fifty, and with an authoritative air with which Mandrake readily identified, answered his knock. The man's wide nostrils flared, as if attempting to detect with primeval sensibilities the scent of danger or friendliness. Then, as if having arrived at a conclusion, "Yes?"

"Mr. William Wheelwright?"

"Yes." His brows knitted. Becky's brother was dressed in a black frockcoat, apparently for Sunday services. Becky had mentioned he was a deacon at the First Union Missionary Baptist Church.

Mandrake removed his felt hat. "Mandrake Jarvis, late of the Tenth Cavalry, Buffalo Soldiers. May I please have a word?"

A smile creased the broad face. "Captain Jarvis. Becky has spoken of you."

"No longer a Captain, Mr. Wheelwright. After the required thirty years of service, I have retired."

"Billy. Call me Billy. And come on in, please."

"I trust Miss Becky Wheelwright spoke of me in favorable terms."

"Most favorable. Have a seat and I'll call Natty. She's just pinning on Cora's hat—our granddaughter. We take care of her. Would you like some coffee? Tea?"

"No, please. I don't want to delay you." For a man accustomed to being in command, this was proving more difficult than he thought. "With you being Miss Wheelwright's next of kin, I have come to ask you for her hand in marriage."

Billy rubbed his jaw. "If you have retired, then what are your prospects?"

"I have none—other than my retirement pay. That is, unless you would be willing to hire me as a freight handler for Paladín Freight Yards." He knew that labor unrest had become a big problem at the wharves. "I have worked hard all my life and I have a strong back and can load cotton bales as easy as anyone on your payroll."

Billy eyed him up and down. "To answer your second question—yes. I will find a place for you one way or another on the payroll. As for the first question, I would advise you to catch the next train back to Houston and ask Becky yourself. Be sure to tell her you have my blessing."

Blessing or no blessing, Mandrake still had to convince her that it was to her benefit to wed with him.

AUSTIN
FEBRUARY 1899

Griffin considered himself, if nothing else, a practical man.

Despite Galveston's helter-skelter growth, the beachfront town was fast achieving world-class port status and housing was hard to come by. Cognizant of the Gulf's occasional fierce storms, he had finally finagled a two-story house built on a woodland of stilts near the middle of the island, yet within walking distance of Nicholas Clayton's architecture firm.

If only he could finagle more assignments from the firm, but he was considered an upstart with little architectural experience.

Something else he had not finagled was Giselle's hand in marriage—and that was also due to his being a practical young man, or so he told himself.

She had before her a reporter's coveted story of a lifetime with her coverage of Cuba's *reconcentrado* camps and her detailed revelation of them in a four-hour-long in-depth interview with President McKinley.

If he robbed her of the fame and glory resulting from newspapers and magazines around the globe picking up her stories, then he was certain she would be forever discontented. The journalist's invaluable 'what if?' would haunt her and him alike the rest of their married lives.

Before she could reply to his final proposal, he had cut her off. "I am giving you six months to make sure you want to be Mrs. Griffin Paladín."

He was absolutely certain he wanted her at his side for the remainder of his life. Adventurous and fearless, she challenged him to be a better man when with her than he was without her.

"Six months," he had said, "or, let's make it Valentine's Day, most romantically appropriate. At high noon. If you want to be my wife, Giselle, meet me where all this first began—in the supply closet of the Capitol. Marry me there and then in Austin, without any pomp or ballyhoo. Because that's the only way I'll know it isn't just another of your adventures—a socialite wedding of the year. Or, say, like First Lady to the President of the United States. That it is me you want, not a headline."

And now six months later . . . well, how was he to know that beginning three days ago, on February eleventh, the entire south would suffer the lowest temperatures on record. That morning's *Austin Statesman* had reported that the day before, the thirteenth, the port of New Orleans was completely iced with floes floating out of the Mississippi into the Gulf—and that snow was piled on Galveston beaches. Meteorologists were predicting negative two temperatures for Austin today.

His waterproof Inverness cape collar turned up, he leaned into the arctic sleet needling his face and the wind buffeting the derby he clamped on his head during the thankfully short walk from the depot to the Capitol.

The pink granite Revival Renaissance building he had once sketched so eagerly felt empty. A few guards and die-hard politicians, none whom he recalled from his father's gubernatorial terms, roamed the halls on predetermined missions.

He pulled his watch fob from his vest pocket and glanced at the time—eleven-fifty.

He went unchallenged as he strode through the corridors, unerringly finding the tucked away supply room. Closing the door behind him, Griffin fumbled in the dark of the musty place, finally twisting the socket key to turn on the pendant light.

The room seemed even smaller. Perhaps because more items were stored in it—wooden file cabinets, bookcases, desks, and chairs. He pulled out one of them, wiped the dust from its seat, tugged off his leather gloves and hat, and prepared to wait. If anything, Giselle, unlike his cousin Pearl, was always on time.

He checked his pocket watch. Twelve-o-five. Well, the weather *was* ferocious.

He reached over and selected one of the law books, an early calf-bound edition of *Blackstone Commentaries*. Thumbing through it brought back memories of his law school days at Baylor.

He had rejected the terms of his Grandpa Niall's will—to run Gorman Transports, which would become Griffin's upon graduation, because he had wanted to build. And now he could foresee a great state's potential to be built into a worthy empire like Sam Houston has once envisioned. Griffin suspected he had a hell of a lot more of his father's political leanings than previously imagined.

However, he was only one-half of that equation. Giselle would have to want it, as well. That was, if she even wanted him.

He put the law book back and once more fished his watch fob from his vest pocket. Twelve-twenty-five.

With a sinking feeling, he pulled out another book, this one a volume of the *Encyclopedia Britannica.* Unseeingly, he riffled through its pages.

His took out his pocket watch again. It read twelve-thirty-two.

She was not coming.

He rubbed the back of his neck, took a deep breath, and returned the book to the shelf. He reached for his gloves and hat. The practical side of him said he just needed to bite the bullet and make the best of it.

But something inside him whispered that there are certain things that change one's life irrevocably and not always for the better—like the last time he opened the supply door and reporters outside created a hullabaloo that sent his and Giselle's lives in different directions.

It all seemed so long ago. So much had happened since

then.

Sighing heavily, he opened the door . . . and there she stood. Her hair wind-lashed from beneath her toque hat, her cheeks and nose rosy behind her veil. She was breathing hard. "The ice snapped the trolley line . . . I ran the rest of the way."

He caught her against him, kissing her temple, so she could not see his glistening eyes.

Nevertheless, she tilted her head back and framed his jaw with her gloved hands. "Griffin, I don't want to be merely Mrs. Paladín. I want to be the First Lady to America's President Paladín. But wife to Galveston's Mayor Paladín will do for a start."

CONROE'S SWITCH, TEXAS
MAY 1899

Knowing he needed income to live on, Drake did what he thought his old man would have done—he diverted some of the profits from the sale of his lumber mill to the purchase of a struggling cleaning and pressing shop in Conroe's Switch, at a rock bottom price.

Once again, he hired Monty as manager. The gold-toothed Cajun was trustworthy and utterly capable. In the three weeks the shop had been open, Monty's garrulous, easygoing charm had brought in more customers each day. Most of them female, naturally—eager to offer their nurturing to the crippled man.

"Got my eye on a pretty filly from nearby Montgomery." The two of them sat in the small pressing room in the back of the shop and drank stale coffee at the ironing table. "Hired her to do the ironing and sewing. She starts tomorrow."

"Great news." Drake was coming in twice a week to treat clothing stains with the chemical perc and detesting every minute of being closed in the room with the nauseating solvent.

He had tried his hand at pressing and had scorched far too many garments. Monty had temporarily taken over that duty, as well as the front counter. If the cleaning and pressing shop were to stay afloat, Drake figured he needed to stay out of it.

The ringing of a bell announced a customer and Monty grabbed his crutch, propped against the wall, and hobbled out of the office to the front counter. Barely had Drake taken another swallow of the god-awful coffee, when he looked up to find Angel standing in the pressing room doorway.

His grimace hid his pleasure in seeing her. Her antics were a diversion in the tediousness of his drilling efforts. Seven-hundred feet and nothing. "You've got that look on your face. What prank have you pulled now? And what are you doing here?"

One hand held a portmanteau, the other a fistful of folded papers. Her grin was impish. "Signed, sealed, and delivered—your official deed to Paladín Pressers."

At the rate he was going, he would have to sell the shop

before the ink had time to dry on the deed. "You could have mailed it."

"I could have." She slid into the seat, vacated by Monty, who had conveniently disappeared. She dropped her portmanteau next to it. "But I have something else I want to show you."

He groaned at her exuberance. "I should have expected this. What?"

She leaned over, unlatched her traveling bag and rummaged through it. He noted her abundant hair caught up beneath a little, perky hat with black ribbon bows and the sunshine-yellow wisps that spiraled down her neck. So fragile, while the girl seemed so strong. Strong-willed, head strong, and unshakable.

He had always thought of her as a kid, but the memory of her small palm in his, kissing that soft hollow, had altered that image irretrievably. He had always felt comfortable around her, but now another element had been added. Gone now was their easy camaraderie. While he lusted after quite a few young women, he most certainly did not want to lust after Angel.

"By the way," she mumbled, still digging in the bag, "Griffin sends his warm regards and an invitation to his marriage next month with Giselle—an intimate family affair to be held at The Barony."

So, his nephew, the same age as he, had succumbed to cupid's poisonous arrow. "Nope. Now, what is it you have to show me?"

"Behold!" she erupted with fanfare, holding up a

bizarre-looking object. He arched a skeptical brow. "What is it?"

"It's a stereoscope. Look, hold this part up to your eyes and tell me what you see."

He slid her a decimating stare, but, plowing back the swath of hair that had tumbled onto his forehead, did as she ordered.

Darkness. He raised his head. Over the gadget, his eyes narrowed on her angelic expression. "Nothing."

"Oh, wait. I forgot to drop in a slide."

Intrigued with the novelty, he watched as she produced a large package of cards, thumbed through several, selected one, and dropped it in. "Now try it." He peered through the viewer again, this time seeing a three-dimensional picture of a man in a brown tweed Ulster coat with a cane, embracing a woman in her boudoir.

"The caption beneath the illustration," Angel purred, "says 'Love's Token, Freely Given.'"

His amusement palled and he sobered at her maddening self-assurance. He set the viewer down, cut his eyes at her, and nudged it back toward her. "Another one of your subtle suggestions?"

She dimpled. "I do think I should like to try that with you, but that is not why I brought the viewer. My college ophthalmology department has started using the Keystone Stereoscope to help those diagnosed with certain vision problems like yours."

"Did you say Keystone?"

Puzzled, she cocked her head to one side, birdlike, then

nodded. "Yes."

He was not a superstitious man, but he did believe in signs. "I'll give it a whirl." He flicked her another grudging grimace.

She threw her arms around his neck and rubbed her lips gently against his, just like the woman had bussed the man on the viewer card. Angel was just a leech that would not let go.

DALLAS
JULY 1899

"Sales are down again." Walter Cleef shook his head. He had stopped by the Emporium to refill his trunk with samples.

Claire, kneeling before a stationery shelf she was stocking, glanced up. "Perhaps it's the heat. People don't want to get out and shop when it's so hot."

Walter peered down at her steadily through his spectacles. "Yeah, perhaps it's the heat."

She knew he didn't believe her. They both knew it was the Obregon Department Store.

Complaining about the competition did nothing to alleviate their problem. Yet she suspected most suggestions, either his or hers, merely frustrated David.

Patiently, he would explain the logistics of the mercantile business and why a particular idea of hers to increase sales or decrease overhead would only backfire. Most of the time, David proved himself to be right. He never said I told you so, but she would always manage to feel like such an incompetent nitwit.

"During this hot weather," Walter grinned from behind his eyeglasses, "maybe we could give away fans for each customer purchase."

He had beautiful white, even teeth, and when he smiled, she thought he was downright handsome. "You know, Mrs. Solomon—maybe some eye-catching chartreuse fans. And to save cost, the fans could advertise Dallas Emporium on one side and, let's say, a funeral parlor on the other, with a slogan like, 'Dead Special - Casket Used Only Once.'"

Laughter pealed from her. "Oh, Walter, Obregon Department Stores would love that idea!"

"Here, let me give you a hand, Mrs. Solomon." He reached for the box of Waterman fountain pens atop a stack of cases but fumbled and dropped it. Pens scattered everywhere. Then, when he stooped to collect them, his eyeglasses slid off and he stepped on them, crushing the lenses.

"Tarnation," he muttered but cast her a sheepish grin as he knelt in front of her to retrieve the frames.

"I'm so sorry, Walter—about your eyeglasses and about laughing." Still kneeling, she admitted, "How positively rude of me. But you do have a way of making me laugh."

"I like it when you laugh, Claire."

He had never called her by her given name. She should have reproved him, but his humor made her lighthearted, and, besides, it was such a negligible incident—until he dropped his glasses again, this time purposefully, and grasped her shoulder to draw her against him in an ardent kiss.

The unexpectedness of it stunned her. Then, as his mouth moved hungrily over hers, a lassitude settled over her that she had to fight hard against. David might be having an affair with Ruth, but did that justify her own straying? She and David still participated in a relatively good sex life.

Relatively? What in the hell did that mean, when it came down to the holes in the heart?

GALVESTON
SEPTEMBER 1899

Classes were late getting started that fall, and Angel was inveigling Pearl to spend the day at the beach. "We can rent bathing suits at Murdoch's Bathhouse and afterwards have dinner at the Beach Hotel."

"No," she muttered.

Angel, pinning up her hair, stared at her in the mirror. At eighteen, Angel had blossomed into a striking young woman. A froth of gold-spun ringlets framed a perfect oval face dominated by lively eyes as green as shamrocks. "Why, not, Pearl? You've always liked the beach."

"It's too chilly and windy today." That was the truth. The past winter had been a deadly, record-setting bitterly cold one. This spring and summer had been cooler than usual, a harbinger, she feared of worse weather to come.

But the excuse of chilly weather was only partially the

truth. The Beach Hotel secreted ghostly memories of that first afternoon Pearl spent there with Nicolas. A year had passed since she had returned from Cuba. He had kept his promise that he was finished with the Paladíns.

She only wished she could be finished with him. Unbelievably, she had spent most of the war aboard the *Relief,* where thousands of men came and went. Yet none of them had captured her fancy, although she had had countless offers of marriage. None of them challenged her the way Nicolas did. None of them possessed that wherewithal to offer a safe anchorage in a storm that he did.

She gathered her parasol and reticule. "Besides," she told Angel, "I want to stop by the Freight Yard—call Momma and Papa, and then check in at John Sealy."

With her war experience in fluoroscopy and skiagraphy and Dr. Gray's Letter of Recommendation, the nursing school had grudgingly offered her a one-year contract last January. Yet, she felt as if she were walking a tight wire.

When Rod Obregon learned of her appointment, as he invariably would, when next would he strike, cutting her off at the knees?

She could have taken the trolley to the Freight Yard, but she preferred walking. It cleared her head.

The Freight Yard was just down the street from the depot and between the Galveston, Houston & Henderson Railroad and the Gulf, Colorado & Santa Fe Railroad yards. An ideal location. The Paladín Freight Yard should have landed the contracts for handling railroad freight moving in and out to the mainland. But something—someone—had intervened. And she had a good guess who was responsible.

As it was, Paladín Freight Yard got the leavings from the cargo business Billy could scrape up from the harbor front. Becky's brother was on the Board of Aldermen, representing Ward Twelve on the east end of the island. The Board had made it possible for colored men to work as stevedores on the wharf

Since the boarding house telephone was out of service, she was planning to use the Freight Yard's telephone, which was nearer than Griffin and Giselle's home. She wanted to place a call to her parents, letting them know she would not be home for Thanksgiving after all.

As usual, the Board of Lady Managers, of which she was no longer a member, believed—as did the infamous Galveston Cotton Mill, which worked women and children sixty-six hours a week—that giving Christmas Day off was sufficiently generous. Any additional days off bordered on the preposterous.

Several freight handlers were hefting bags of coffee and rice, barrels of sugar and flour, and boxes of tools and firearms for loading. She found Billy in the small, dusty office, closeted with Nicolas. He looked as surprised as she felt, but he recovered quickly, tipping the brim of his pearl gray derby. "Miss Paladín."

She dipped a slight curtsey. "Mr. Cordova."

Billy tipped his felt cap, revealing his grizzled, tightly curled hair. "Miss Paladín."

From beneath half-cast lashes, she peered at Nicolas. He was watching her, a sardonic smile doing nothing to ease his rough-cut features. Her mouth felt dry. Her heart was beating so loudly in her ears she feared he could hear it. "I didn't realize you visited the Paladín Freight Yards, Mr. Cordova."

"Why, he has shares in—" Billy began but Nicolas cut him off.

"Billy tells me Becky says you acquitted yourself valiantly in Cuba. Not so squeamish anymore?"

A lady was never bold or brazen, but she looked him directly in the eye, hoping he could read the answer to his unspoken question in her eyes. "No, not at all." He was a proud man. What if he no longer had any interest in her?

It seemed he waited far too long to respond. Then he merely tipped his hat, tucking his cane beneath his arm. "Enjoy the day, Miss Paladín, Billy."

Anew century.

Eyes closed against his throbbing headache, a result of the New Year's Eve dissipation, Rod Obregon considered the future. What would the next year bring? Certainly not peace to his soul. Not until the Paladíns suffered as much as he.

Holidays stretched before him like a line of upright dominoes, falling with a thud, one rapidly succeeding another . . . and then nothing but deadly quiet. New Years . . .Valentine's Day . . . Easter . . .the Fourth of July . . . Thanksgiving . . . Christmas. Times for family get-togethers. But not for him.

And no reparation for Paladín injustices.

According to the Pinkerton's report, Angelica was aiding and abetting the Paladíns. Specifically, Drake Paladín, a ne'er do well. The deadbeat was now wildcatting, In the most unlikely of places to find significant oil. And with a fly-by-night cleaning shop on the side.

Angelica had always been precocious. Smart as a whip.

Why couldn't she see that Drake's kind was not the marrying kind? She was throwing herself away on a taker. Because that was all the Paladíns were. Takers. They had taken land from the *Tejanos.* They had taken land that should have been his. They had taken his father's life. And they had taken his sister and daughter.

Feeling every bit of his fifty-three years, he slipped from beneath the bed-coverings a still well-honed body, thanks to the new natatorium in El Paso.

He was careful not to awaken Adele, El Paso's stunning socialite, curled next to him. He was not up to reassuring the divorcee that, at thirty-five, she was still undeniably desirable. She was as miserable as he in her solitude.

He padded down the stone stairway, where Emilio greeted him with a toothy grin that could have sculpted President McKinley's glowering profile into the Franklin Mountains.

"Jugo de naranja y café, Señor?"

"On the terrace." It overlooked both El Paso and Ciudad Juarez, Mexico, across the mud-brown Rio Grande. He blinked at the glaring morning sunlight. "And a glass of vodka and tomato juice."

The morning was chilly but invigorating. Alice's bared fangs were little better than Emilio's grin. The iguanas' tail swished a lazy greeting.

Sitting himself at the pigskin table, Rod shook open the *El Paso Times.* Even the rustling of its pages made him wince. Hand at his brow, blocking the blinding morning sunlight, he scanned the headlines and accompanying articles.

> *El Paso Saddlery Company wishes all its patrons a Happy New Year. A grand bullfight is being held for the benefit of Alberto Zayas on Sunday, January 7th, '00. Four ferocious bulls have been selected for the occasion, regardless of expense.*

> *News has reached Canton, China, that French soldiers and Chinese natives engaged in battle near Wangchanan. The Chinese routed the French, killing 30. Chinese losses were not given.*

> *Miss Herndon, of San Antonio, will have her art studio at the Center Block. Pupils solicited in all branches of art.*

> *The last New Year in the 19th century was celebrated last night in El Paso by the blowing of whistles and ringing of bells.*

Interested, he focused blood-shot eyes on the paragraph and read on.

> *One hundred couples participated in the grandest social functions of the year—the Grand March, opening the Border Rifles' grand ball in the Orndorff Hotel, which was handsomely decorated. With clash of rifles and trumpet's bray, the grand march of the first and very successful military ball of*

the Border Rifles was led off by Mr. Rod Obregon and Miss Adele Bliss. The proceeds will be devoted toward fitting up the new armory donated to the company by Mr. Obregon's Lone Star Smelter Company.

Well, that was good for business and public relations. Then he read the last paragraph in the column.

Mr. Griffin Paladín of the famed Barony Ranch Paladíns and son of former Texas governor, Kerry Paladín, has announced his candidacy for mayor of Galveston.

Rod knew something drastic was called for. But what?

GALVESTON FEBRUARY 27T[H], 1900

Sister Elizabeth Ryan, one of ten sisters at St. Mary's Orphanage, grinned up at Nicolas as he alighted from his brougham. Her bespectacled eyes took in his red demi mask, red vest and cape, breeches of black silk velvet, patent leather shoes and top hat. "Why, Mr. Cordova, I almost didn't recognize you."

"Beware the devil in your midst." He flashed what he imagined might pass for a demonical grin. With his driver, old Marcus, he began unloading the cardboard cartons.

"A devil of a man bearing gifts of food is always

welcome at St. Mary's"

"While I would like to stay, Sister, I have another destination."

She peered at him over her spectacles. "Ahh, yes, that Bacchanalia, where one attempts to satiate the desires of the flesh."

"I sincerely hope I do, Sister." For five years now, Pearl Paladín had been a desire of both his flesh and his soul.

Mardi Gras in Galveston was a combined Charleston, Mobile, and New Orleans revelry done Texas style. However, by 1880, street parades had proved too extravagant and expensive to continue. Nonetheless, masked balls continued to flourish with exquisite costumes and lavish Carnival celebrations.

All the mischief of the event was throbbing with anticipation. Fun, frolic, and masquerading as mermaids, monks, and satyrs was the order of the night. Up and down the Strand, wild shouting, singing, laughing, drumming, fiddling, and tossing of glass beads took place as merrymakers wended their reckless way toward what would later be semi-oblivion.

That evening, the luxurious venue for the exclusive masked ball, a black-tie affair, and crowning of the Duchess was to take place at the Tremont Hotel, renowned as one of the grandest in the nation. Young ladies 'of family' from all over Texas vied to become coroneted duchesses, and the event was even reported in the society pages of the *New York Times*.

The Tremont's European-style showpiece lobby was

already packed with the arrival of masked guests, waiting on the Otis passenger elevator to descend once more. The hotel was the only one in the world to boast that innovation.

While human bodies were regaled with the sedate opulence of High Court Dress, above a ruff at the neck or a modest décolletage might be seen heads of beasts and birds. Everywhere could be observed gold lame sequins, dazzling rhinestones, and extraordinary plumage.

He shouldered his way past the guests clustered at the elevator and climbed the curving marble staircase to the Grand Ballroom. Beneath its magnificent chandelier dappled with shimmering soft light, revelers were already seated at white damask covered tables. Buntings the colors of Mardi Gras adorned the walls—purple for justice, green for faith, and gold for power.

A buffet supper, served from tables laden with gold plates, was being readied, and photographers and reporters with passes were already admitted. Liveried waiters moved among the tables, dispensing champagne. The orchestra was tuning up.

At a hundred dollars a person, he had reserved a table for four—himself, Giselle, and Griffin. That left a fourth chair at his table. Empty.

He had mentioned to Griffin that the table was for four and the extra seat was available should Griffin's cousin Pearl desire to attend the festivity. Nicolas could have invited her himself, but he wanted her to come of her own accord.

Those damnably proud Paladíns. Not that he was without pride. As a child without family or home, pride had become foremost for him.

But for once, Pearl would have to put aside her own highly valued pride and declare she needed him. Needed the Mexican orphan, Nicolas Cordova. Persuasion, at which he was exceedingly accomplished, would not serve in this case.

Griffin and Giselle, looking resplendent in a pink gown and demi-mask, arrived moments later, both looking radiant.

"Can't tell you how much we've been looking forward to this outing." Griffin shook his hand.

"Congratulations on your marriage." It was all he could do to refrain from asking if Pearl would be coming to the Mardi Gras gala or even if Griffin has passed along the casual invitation.

Griffin's eyes, looking out from a black demi mask, reflected sincerity. "I am most appreciative of this opportunity, Nicolas."

He had offered to introduce Griffin to Galveston's elite—government officials, members of the legal profession, naval and military leaders from nearby Fort Crockett, principal members of the medical and arts professions, prominent bankers and members of the Stock Exchange, as well as those engaged in commerce on a grand scale.

In short, most everyone he knew. He genuinely liked and trusted the young Paladín heir and felt the innovative Griffin would be great at leading Galveston into a new century as its next mayor.

And, still, Nicolas chaffed at Pearl's absence. For all his self-sufficiency, he could not rid himself of this voracious need of her.

Dignitaries came and went from his table, each of whom he and Griffin glad handed. Later, Griffin and Giselle danced, looking at one another with such adoration that Nicolas had to turn away from the loss and hurt that gnawed at him.

Young damsels preened from behind lace and feathered fans as they passed his table, where he sat smoking his cheroot or sipping from his flute. Several of the beauties he had bedded. They all paled against Pearl's wild, extravagant beauty and exotic grace.

And then, as if he had conjured her through mere thought, she was there before him—in satin and silk with her pearl-beaded train, which had to weigh over fifteen pounds, draped over her left arm. White—the color of sunlight, snow, milk, polar bears, and the Taj Mahal—gift wrapped her dark beauty in breath-taking luster. Her hair sparkled with what had to be silvery fairy dust.

"I should have known you would be late," he told her, trying to damper his elation. He strove to remain outwardly impassive, while inwardly he was flooded with exultation.

From behind the sequined white mask, she stared down at him. "Well?" She was biting her lower lip. "How do I look?

He stood, looking down at her. His stomach knotting and twisting, the hollows of his jaws pulsing, he answered foolishly with what first came to him, "Like a bride."

Eyes aglow with sheer intensity, she looked unblinkingly at him. "Yours?"

His grin was as silly as any Court Jester's. "Would six months—say September—be sufficient time to prepare for a wedding?"

"I thought the bride got to select the wedding date."

"Not a chance. If I don't take control of our wedding, you would be late for it, as you are to all other occasions."

Later, when the traditional King Cake was cut, his piece contained the gold doubloon. Some claimed it was lucky. Others claimed that it was unlucky, since you had to provide the cake the next year. It had both its privileges and responsibilities.

DALLAS MARCH 1900

Claire set the letter on her desk next to the company ledger. The letter—from the French wife of Claire's grandfather, had shaky penmanship that betrayed Thérèse's eighty-one years. Yet in Claire's memory, Alex and Thérèse Paladín seemed ageless and indestructible.

Claire missed her family terribly and wished some bond could be established between them and David. But he was adamant about making any kind of conciliatory overture. Thanksgivings were the worst, when she knew the family would be assembling at The Barony from all parts of Texas.

Thérèse wrote that Griffin had announced last Thanksgiving the news that he had accepted an architectural position with the prestigious N. J. Clayton and Company out of Galveston. The company had designed Gresham's Castle, the Beach Hotel, the Garten Verein, and the John Sealy Hospital. Thérèse also mentioned in her letter that Sarita had shared the news that Becky had become engaged to a fine, retired army officer who had seen duty in the Spanish American War.

Claire laid her hand atop her stomach, still concave. But then, her lanky frame had not shown evidence of her last child she had carried until she was further along. How she would love to share her own news, but a fear of another loss kept her silent—from all but Lila Bradford.

She had confessed to her friend that she was barely six weeks into motherhood. She had wanted to confess more, but that particular cross her soul would have to bear in silence for the rest of her life.

Lila Bradford announced she wanted to have her Baptist Women's Mission Union knit baby clothing. "Forget Butterick patterns. I always like it better when someone else makes my clothing."

Claire suspected David would be terribly worried how he would support another mouth. She, too, worried how they would feed and clothe a child when she herself often skipped meals to conserve the little cash they had.

Trying to compete with the giant that Obregon Department Store had become was draining David and draining the Dallas Emporium, which was wheezing on its last breaths. Inventory was gathering dust. Both the power plant and telephone company were threatening to cut off service. And customers were few and far between.

With over a hundred thousand soldiers returning from the war to find too few jobs, the economy was fragile yet dynamic. American investors poured billions into Cuba, Latin America, and the Philippines in projects like railroads, mines, and sugar, banana, and coffee plantations—but diverted little of their funds to homeland projects.

She opened the ledger and sighed at the dismal figures penned in red ink. She was now bookkeeper, salesclerk, and cleaning lady. But not seamstress. As money became scarcer and debts grew deeper, David had been forced to let go of Walter Cleef and the sales staff—but he had kept Ruth Warsaw, the seamstress.

And that thought led back to Lila Bradford's remark earlier, that she liked it better when someone else made her clothing. Claire wasn't certain if it was the baby kicking for the first time or excitement about her idea that triggered a tingle inside her.

Late that night, when David finally closed the store doors and they retired to their sixth-floor living quarters, she waited until they were abed to broach the subject that had been tapping relentlessly inside her, demanding his response.

As usual, she snuggled against his side, her head pillowed at the juncture of his chest and shoulder. Her fingers threaded through wiry hair matting his chest, feeling the steady beat of his heart and heat of his skin. She loved the smell of his skin, citrusy and fresh. So many times, early on, at the devastating thought of his betrayal, she had wanted to bolt. But it was the many intimate times like this, merely his simple scent, that cemented her to him. Foolish, she knew.

"David, instead of stocking household goods and farming tools, what do you think about adding an inventory devoted to women's apparel—you, know, lingerie and accessories, and children's clothing, too?"

"I think it's an outlandish idea. You know we don't have the money to add more inventory."

She raised on one elbow. "Regardless of what is bought, it is the women who do the shopping for their men and children. I think we need to be catering to women, David. We need to stock clothing of a sophistication—not generally offered here in the Southwest—and to furnish our store lavishly."

His voice was harsh with sarcasm. "And just who can afford to pay for the latest styles from Paris, New York, and other fashion centers?"

She smiled dreamily into the darkness. "People with money—like the Obregons of the world." And the Bradfords. Just maybe, Lila Bradford would "Drake, if I can get the money—"

He caught her hand, squeezing it tightly. "No! I will not allow you to go to your family for a loan, Claire."

The asperity in his tone was like a fingernail on a chalkboard. She drew away. A first for her. She had always tried to be the submissive wife. "I need a husband, not a jailer!"

"Maybe you don't need a husband even. Maybe you just want to run home to your family."

"Maybe you would like to be Ruth's husband."

He yanked her down against him. His other hand came up to capture the back of her head, his fingers anchoring in the mass of her hair. In the darkness, she could see the frustrated flash of his eyes. "Listen to me, Claire. We have to stop hurting each other like this. We're all each other has."

She gulped back the burning tears. "So you don't deny that you still have Ruth."

He looked stricken. His words eked out hoarsely. "All this time, you . . . you knew." It was a statement, not a question. "Damn't, why didn't you say something?"

Her laugh was as brittle as bone china. "Like stop or I'll leave? Didn't I tell you at the beginning of our marriage that I wasn't a runner?"

Shaking his head, he scrubbed his eyes. "God, Claire . . . I'll fire Ruth. Whatever it was that was between her and me—the sexual heat, the Jewish connection—it has long since faded. You have to believe me." He looked up at her from reddened eyes, his gaze raw with desperation. He caught her hands in his larger ones. "I am so sorry. Please . . . please tell me you will forgive my . . . my indiscretion."

God, could she feel any worse? "I do, I do," she rasped, trying to choke back both tears and fears. Because tears were weakness. And because she feared, though Walter Cleef was long gone, she carried his baby. If she did, it would be a secret she would have to carry to her grave.

GALVESTON APRIL 1900

In 1528, when Cabeza de Vaca was shipwrecked on a sand barrier one and one-half to three miles wide in the Gulf, he called that strip of sand Isla de Malhado, Island of Misfortune.

If Max Von Hesse-Lippe's son-in-law Griffin managed to avoid the island's damning reputation for misfortune and won Galveston's mayoral race, he would be a giant in Texas politics, both literally—standing six foot three—and figuratively, as the champion of the average Joe.

Already a state-wide renowned architect and lauded for his selfless public service, Griffin, was managing to appeal to the common roots of the island. This, despite his burden—his elite heritage of both The Barony wealth and Paladín politics, with his father Kerry serving yet another term as governor of the Great State of Texas.

The young man believed that good government combined with big business could be agencies for good and for change; that Galveston's affluence was meant for more than just railroad barons, shipping tycoons, and oil magnets.

Max and his stepfather Karl, who had represented the Paladín's legal and financial interests for more than sixty years, knew how naive that sounded.

Max's daughter Giselle had canvassed the island, requesting signatures for Griffin's petition to run for mayor. That obstacle hurdled, his campaign manager, his Uncle Wade, who owned a freight yard in Galveston, had been clever in appealing to various City Commissioners to vote for whomever they wanted on the first ballot but beseeching them to vote for his nephew Griffin on the second.

So, out of nowhere, came this upstart who was not even supposed to be nominated—and later the next day had come the yellow telegram, informing Griffin et al that he had won the nomination.

Next month, in May, Griffin stood an excellent chance of being elected, at twenty-seven-years-old Galveston's youngest mayor. At least, he had stood an excellent chance, until the *Galveston Daily News*, the oldest newspaper in the state, published this small paragraph in the "Galveston Gossip" section.

Our mayoral candidate, Griffin Paladín, may have a streak of lavender about him, as the register of Bolivar Peninsula's deluxe Sea View Hotel indicates the scion of The Barony Ranch shared a bed with another man recently.

And because of this news item, both Griffin and Wade had summoned Max from Austin for this pow-wow.

"What stuff and nonsense." Wade tossed the newspaper onto the marble-topped mahogany table from where he sat on the scrolled armchair. "Nonetheless, the damage is done."

At sixty and fit, Tara's brother Wade made Max, at fifty, feel flabby. His high-powered and high paying position as one of Texas's most successful attorneys had confined him far too often behind the desk.

Then there was Tara. Her position, running The Barony Ranch, had kept her in quite admirable shape. Nearing sixty, she was even more desirable than she had been at twenty, when he had been sorely tempted by her raw looks and freshness. Character and time had only polished her beauty.

And Ingrid, the young woman of wealth and refined beauty he had taken to wife instead, she was a jar of lard stirred with perplexing fits of mania. What a fool he had been. But then, once you've made your bed, you're forced to lie in it.

Griffin, hands locked behind his back, paced the parlor of his two-story house—a house Max found warm and welcoming.

Perhaps Max felt comfortable in the home because of his daughter's preference for classical and renaissance decorating, so evident in her choice of wallpaper and furniture. Or perhaps it was because her and Griffin's house reminded him of his own father's birthplace in Germany, with all its gingerbread mansions.

Griffin halted at the room's far end, before the two glass-doored bookcases, and faced him and Wade. "I was stumping on the peninsula, when a storm came up, damn't, and stranded us ferry passengers. We all ended up forced to share rooms and beds. I don't even remember the man's name I shared a bed with, but he was a piano tuner and snored like a walrus. I didn't sleep a wink that night."

In the 16th century, other Spanish arrivals had named that strip of sand Isla de Culebras, Island of Snakes. Max was of the strong opinion that Galveston Island harbored a deadly form of vipers in the guise of the members of the City Club. It had been organized around the interests of a select cadre of elites, lobbying for electoral reforms to limit the power of the working and middle-class constituents.

"Listen," he counseled, hands clasped beneath his bohemian goatee, popular in Paris at the moment. "From the little information I have been able to ferret, this hoax was planted by your Republican opponent." Oliver Baughman was the director of the City Club and sometimes called the Boss of Galveston.

"I'll nail him inside his coffin," Griffin muttered.

"Baughman did the best thing by you, Griffin. Think about it. Lincoln was repeatedly accused of the same intimacy, of sharing a bed with male companions throughout his life and look where that took him—all the way to the White House."

Griffin turned his eyes up to the barrel-vaulted, wood-paneled ceiling and sighed. "Just what your daughter has in mind for me, sir."

GALVESTON SEPTEMBERS, 1900

The sky was, absurdly, a mother of pearl color.

Above St. Mary Cathedral Basilica, the cradle of Catholicism in Texas, the fifteen-foot statue of Mary, Star of the Sea, and highest point on Galveston island, looked out over a turbulent Gulf.

A robust wind whipped waves against the foundation of St. Mary's Orphanage. In the city's earlier years, the orphanage had been built farther down the beach among the sand dunes to prevent the children from coming in contact with rampant yellow fever. Inside at that moment, ninety-three orphans thrilled with delight. Storms were always exhilarating.

Gray clouds boiled on the horizon, promising rain squalls. But then, did superstition not hold that rain was a lucky omen on a wedding day? Besides, Galvestonians were accustomed to storms and took them in stride.

Fighting exceedingly hot wind blasts, Nicolas arrived early at the gray-plastered brick cathedral—at eleven o'clock. The wedding was not until noon, with the reception scheduled for two at the Tremont Hotel.

But this was no mere wedding. For him, this was the creation of the family he hungered for. And what a family the Paladíns were.

Griffin, his best man, was already there. With a grin, his eyes assessed Nicolas's de rigueur wedding attire—morning dress in silver and gray with kid gloves and a silk top hat. "When my Giselle sees you, she may change her opinion about my being the most handsome man this side of the Mason Dixon Line."

"Where is Giselle?"

Griffin's mouth crimped in a wry smile. "Back at the house, tossing up breakfast. That aspect of motherhood has nearly become a morning ritual. But Max and Ingrid are with her. I knew you would be needing me more here to help you prepare to surrender your bachelorhood."

Nicolas mentally ticked items off his nuptials list. The sacristan had laid the carpet on the church's stone floor and put up the awning, but the wind was whipping it mercilessly. Nicolas had also stationed a man outside to assist the three-hundred invited guests from their carriages and maintain order among the reporters and photographers, while another man was at the door to check invitations. In addition, Nicolas had enlisted a policeman to keep away uninvited guests.

In his mind's eye, Nicolas placed each family member. Angel, as maid of honor, was at the boarding house, helping Pearl finish with her bridal preparations. This was one appointment for which he fervently desired Pearl to be on time—a rarity for her. Marcus had been dispatched in the brougham to deliver the two to the church.

Pearl's parents, Wade and Sarita, should have arrived already by the first morning train from Houston and, hopefully by now, checked into the Tremont. The rest of the family had already checked in—Alex and Thérèse Paladín, along with his son Kerry and his wife Catarina and Alex's daughter Tara and her husband Buck McHenry.

Karl and Rafaela von Hesse-Lippe had opted for rooms at the Hotel Grand, as had their son Max and his wife Ingrid. Less opulent than the Tremont, it nevertheless was quiet and sedate with old world charm and was adjacent to the internationally famous Galveston Opera House.

Nicolas had invited another family member, more specifically an extended family member—Roderick Obregon and his bride, Adele.

The policeman Nicolas had hired was not only intended to keep the uninvited away. He was to keep watch on Obregon. Nicolas meant to protect this new family of his, even more so by bringing the wolf into the fold.

The bigger question was whether the two black sheep of the family—Drake and Claire, along with her husband David—would show up for the wedding. Invitations had been issued, and yet no reply from either.

TWO HUNDRED ROOMS OF THE impressive Tremont Hotel faced the Gulf. Against a coppery dust sky, the ferocious wind tumbled green-gray waves against Murdoch's Bathhouse and Pier, jutting into the sea. More than twenty-feet high, they poured over the pier's lamps suspended from tall posts to illuminate naked night bathing.

Despite the weather display tower at the island's east end that flew a red and black storm flag, excited spectators traipsed to the beach to watch the spectacle of nature's power.

While Adele readied herself for the wedding, Rod stared out their room window, totally absorbed in the battle the wind was raging with the sea. Another type of battle was being raged within himself. A mindless fury that he knew was destructive.

After all these years, he would come face to face with Alex Paladín. Retribution was required, yet in taking it, he knew he would lose his sister and daughter, for all time. His anger at their betrayal gnawed at him day after day. A part of him demanded they seek his forgiveness—and a bigger part of him was afraid they would not.

WATCHING THE RAIN PELT THE hotel window like bullets threatening to shatter it, Alex felt every one of his ninety years. The train trip from San Antonio the day before had exhausted him. Griffin had met him and Thérèse at the Santa Fe Union depot with both welcome and unwelcome news.

The welcome news—Giselle was in the family way,

which meant the first great-grandchild for Alex. And more welcome news, Nicolas Cordova had invited both Drake and Claire and her husband to the wedding. For Alex, who had learned from Fiona the value of family, this might possibly be his last chance at a ceasefire with his son and granddaughter.

The unwelcome news—Nicolas had also invited Rod Obregon, who had already registered at the Tremont.

Ruefully, Alex admitted to himself that he was far too old to fight a duel with pistols. His sight was not what it used to be, and his right hand tremored with palsy. Yet that youthful spirit still resided in his aging body and sprang ever ready into familial protective action.

Before his eyes, another action was taking place. Astounded, he watched the immense waves overtake the Murdoch Bathhouse.

THE GALVESTON, HOUSTON, and Henderson railroad had chugged out of Houston early that morning—the first train Galveston-bound for the day. Inside the muggy coach, Drake was thinking how foolish of him to decide at the last minute to attend the wedding.

He was sweating—maybe because it was extremely hot with so many businessmen, tourists, and returning Islanders crammed shoulder to shoulder.

Maybe he was sweating because his well's rotary drill bit broke and he was running out of money.

Maybe he was sweating because after all these years, he would be coming face to face with his old man, meeting him as the failure his old man has predicted.

Or just maybe he was sweating because he would be seeing Angel again. That last time, when she had kissed him, although a mere brushing of the lips . . . then and there his gut told him that had been her final assault. He knew this weekend he either capitulated or learned to live without her palavering and no-quarter-given sieges.

But at that moment, it was the view of the blood-red sky from the train window that diverted him. Rain sluiced down the windows on the train's north side, but strangely, on his side—the side facing the ocean—the train's panes were dry.

The coach, joggled by wind gusts, rattled across the trestle over Galveston Bay. The surf was skyrocketing gigantic combers against the flimsy trestle. The three miles it took for the train to clatter across from Virginia Point— the last railroad stop on the Texas mainland—to the island seemed more like thirty to Drake.

When the train at last wheezed to a halt at Galveston's Santa Fe Union Depot, he should have been relieved, but he looked out again and saw the fifteen-passenger horse-drawn Tremont bus waiting to take its arriving guests to the hotel—and realized the horses stood in water inching up toward their bellies.

COLD WIND WAS WHISTLING through the boarding-house's door and window slits, but Angel and Pearl were both trying their best to ignore it.

"I have never seen anyone more beautiful." Angel smiled while arranging Pearl's train, which was more than seven feet long. Its borders were rose-leaves tied by true-lover's knots.

True love. Did such a thing really exist? At eight-years old, she had thought so. Those feelings had not been something as superficial as infatuation, lasting only a short time. No, as the years passed, those feelings for Drake had only intensified. So much so that when she was in his presence, the yearning was a sweet agony—an agony that was becoming almost unbearable.

If he couldn't feel the same way about her that she did about him, then it was better she pursued a life without him. Except that life without him was not a life. It was only existence. And existence equaled for her a dragged-out death. Better a quick and merciful one.

Pearl pirouetted. "This gown must have cost a fortune, but Nicolas insisted on buying it."

The gown was a fairy godmother creation Angel dreamed of wearing for Drake. Of soft, rich cream-white satin, it was covered with flounces of point d'Angleterre wrought with pearls and tiny silver spangles. A wreath of orange-blossoms and a tulle veil accented Pearl's dusky beauty.

"Queen Victoria would be jealous. And, lest I forget," she said extending her palm, "a pearl necklace—for Pearl and Nicholas."

Smiling broadly at both the wedding gift and the juxtaposition of the two phrases, Pearl turned around so Angel could fasten the necklace. "You are impossibly clever, my precious and precocious cousin."

"But not clever enough to attract the likes of Drake Paladín," she bemoaned and finished fastening the necklace around Pearl's throat. She lowered lids over eyes bright with misery. "He wouldn't come any closer to me than he would a pole cat."

Pearl turned and caught her hand. "Angel, Nicolas has invited Drake to our wedding. I have vacillated about telling you. I don't want you to be disappointed if he doesn't come."

She knew her grin had to be stretching from ear to ear. "Let's get you to the church on time!" Pearl's being on time for anything was something all the Paladíns knew was unimaginable.

Angel collected her silver compact purse, slipping her wrist through the chain so that she could manage the umbrella against the pelting rain. Hopefully, Marcus would have the brougham at the curb in front of the boarding house. With that bridal train weighted by water, Pearl would barely be able to walk down the aisle.

Outside, the dragon winds had other plans. They fileted the umbrella's ribs so that she and Pearl were instantly soaked. The air had turned chilly, the rain icy cold.

But that was not the worst. Brown water coursed between the street's three-foot-high curbs like a river through a gorge—and it carried not rain water but the Gulf itself into the city.

The water was cresting just beneath the waiting brougham's doorstep. "Careful!" a drenched old Marcus warned, assisting first Pearl, then Angel into the coach.

Children, dressed in their Saturday 'rough' clothes, were deliciously delighting in the phenomenon, wading and floating in improvised vessels like wash tubs, picnic hampers, and even dresser drawers.

The wind-jostled carriage got as far as Church Street when a policeman yelled, "Turn around! You can't get through—there's an electrical line down!"

BLESSING THE NUECES RIVER AND one of its walnut tree's swinging ropes that had taught him to sink or swim as a boy, Drake tugged off his boots and waded toward the St. Mary Cathedral Basilica, which, at the center of the island, was barely six feet above sea level.

Submerged objects bruised and cut his stockinged feet. The wind drove slivers of rain at his face so that, lids nearly closed, he could barely see the few other souls who had risked getting out and were wading to the safety of higher ground.

Debris bobbled past him—shoes, a rocking horse, a banjo, and even a couple of snakes. At last, he made out the large gray cathedral, the highest point on the island. Soaking wet, he staggered against the driving wind, which snatched his hat. He reached the great wooden doors and yanked hard to get one open.

Inside the nave, the water was already close to a foot deep. Scores of people, perhaps some of them wedding invitees, had already taken shelter there. They hovered in terrified groups. Some were praying, others wailing, still others telling their rosary beads.

Near an aisle pillar, Nicolas and Griffin stood talking with a gray-tonsured priest. Their arms waving, they appeared to be arguing, almost shouting, though the wind howling outside blunted their words until Drake drew quite near.

At the sight of him, Nicolas gaped. "My God, you made it through this!"

"If he can, then I can," Griffin said with not even a 'glad to see you, uncle.'

"Where are the others—our family?" Instantly Drake wanted to recall that last word. *Family.* Yet they were, like it or not, his family.

"Your father and mother are at the Tremont Hotel, along with Kerry and Catarina and Tara and Buck. The rest should have started arriving here by now."

The old priest shook his head. "The cathedral and the Tremont are the safest places, my son—the center of the island."

"And the places where we all would assume to rendezvous," Nicolas said.

Griffin shook his head. "Giselle could still be with her parents at our house. I'm going for her."

"Not a good idea," the priest counseled. "To leave here

is to risk being drowned. Your wife needs her husband."

With the back of his hands, Drake swiped away the water that was dripping from his hair into his eyes. "Angel?"

"She was with Pearl." Nicolas's face, a study in power, was tense. A vein flicked in his jaw. "I sent my driver to pick them up at the boarding house. They should have been here already."

"I'm going for Giselle." Griffin, obviously impatient with the jawing, turned and headed for the basilica's heavy double doors.

Drake swung away to follow in Griffin's footsteps. "I'll find Angel."

Nicolas grabbed his arm. "Wait. We can't go off half-cocked in this hurricane. We need a plan. I know the island. The boarding house is on Avenue O and 17th Street. There would only be two main streets Marcus would have driven between here and there—18th or 20th. You take one. I'll take the other. We meet up back here in an hour."

Outside, the water was rising rapidly over the three-foot-high curb. The torrent moved west at tremendous speed. This time, Drake noticed that among the debris deposited at the cathedral's doorstep, the water had also beached the body of a baby.

AS HE LACED UP HIS shoes, David heard the groaning of the Hotel Grand. The wind shrieked and swirled about, swaying the hotel on its very foundations. Sweat popped out of his pores. He had been through this before, at fourteen, when the horrific hurricane had wiped Indianola from the map.

Damn, he should not have agreed at the last minute to attend the wedding of Claire's cousin Pearl. His stiff-neck pride, which he readily conceded, could only bend so much. He realized that it would be his fear of losing Claire that would drive her from him and back to her family. So, if keeping her meant stomaching the Paladíns prejudice for the rest of his life, then that he would try to do—if he did not kill Claire's father first. The bigot Buck was nitroglycerin to David's gunpowder.

He had cabled ahead and reserved a room at the less prestigious and much older four-story Hotel Grand rather than the newer, internationally famous Tremont. Both were in the center of town and its financial and entertainment district, but most of the Paladíns were staying at the Tremont.

With an awful foreboding of the monstrous weather yet to come, he called out, "Claire!"

She opened the bathroom door partially, peeping from where she was dressing for the wedding. Theirs was one of the fifty suites on the top floor that had their own private baths, which he and Claire could ill afford. She was smiling, but he could tell she was almost as apprehensive as he about the shrieking storm. She could have no idea of the havoc a hurricane could wreak.

"Yes?" She wore a bell-shaped skirt and a heavily frilled

blouse that was pulled forward over her bulging waist.

He opened his mouth to yell at the need to leave—and was stunned that nothing but a croak came out. Fear was paralyzing him. He tried again but only stuttered. "Danger . . . dying . . . ."

Her fingers left off rapidly buttoning her blouse. She crossed to him and framed his trembling jaw with her palms. "Look at me, dear."

He forced himself to fix his gaze on her unwavering one. He could see her fear, as well, but something else— something stalwart.

What a weak and blind fool he had been. Even from the beginning, he had not recognized her strength. That first night on the Paladín veranda, he had worried about moving too fast, afraid to scare her off and yet afraid to lose that fateful opportunity if he did not blurt his marriage proposal.

"If I have to die today, David, then there is no other place I want to do so than here in this room, in your arms."

Without a doubt, he knew that in their seven years of marriage, he had been keeping Claire on a tether, always afraid the day would come when she would weary of the constant stress exerted upon her as the wife of a Jew.

Nevertheless, despite the snubbing's, the harassments, even the arsonist-set fire and the loss of their child, she had remained incredibly constant and strong. His bruised male ego had airily dismissed her suggestions for improvements to the Emporiums operations. Yet, all along, he had sensed her opinions for the store were well conceived and practical.

Worse, his bruised male ego had relied on the familiar

comfort of his own heritage offered by the grateful and love-starved Ruth. Yet all those years, it was both Claire's unique qualities and her faith in his abilities that had stimulated him to reach beyond what he thought was his capacity for success.

He brushed his lips over hers. Finding his voice, he grabbed her hands. "Forget getting ready, my love. We're leaving. Now."

"But my suit jacket."

He grabbed her hand and yanked her behind him. He had to get Claire to shelter that would better withstand the wind. In the Indianola hurricane, he had watched the pummeling wind corkscrew the three-story newspaper building with its heavy presses before sweeping it out to sea.

Her unwieldy body was hampered by the cumbersome skirt, and he helped her negotiate the steps as quickly as possible. He plunged them down three flights of the circular staircase, past the gathering of alarmed guests, and through the door, nearly torn from its hinges by the wind.

Debris hurtled through the air like death-dealing missiles—brooms, banister slats, gallery planks. Still, he had not anticipated the fullest potential of the looming catastrophe.

A Norther was blowing bay water onto the island, while keeping the brunt of the hurricane's huge tidal surge out in the Gulf, on the island's south side—until the wind shifted and only Yahweh knew when that might happen, but when it did, David knew Galveston Island would be as lost as Atlantis.

★ ★ ★

"NATTY, WHY DON'T YOU PLAY the piano," Becky's brother Billy suggested. "Cora," he told his six-year-old granddaughter, "you turn the pages for your grandma."

Over Cora's head, his eyes met Becky's and she nodded almost imperceptibly. She, too, knew this was no mere passing storm. "Don't think we're going to make it in time for you to play for Pearl's wedding, Natty," she gave a forced smile for Cora's sake, "so you might as well play 'Ave Maria here.'"

Hands clasped behind his straight back, Mandrake stood at the window, looking out toward the Gulf only a few blocks away.

Becky crossed to her husband, wrapping her arms around his corrugated stomach. Quietly, she whispered against his ear, "Best you stand back from the window, honey."

Although between the roar of the wind and the pounding of Natty's piano keys, her words would have been obliterated from the others in the room.

He nodded toward the house across the street. "Water's rising fast. By my estimate, four feet in four seconds."

Even as they looked on, all the while watching the water rise, the neighbor's frame house seemed to lift off its perch of stilts, then settle back. Unbelievable! Then, both she and Mandrake glanced down, seeing the water seep beneath Billy's front door.

"Get everyone up the stairs," he ordered.

Abruptly 'Ave Maria' ceased.

As Mandrake began to hustle her, Natty, and Cora, up the stairs, she saw Billy disappear into the kitchen and reappear with an axe.

Seeing him chopping holes onto her grandma's cherished and highly polished parquet floor, little Cora shouted from the first stairstep, "Grandpa, no!"

Becky realized he was hoping to prevent the house from being washed away. But it was not the water she feared would dismantle the house but the shrieking gusts, pummeling it on its southern side with each accelerating gust like a giant sledge hammer.

The wind had shifted.

WADE CHAFFED, WAITING FOR THE relief train on the adjacent tracks. Because of the storm battering Houston, he and Sarita had just barely made the last Galveston-bound train, packed with passengers. Then the train had chugged to a halt just short of Virginia Point and a signalman lugging a railroad lantern against the eerie midday darkness climbed aboard their coach. "Sorry folks. Tracks are washed out ahead."

Passengers, he explained, would be shifted to another train that would take them instead to Bolivar Point and from there the big Charlotte M. Allen ferry would take them to Galveston Island.

At first, Wade was frustrated that he and Sarita might miss their daughter's wedding. But within the hour, the relief train arrived. He, Sarita, and ninety-three other passengers, buffeted by wind and pelting rain, hurried across muddy ground to climb aboard one of the two relief coaches.

When the train came to a halt at Bolivar Point, Wade looked out the window. In an interval between blinding sheets of rain he caught sight of the ferry. Giant swells tossed it aloft before plummeting it into troughs. Even before the conductor entered their coach with the news, Wade knew the ferry wouldn't be able to make the pier.

Yet, as the engine backed up the coaches, water overflowed inside. Wade looked out again—his gaze locked on the lighthouse a quarter of a mile away on higher ground. Between it and the train, only water could be seen. Plumes of water slammed against the lighthouse's Gulf side.

When the next blast of wind rocked the big train coach on its springs, he turned to Sarita. "We're getting off."

In the row behind them, an old man in a battered Confederate cap shook his head. "Are you crazy? You're safer here than outside."

Wade glanced at Sarita. A steamboat child, she was accustomed to navigating storms on the water. Yet her face was ashen. "I don't like the way the water's running," he explained to her. "It's not just rising, it's rushing."

She nodded and put her hand in his. "Nearly forty years we've shared together. We'll do this together, too."

She had such faith in him. What if he was wrong?

Of the ninety-five passengers, they were the only ones to get off. With Sarita on his back, he fought through the whooshing water. Wind slapped waves as high as his chest, staggering him. At sixty, he was far too old to be piggybacking, even as light a weight as Sarita was. But somehow, slowly forging forward, he sloshed toward the lighthouse.

At last, he stood, utterly exhausted and ankle deep in water in its doorway. He didn't know what surprised him more. To look inside up its spiral staircase, lit only by one window high above, and see nearly one-hundred pairs of eyes of marooned people, seated on each step, peering down at him. Or to glance back at the departing train, black smoke from its stack whirling

upward into the equally black clouds, and watch in horror as it was tumbled, like a child's toy train set, off its submerged tracks.

GALVESTON

Only a few blocks separated the Hotel Grand from the Tremont, but negotiating those blocks took all the strength David possessed. With Claire clinging to his waist, he winched the two of them from lamp post to lamp post, even latching onto a barber shop pole. As the wind accelerated, it became doorknob to doorknob—anything, including a hitching post, that he could clutch to keep them from being swept away.

All the while, the water kept rising—it was above their hips now. Powerful gusts were blasting through at lesser intervals and with greater intensity. Claire's hair had long before been snatched from its pins and streamed behind her like a brown wind-whipped flag.

Worse was the rubble—deadly projectiles—spearing through the wind blasts. Unbelievably, he saw a 4"x6" twelve-foot piece of lumber impale a milk wagon. The mule pulling it had been floundering desperately in the surging water. Both were swept away.

Just ahead, he saw bricks flying off the Tremont Hotel,

his only hope for their safety.

With his eyes on the hotel, David never saw the hurtling sterling silver coffee pot.

SOMETHING LARGE THUMPED hard under the floor of the second story, where Becky and Mandrake, along with her brother and Natty and Cora, had escaped the water rapidly rising from the first floor below.

"Grandpa!" Cora cried, clutching his hand.

Becky glanced questioningly across the bedroom, dimly lit by its window's shaft of ghoulish yellow phosphorescent light.

Billy caught her worried look. "The piano," he shouted to make himself heard. He had chosen that bedroom because it was on the windward side. Should the house be capsized, they stood, at least, a chance of being above the water.

Even at that moment, the houses timbers could be heard creaking. Becky leaned into the shelter afforded by the arm Mandrake wrapped around her.

How did one prepare to die? The Lord already knew she was sorry for all the wrongs she had done—especially her penchant for thievery, which she had committed early in her life. And oh, so many regrets. The petty grievances she had harbored, the hurting words she had hurled, friendships she had lost because of her quick temper, which just as quickly receded—as she hoped the water would below them. But that did not look likely. No, it was only going to get worse.

Her biggest regret would be she would not live to give birth to the child she carried.

Mandrake released her and crossed the room to the trembling Cora. Sliding his hands beneath her armpits, he hoisted her up onto the bureau. Standing up there alone, the girl's terror shone in her eyes, large and deathly white against the darkness of her face.

"You get up there, too, Mrs. Wheelwright," he called out to Natty.

Billy's wife nodded and, despite her age, agilely scrambled to heft herself on top.

Ever in command, he spun next to Billy. There was an exchange of words that even in the lull between gusts of wind Becky could not distinguish. But Billy went to the closet door and began jerking on it, unhinging it.

Mandrake rejoined her and inclined his head next to hers to make himself heard. "No telling how high the water's going to rise. Get on the bureau. But if the wind takes the house, we want you and Natty and Cora to be ready. Hold fast to the doors. They're your life rafts."

Her heart lurched. "What about you and Billy?"

He ignored her and turned to the bedroom door, instead, grabbing its knob and wrenching.

At that same instant, the wind tore the roof off its frame.

WITH THE SHIFT OF WINDS from the north to out of the south, the already giant and steadily building tidal wave out in the Gulf was, at last, released to hurl forward its wrath and meet in the island's center with the already surging bay water from the norther.

Giselle sat beside her mother, curled in a fetal position on Giselle and Griffin's bed, and held Ingrid's withered, quivering claw of a hand. All the years Giselle had feared her mother's unpredictable anger. The woman had seemed huge and overpowering. Even when Giselle had reached adulthood, her mother had possessed that formidable power to intimidate her.

"It's going to be all right, Mama. The hurricane will eventually pass over us and all will be peaceful again."

Not that Giselle believed what she was saying. One had only to look out the upstairs window at the damage already done and know nothing would ever be the same again. Despite their house being towards the island's center, water had already reached its lower floor level.

She thought of Griffin, waiting for her at the church, of the baby she carried, of the grand adventures neither she nor their baby would ever experience. She could only hope that somehow Griffin could survive through this ordeal.

He would. The Paladíns were survivors.

"Giselle!" Her father, his expression horror-stricken, beckoned her to the window.

She deserted her mother momentarily to join Max and saw with astonishment what was swiftly bobbing like a battering ram into a collision course with her house—a section of a train trestle.

CARCASSES OF HORSES and corpses of mangled humans bobbed along in the street like toy boats. Karl swung away from their Grand Hotel fourth floor window and began tugging the mattress from its frame.

"What a wonderful adventure our lives have been," he told Rafaela, hoping to ease the tension so evident in the way her tall and still taut body was moving. At his instructions, she was ripping sheets into strips.

She was not panicking. As long as he had known her, since she was the young bride of one of his best friends, she had behaved with calm purpose. One would never have suspected the whirlwind of passion that rippled just below her cool, classical exterior. But then he had never suspected his career-focused, analytical mind could ever have been so diverted by his passion for her that he would put everything else aside to have her for his own.

"Lie down," he told her, taking from her the long linen strips he would use to bind her to the mattress.

"No." Eyes as warm as *cafe au lait* looked out of her patrician features. "We have shared but one bed together all this time, Karl. We shall continue to do so."

He knew how adamant she could be and there was no time to argue.

As it turned out, there was no time at all.

FROM HIS FOURTH FLOOR Tremont window, Buck gaped in horror as the wind sheared off the fourth floor of the Grand Hotel as neatly as a carving knife slicing ham. If that could happen there, the Tremont could be next.

Then the lights went out. The hotel had its own electric power plant in the basement, but it must have been flooded.

He turned to Tara. "We might have to evacuate. I'm going downstairs to check the lay of the land."

She placed her palm, damp with anxiety, against his scruffy face. Her limpid eyes looked pleadingly into his. "Don't go."

The ranch woman was still beautiful to him, despite her near sixty years, thickened waistline, and eyes fanned by sun wrinkles. And she still loved him . . . regardless of his ornery nature. She deserved a better man than he. "I'll be right back. I promise."

He might be old, his body growing decrepit—after all, he had prematurely grayed in his thirties. He might be set in his crabby ways, but, by God, his gut instincts were up to snuff. If nothing else, they had been honed even sharper with age. They told him he had to go downstairs. Now.

With the electricity gone, the elevator was out. Like a freight train, the sound of wind roared up the staircase. In the dark, feeling his way down the marble stairs, he was stalled at the last landing by a hundred or more men, women, and children huddled on the steps below—and below them, the Italian marble floors of the famed grand lobby were awash in water.

Something caught his eye. Out one of the lobby's plate

glass window, he could swear he had caught a glimpse of Claire, large with child. But that could not be, could it?

The rain sluiced away the image—and a second later, some hurtling ricocheting object shattered the glass into a thousand splinters. Inside, people screamed.

Instincts won out against caution. Immediately, he picked his way downward among the dozen persons clustered on each broad step, reached the bottom, and waded through doors shoved wide by either the influx of refugees or water.

Godawlmighty, his instincts were right! Outside, Claire knelt, clinging with one arm around one of the columns supporting the Tremont portico. With her free hand, she was trying to hold onto her sagging husband by his coat lapel. Blood gushed from a wound somewhere on David Solomon's head, only to be washed away by horizontal rain.

Slight as Buck was, he was nearly blown back through the hotel doorway. Somehow, he lurched across the walkway to his daughter. "Let him go!" he shouted at her.

Vehemently, she shook her head.

He grabbed her arm, loosening it from the column. She tried to yank away. In doing so, her clutch on her husband's jacket slackened. The rapid tide snatched his body. It hurtled toward an overturned black wagon and decapitated horse, lodged against a high curb.

Buck jerked and tugged and shoved her inside the Tremont at last. "Hold her!" he yelled at a stocky man perched on one of the lower steps.

Without waiting to see if the stranger complied, Buck

swung back to the doorway. He was a damn fool to risk his life for a Jew who was probably already dead, anyway.

Nearly pinned to the building by wind that had shifted, he inched along the lengthy stretch of the Tremont, dodging the flying debris, until he reached the wagon. What irony—the lettering on its side read *Montclair's Funeral Home.* Solomon was trapped between the overturned wagon's floorboard and the curb.

Hunkering to loosen the man's limbs from the entangling reins and harness, Buck was nearly submerged himself. Then a wave caught him and sent him tumbling against Solomon. It was all Buck could do to regain his footing. His heart pounded excruciatingly. Pain shooting down his arm, he somehow managed to tow Solomon, yard by yard, back down the length of the Tremont to its entrance.

At the sight of him and her husband, a sobbing Claire broke loose from the stocky stranger. Both waded forward to meet Buck and his weighty cargo. Short of breath, he could only nudge the limp body toward them—and then felt his own body go limp, as if the wagon had overturned on him instead, crushing his chest.

MARCUS GOT OUT TO TUG the carriage's balking horse forward—and sank from sight, only to surface moments later, arms flailing to stay afloat.

Pearl stared aghast, then flung open the carriage door.

The wind fretted her veil about her.

Angel grabbed her wrist and moved to rise. "Stay here—your bridal gown is heavier than an anchor."

She shook off her grasp. "No, you can't swim."

Quickly climbing down, she gripped the door handle to steady herself against the turbulent current while she first blindly shoehorned off her silk slippers with one foot then the other. She tugged off her veil, then ripped away her court train, fastened to her shoulders and attached to her skirt below the hip. If she was fortunate, she would live through this to mourn the destruction of the expensive gown.

Gripping the carriage's trace for support against the wind and hip-high water, she splashed along the oyster shell-paved road toward what she discovered was a quicksand sink hole. Driving rain needled her face. The colored man surfaced again and reached a frantic glove hand to her. She grabbed it, trying to pull him over the rim of the hole. His terror manifested in his grip.

She teetered over the abyss.

They said one's life passed before the eyes just before death. An image of a swimming hole on Buffalo Bayou displayed before her eyes like a viewer's slide. Naked as the day she was born, she had learned to swim there. Another slide, of Nicolas's swarthy naked body, poised above hers, dropped into her memory's viewer. If he did not survive this maelstrom, she did not want to either.

Then Angel was there, tugging and yanking her back. Marcus's hand slipped loose. "Oh, God, Angel!" Pearl gasped, aghast at the empty glove she held.

Clutching one another, both stared—watching, waiting—for Marcus to surface. Nothing.

Now the water was rising so fast that keeping one's balance was impossible. Together, they lunged through the water toward the nearest house.

The three-story Victorian Gothic stone structure on Bath Avenue near Avenue 0½ was not far from the Gulf of Mexico. The home, built only four years earlier, had recently been renamed the Letitia Rosenberg Woman's Home and housed elderly women.

Only by banging on the door unrelentingly had Pearl summoned the pinched face matron with severely drawn-back hair. The woman's marionette lines bracketing her mouth deepened. "The rooms are already full," she shouted at them and tried to close the door.

"Please," Pearl begged, "we were on our way to my wedding when we had to turn back. Surely, you can squeeze us in somewhere."

Twenty minutes later, from the third story dormer attic of the Woman's Home, she and Angel looked out over the city—all of it but a few spires and fortressed stories swiftly submerged. Wind was cannonading the brick house like deadly shots from nearby Fort Crocket.

Odds were increasing that she would not survive this tempest. Still, she had a wedding to make and she was not going to give up yet. She opened the closet, rummaged around, and dragged out an ironing board. "Take this, Angel. Hold onto it. No matter what."

"What about you?"

She pried open the old trunk and began emptying out its blankets and linens. "I always wandered about the nursery rhyme, 'Rub-a-dub-dub, three men in a—

But she never finished her sentence. Plaster crumbled, timbers buckled, and windows burst with wickedly lethal shards.

This time Pearl tumbled into an abyss without top or bottom, beginning or end.

WITH A LINGERING LOOK OF concern, Thérèse closed the door to Tara's hotel suite and only then did Tara turn back to the bed where Buck's body had been placed. Removing her shoes, she climbed into bed and stretched her long length next to his shorter one. As the wind reaped its destruction outside the vibrating window panes, she slipped her arm beneath Buck's sunbaked neck to cradle his head alongside her jaw.

What a marriage theirs had been. He, a famed hard-bitten Texas Ranger, content with his solitary life. She, a dried-up old maid of thirty-four, content to run the famed Barony Ranch. They had fought and loved their way back and forth across Texas.

She brushed away her tears that fell on his beard-stubbled face. "You conducted yourself today like a true Texas Ranger. I will always love you, you old coot." As if to reinforce her declaration, the shattering windows sounded like a thunderous applause.

THE CITY OF GALVESTON WAS entirely cut off from the world. All vessels were gone, with ships most likely as far flung as other counties. The mainland railroads would undoubtedly be inoperable. The water was so high, evacuees would be unable to flee across the bay by way of the world's longest wagon bridge—even were the wagon bridge still standing, which eyewitnesses in the Tremont's lobby below said it was not.

As Texas governor, Kerry was used to being in charge. Once this hurricane had passed, the full extent of its destruction would be known. Word would have to be gotten to the mainland, to the nation's major newspapers, of the city's tragedy.

A central committee would have to be established to direct the city's recovery efforts—to designate chairmen to organize hospitals, morgues, finances, relief services, and donations. Clara Barton's Red Cross workers would be needed to help distribute food and clothing.

But the central committee's most urgent and immediate task would be to dispose of the remains of the victims for health reasons—and Kerry's fear that his family members would be among the victims reduced his hard-ass core of leadership and command to the gelatinous composition of a jelly fish.

However, at the moment, he had more pressing

problems. His gaze followed the direction of Cat's eyes, wide with disbelief. The hotel room's seams between the wall and the ceiling were separating to display a view of the cloud-writhing sky.

AT SIX-THIRTY SATURDAY EVENING, with the power plant ruined, the city in darkness and the wind still raging, Alex struck a lucifer. Its light was feeble, but outside was a bright eerily green. He watched as the Gulf's waves receded from the beach and their dense yellow foam carried away the Murdoch Bathhouse like it was a pile of matchsticks.

"Get in the tub," he told Thérèse. "It may very well just float should the hotel collapse. I'm going to check on the others."

Fist on hips, she looked at him as if he had lost his mind. "You crazy old geezer. *Non!* You are so frail you could not win a battle with a gnat!"

He caught her veined hand. "Thérèse, I have to. Members of my family are out there, somewhere in this storm."

Her lips trembled. Her face seemed to crumple, but she only said, "Alex . . . I love you. I always have. All these years."

Amazing. He had thought it was not in him to love anyone, and here he had come to love two women with the fullness of a heart he would have sworn he did not possess.

If one was lucky to live long enough, one could see the golden thread woven through life's tapestry from the vantage point of the accumulation of those years. Then, at last, life's journey made some sense.

Yet at that very moment, it made little sense. Little sense at all for it to end without a farewell to his family. All of them. At least, Drake was safe in Conroe's Switch and Claire in Dallas.

He got no further than the end of the hallway, when a tremendous blast rocked the building. With the unprecedented fall of barometric pressure, decompression exploded the hall window outward, sucking him toward it.

ROD'S EARS WERE POPPING, AND he knew that something catastrophic was about to happen. "Get back from the windows!" he shouted at Adele.

He yanked open the hotel suite door to relieve the room's pressure just as glass burst—and he collided with a hurtling body. Both of them were grappling with the window frame and each other as they tried to outlast the powerful suction. When it ceased seconds later, they both collapsed onto one another.

The other, an ancient, reed-thin man, could barely haul his creaky bones erect. Flicking off splinters of glass from his dress coat, Rod gave him a hand, levering him up. Only at that moment, did he realize his own forehead was badly bleeding. With the back of his sleeve, he wiped away the dripping blood.

Roaring wind whipped the elderly man and Rod, making standing a herculean effort. He had to shout to make himself heard, even though they were standing mere inches from one another. "That was a close shave, my friend!" The old man, quite dignified in his hawkish look and manner, offered his hand. "I think I owe you my life. Paladín is my name. Alex Paladín."

For as long as Rod could remember, this man had been his bitter enemy. And here he was, at last, confronting him . . .this frail, old man.

Rod took Paladín's outstretched veined hand and glanced at the maelstrom out the window.

How fitting—and no one to witness.

In that blinking of an eyelid, he saw his own hand, reaching out to his father, reaching for approval and love, and encountering only and always his old man's all-consuming anger with the Paladíns.

Rod knew he had to let go.

When the wind and rain ceased, and the sea finally begin to recede, survivors emerged from their shelters. Dawn's early light of the next day revealed something out of Edgar Allen Poe's macabre imagination.

Mouth agape, Griffin stared at the horrific sight. Bodies littered the decimate landscape. A dozen or more were caught up in the slots of a remaining section of the trolley trestle. Others hung from trees like branch-caught kites.

But most of the victims were buried amid gigantic windrows of rubble covering the entire city. One pile to the south resembled the ragged tail end of the Rockies. Two to three stories high, the debris stretched for miles.

Because that wreckage had kept piling up, it had absorbed the direct impact of the giant tidal wave that crashed against the city at seven-thirty the night before and kept the buildings to the north from collapsing. Nevertheless, the entire city had suffered horrendous wind and water damage. The Gulf had also contaminated the city's drinking water.

Ironically, Griffin himself might have become a victim, had it not been for the wind. The handle of a metal frying pan clipped the side of his head. Stunned, he would have sunk beneath the tide had not the force of the wind from behind held him upright. As it was, a kind soul of a waiter dragged him through the doorway of Toulouse's Bar to wait out the storm—crouched atop its marble counter.

His architect's eye scanned the horizon for landmarks and found few remaining. Gresham's Castle. The Tremont Hotel. St. Mary's Cathedral Basilica. If Giselle survived, she might have gone on to the cathedral.

And if she had not?

That horror took his breath away. She was his breath. Images of her smote him with his loss—her parading the protest sign through the senate chambers and striking old fuddy-duddy Harrelson on the noggin. Her in her bloomers, falling off her bicycle into the World's Fair lagoon. Her lying beneath him on the Cuban beach while butterflies and bullets danced around them.

He swallowed hard. He would find her . . . alive or dead. But he would not rest until he did. Even if it took him a year to search through every tangled piece of the devastation.

But where to start?

Someone had mentioned the first temporary morgue had been set up in a nearby warehouse, on the Strand. He found it between 21st and 22nd street. And thus, found a living hell.

Holy Mother of God.

Bodies stretched out, row after row. Some were covered by blankets, others naked, their clothes having been ripped away by the storm. Many had necks, arms, or legs twisted in grotesque positions, some had mouths open in an 'O' shape, and many stared back with dead eyes full of dismay.

A tropical day was already heating up the warehouse and because of the powerful stench of already decaying bodies, searchers were tying handkerchiefs saturated with camphor over their noses.

It was all he could do to keep from retching—and all he could think of was how badly he wanted a drink of whiskey to dull this horror.

Sighing with relief that he found neither Giselle nor any of his family among the morgue's corpses, he almost turned away when he spotted a handkerchief-masked face among the searchers.

The young woman was shoving filthy, blood matted hair straggling hair from her face, but he would have known those eyes anywhere. They had laughed at him and with him. Now they wore a dazed look.

"Giselle!"

He had thought he had yelled her name, but it came out as more of a rasp. Nevertheless, her head swiveled toward him.

Then she was running toward him. "Griffin! You're alive!" Her words were muffled by her face handkerchief. Frantically, her fingers traced the blood dried gash above his sideburn, as if by touching the wound they could heal it.

Yanking her handkerchief from her face, he wrapped an

arm around her shuddering frame. "You are all right? Our baby?"

She looked up at him, nodded. "Yes." Her hand dropped to her stomach. "Both of us. But Momma and Papa . . . they didn't make it."

With faltering words and a tear-choked voice, she recounted her miracle. She had latched onto a green wooden shutter that had floated her first out to sea and then hurtled her back to collide with a grain mill before breaching atop accumulated wreckage. "After the water receded, I picked my way down from the mound."

Framing her bruised and lacerated face with his hands, he ran his thumb across her cheek, wiping away a tear. "Your parents will live on through our child. He or she will bear their names."

At that, a wan smile eased her grief-etched features. "A boy by the name of Ingrid?"

"Why not?" He grinned. Elation filled him. He and Giselle and the child she carried were alive. And a city would need an architect to help it rebuild— an architect with the mind of a mayor.

★★★

LIKE A DRUGGED MAN, NICOLAS staggered, exhausted, along the corpse-littered beach. His wedding attire looked like something a farmer hung on a scarecrow. He was barefoot. While searching for Pearl during the brunt of the hurricane, he had removed his shoes to tie around his head as a helmet.

Not a single house was left standing between the Gulf and O street, where he could last place Pearl, so he made his way first to the beach to search. Bodies were still floating ashore. After the first thirty minutes, he thought he was inured to dismembered body parts and other ghastly sights.

But when he stumbled, catching a bleeding foot on a dock chain half buried in the sand and tugged on it, he popped up one child's body after another, tied by a length of rope clothesline to the cincture at the waist of a nun. Eight of them. Despite what must have been Sister Camillus's good intentions, the orphans had become entangled in underwater rubble.

He fell to his knees and wept.

At last, he struggled to his feet. Damn't, if he had made it through the hurricane, Pearl could have. Her personality was so intense he could not imagine her among the dead littering the beach like seaweed. She was a Paladín, was she not?

He turned his steps toward St. Mary's Infirmary in the center of the city and the closer of the two hospitals. A mountain of debris wrapped itself around St. Mary's three stories, then snaked south of the city center. Buried inside the mountain were demolished houses, fragments of furniture, skillets, pots, dogs, cats, and horses.

And men, women, and children, who were dead or dying.

Outside St. Mary's Infirmary, despite the sun's already

searing heat, two Sisters were drying over a small fire water-soaked crackers, cookies, and bread they had salvaged. Inside the infirmary, the injured and those who had nowhere else to go—there had to be more than a thousand—occupied the rooms and halls. A line of mud near the ceiling recorded the water depth during the hurricane.

When he didn't find Pearl at St. Mary's, he realized he should have thought of it sooner—the place where she had worked, John Sealy Hospital.

All through its rooms and corridors, dripping with condensation from the heat and humidity, stunned and wounded people were sitting or standing, waiting for help. He found Becky, kneeling on the bare floor, tending to a sheet-draped Chinese woman, whose shoulder had been staked by a flying fragment of wood.

From Becky, he learned she, Mandrake, and Billy had been able to climb aboard their house's inverted roof. Mandrake and Billy were still searching the ruins for Cora and Natty.

But Becky had heard nothing of Pearl. With her forearm, she wiped away the sweat glistening on her dark face. "But knowing the determined Miss Pearl like I do, I would bet she's waiting at the altar."

Past grisly sights and dumbfounded people wandering aimlessly, he hurried to St. Mary's Cathedral Basilica. When he reached its flung-wide doors, he stopped short. He was afraid to hope . . . to have his hopes dashed by what reality may wait inside.

Forcing one foot after another forward, he entered the nave's dimness. To his left, something, someone, grabbed his upper arm. "Nicolas!"

He spun. It was Pearl's mother.

"We were so afraid you didn't make it, Nicolas." Distractedly, Sarita shoved back silver-blonde hair into a bird's nest of a knot atop her head. "Pearl sent Wade out to look for you."

"Pearl . . . then she's alive?!" He did not realize his fists had been clenched.

"Yes, by some miracle. Like baby Moses in a basket, she drifted ashore in a trunk near . . . but I'll let her tell you all about it. She's at one of the side altars, to your right—the Blessed Heart altar."

Hundreds of candles lit up the high altar, where survivors were praying and holding vigil. He moved along the aisle until he found the side altar of the Blessed Heart. Amidst gutted candles, a single, flickering candle lit a statue of St. Mary.

Head bent, Pearl was kneeling in the tattered and strained remains of her outrageously expensive wedding dress.

He dropped to his knees beside her and covered her clasped hands with his knuckle-battered one.

She gasped. Her lids, weighted by tear-damp lashes opened, and her gaze swerved to meet his. "You picked one hell of a day for a wedding, Nicolas Cordova!"

"And you were late for it, Pearl Paladín! Late, as always. Just as I had anticipated."

Around them, people were glaring, 'shushing,' and wagging their fingers. It did not matter. He had never been so happy in his life.

WITH SLATE SHINGLES SCYTHING through the air, Drake had taken shelter from the vortex in an ice box swooshing out the door of the Fred Harvey Eating House near the railroad tracks. No bull Drake ever straddled had taken him for the ride that ice box had.

His ride lasted, not eight seconds, but eight terrible hours. At one point, he would have sworn he had floated over the Garten Verein. At last, passing the second story of the Ursuline convent, he had abandoned ship and swum hard to wriggle through a blown-out convent upper window.

The after light of the maelstrom was murky. He knew little about Galveston—the location of the Santa Fe Union Depot, the St. Mary Cathedral Basilica, and the boarding house where Angel lived—all in relationship to the Ursuline Convent.

He was frustrated as hell. He hadn't a clue where to begin to look for her. It never crossed his mind that she would have died in the hurricane. Not a scrapper like Angel.

Where would she have gone? He tried to put himself in her place, to think like her. But no one thought like that gal.

More than half a day was spent, and still he searched. At various intersections, work gangs had built funeral pyres of lumber from destroyed buildings and were cremating piles of bodies. The powerful stench wrenched his innards. Hoping to escape it, Drake veered away, back toward the Garten Verein where he hoped for a respite of fresher air.

A wry smile hitched one corner of his mouth at the memory of Angel tumbling head over tea kettle above the club's spiked fence, their frenzied flight through the garden labyrinth, and the guard searching high and low for them.

Searching?

At that, it hit him that he was going about it all wrong. It was Angel who would be searching for him!

If Nicolas or Pearl had told her he had been invited, and surely, they would have, then his Angel, as the saying went, would not let hell nor high water keep her from him.

The question was, where would she expect him to go? And he knew the answer to that. She understood him so well. She would expect finding his family would be foremost for him—because until the hurricane, he had never realized she was his family.

A BRILLIANT SUN WAS setting on the azure horizon.

Meanwhile, the streets were crowded with frantic, barely-clothed people seeking lost relatives and friends. Gangs of weary, stunned men shoveled aside mud and hauled off wreckage and bodies.

However, the Tremont's lobby was almost empty. A good foot of mud and silt layered its marble floor.

Although Drake knew his family was registered at the Tremont, he did not know which rooms. He took a good fifteen minutes searching each floor. Windows shattered, curtains ripped away, water-soaked walls, and strewn clothing and linens revealed the hurricane had taken its toll at the Tremont, too. Only a few bewildered occupants lingered in their rooms.

By the time he reached the fourth floor, he was out of both breath and hope, wearier than he could ever remember feeling.

Suddenly, from the end of the hall he heard his brother Kerry's authoritative voice booming—something about checking off some list of agendas and names.

Paralyzing fear of what he would and would not confront anchored Drake's feet for a beat. Then, as if trudging through mud, he forced one foot after another. Slowly, he inched down the hall toward the open doorway.

And there they all were—the Paladíns, crowding every square inch of that suite. Plus a benevolent looking middle-aged couple he did not recognize.

There was his father, rising unsteadily from a chair beside a desk where David sat, his head swathed in bed linen strips. David was jotting down notes that Drake's brother Kerry was dictating. A frowning Griffin, as tall as his father Kerry, was scouring some kind of clipboard list.

The old man, tears in his rheumy eyes, spread wide his arms. "We were all waiting just for you, son."

"Drake!" Angel screeched, flinging herself against him.

Gulping, he caught her up with one arm. He kissed the

top of her head, hiding his face in her mass of sun-spun, disheveled hair. His other arm he wrapped around his father's frail body, pulling him close, too.

All around him whirled hollers of enthusiastic welcome. Wade, Sarita, Catarina, Giselle, Pearl, Claire, and a blur of other loved ones hugged him.

And then came his Angel's pleased-as-punch introduction to the unfamiliar couple—her father, Rod Obregon, and his wife, Adele.

Who could or would have believed? It was odd, he reflected. So many times, when he had thrashed at the blows dealt him, life had twisted everything around, somehow tying up all the loose ends, making everything right with age and wisdom.

Later, much later, amid the harrowing yet miraculous tales of surviving the hurricane, he learned of the lost—Karl and Rafaela, Max and Ingrid, and Buck—but Drake also learned how resilient and how courageous all his Texicans were.

ACKNOWLEDGMENTS

I WANT TO ACKNOWLEDGE SEVERAL books that were of enormous help in my research of the Great Galveston Hurricane of 1900, the deadliest natural disaster in United States history, claiming an estimated 8,000 to 12,000 lives and ending the Golden Era of Galveston.

Special thanks for invaluable information provided by Erick Larson's fabulous *Isaac's Storm,* Nathan C. Green and Nathan Green's *Story of the 1900 Galveston Hurricane*, and *The Galveston Hurricane of 1900: Use Deadliest Natural Disaster in American History* by Charles River Editors.

As mentioned in Book II, *The Barons,* Skip Hollandsworth's article "When We Were Kings" in *Texas Monthly* was an insightful source.

In addition, I wish to thank Camille Bryan, Certified Academic Language Therapist (CALT), and a Licensed Dyslexia Therapist (LDT), who graciously and patiently answered my many questions regarding word blindness, known in today's linguistics as dyslexia.

ABOUT THE AUTHOR

PARRIS AFTON BONDS is the mother of five sons and the author of more than fifty published novels. She is the co-founder and first vice president of Romance Writers of America, as well as, co-founder of Southwest Writers Workshop.

Declared by ABC's *Nightline* as one of three best-selling authors of romantic fiction, the award-winning Parris Afton Bonds has been featured in major newspapers and magazines, in addition to being published in more than half a dozen languages.

The Parris Award was established in her name by the

Southwest Writers Workshop to honor a published writer who has given outstandingly of time and talent to other writers. Prestigious recipients of the Parris Award include Tony Hillerman and the Pulitzer nominee Norman Zollinger.

She donates spare time to teaching creative writing to both grade school children and female inmates, whom she considers her captive audiences

Parris would love to send you a free e-book. Visit her website at www.ParrisAftonBonds.com today and claim your free book!